# PREEMINENCE

## THE RISE OF THE PENGUINS SAGA

STEVEN HAMMOND

# ROCKHOPPER BOOKS

This book is a work of fiction. Any references to historic events or real locales are used fictitiously. Any other resemblances to actual events, locales, or persons, living or dead, are purely coincidental.

Edited by Ella Medler
Cover art by Caner Inciucu
Interior layout by Tanya Adams
Find out more at:
STEVENHAMMONDBOOKS.COM

# Dedicated to

Those who know the grass isn't greener, it's just more grass.

# ACKNOWLEDGMENTS

Thank you to everyone who supports me along this journey. It's a long road, marked by countless hours spent lost in the isolated world of creation, and if not for Joy, Cathy, Michelle and Rodney, Lauretta, and my doggies, Buster and Jak, I would have no string to guide me back out of the labyrinth. And thank you to Ella, Tanya, and Caner for your efforts to make these stories worth reading.

# OTHER BOOKS BY STEVEN HAMMOND

*THE RISE OF THE PENGUINS SAGA*
Rise of the Penguins
The Warlord, The Warrior, The War
Crosscurrents
Whispers of Shadows
The Royal Creed
Order of Kings

*THE STAFFS OF OMIA SERIES*
The Talents of Bet
The Journey of Bet

# DRAMATIS PENGUINIS

**Royal Emperors (K'tha)**

Overlord Antaean

General Liutites

Captain Temalus

Lieutenant Diutes

Mearna—Overseer of the rookeries

Talus

Clayfus—Attendant to the Overlord

Lieutenant-General Persus

Ceocilus—Elite Guard

**Basileios (Cu-kisc)**

Lord Saeson—Lord of the Misshapen

# PREEMINENCE

# CHAPTER 1

Overlord Antaean stood on the raised dais, his bulking five-foot frame quivering with rage. "Aperion is dead. Surrender your minions to me and end this conflict." The Overlord stepped toward Lord Saeson, clutching a spear in his rudimentary fist. Antaean's black eyes burned with the prejudice and hatred of a thousand generations toward the Cu-kisc penguin standing before him. The Overlord's seal-skin cloak dragged on the floor behind him, and Leopard Seal teeth adorning a necklace, trophies of long-defeated enemies, rattled through each huffing stride.

Lord Saeson, six feet of bulk, with elongated wings touching the floor beside him, remained steady, unintimidated by Antaean's advance. "Believe what you believe. But my brother, Aperion, is not dead. However, if you continue to threaten me when I come in peace, you will be," he said through a broad, black beak which terminated in a deadly downward curving tip. Equally dark eyes bored back into the Overlord's, matching him scowl for scowl. "But this does not have to be." He spread his wings wide and looked to the chamber filled with Royal Emperor penguins, the K'tha. "Let us live our lives with no demands or threats, and we will work together, and we will strive to make a better world for all penguins. We can end this strife."

Overlord Antaean appeared to turn the thoughts over in his mind, meeting the eyes of each of those under his command who stood firm and ready for the violence they were sure was to come. "You came here, saying you've come in peace, yet it is you who threatens my life." His eyes flashed toward the guards at the entrance of his chamber, then back on his ancient foe. "The time of the Cu-kisc has finally come to an end. Your females are dead and you are the last of your kind. The Misshapen who carry your blood cannot breed. When I root them out of your tunnels below, and when I kill them all, you will be all that is left." He fixed his gaze on Saeson and hammered the end of his spear against the ice. "I will end this strife, as you call it. It ends today!"

"You are a fool, Antaean. The day will come when you'll pay for this folly. I know what the Oracle saw. And I know this could have been avoided." Lord Saeson drew his broad wings against his body and waited, silent and ready. "And I promise you, this does not end today."

"Kill him," Antaean cried, his voice stained with a pleading malevolence, begging for the chance to complete what his ancestors could not achieve—the extinction of the Cu-kisc.

Standing beside the Overlord, General Liutites signaled for the warriors to attack. They moved in on Saeson, joined by elite guards, with spears forward. In moments, it became clear that Saeson, Lord of the Misshapen, had no intention of letting his line end there. Two Royal Emperor warriors charged forward and Saeson easily swatted their weapons aside.

"Stand down. I don't want to kill you," he urged in a final attempt at a peaceful resolution.

When another warrior lunged toward him, the hope of peace ended. Slapping the attacker aside with his long, powerful flipper, he spun to face the next assault. A guard came forward and stabbed at him overzealously, losing his balance. Saeson seized his head in his enormous beak, and bit. The sickly snap of the penguin's neck rang out and Saeson jerked back with the head of his attacker still clutched in his beak. He watched the guard's headless body fall limp and spat the head out, watching it roll to a stop at the foot of the next in line.

The sight gave the warriors pause until Antaean bellowed from behind, urging them onward. Lord Saeson's shoulders sagged, knowing they wouldn't stop their assault. The warriors rushed him at once and Saeson's massive black and white body became a whirl of motion. Powerful flippers swiped the phalanx of spears away, and those caught too close to the strikes were knocked from the melee, dazed or unconscious. Still they came and the mighty Cu-kisc penguin lashed out, tearing flippers from bodies, dragging his curved beak through flesh, spilling blood and intestines across the frozen floor.

In minutes the fighting had ended and Saeson stood, beak agape, his breath coming in tired rasps, long yellow-gold head plumage hanging wildly to his shoulders. He stared at Overlord Antaean, eyes burning with fury. "Your warriors are dead and now you will join them in the Great Sea."

Antaean stood unwavering, bringing his spear up ready for battle. "You will find I will not go so easily to the Great Sea."

"We will see." Lord Saeson moved closer and General Liutites stepped between them. "Move aside, Liutites, or you will join your father in death."

"I will do what I must. However, you will find those of us without the Grip fight much fiercer than those who depend on their weapons." Liutites stared up at Saeson's blood-dripping beak, showing no fear.

Lord Saeson leaned close to the general until their beaks almost touched. "You don't have to die for him. We both want the same thing."

Liutites' eyes shifted almost imperceptibly. A click rose from his throat as he stood unflinching before the Cu-kisc. "I will ascend to the dais my own way," he said, shaking his head with the tiniest of movements.

"So you must," Saeson said. Before he could make his move, dozens of Royal Emperors, led by Captain Temalus, rushed into the Overlord's chamber. Saeson slapped Liutites, sending him sprawling to the ground, then turned to face the new threat. He threw a glance back at the Overlord. "Your time will come, Antaean."

"My time is now. And your time is over," the Overlord said, then called for his warriors to attack.

Lord Saeson rushed toward the line of warriors. Before reaching Captain Temalus, he dove to the ice floor and propelled himself forward on powerful clawed feet, knocking Temalus away and plowing through the line of surprised Royal Emperor soldiers, barreling them aside as he tobogganed on his stomach into the corridor, making his escape.

"After him," Antaean roared, rushing forward, knocking Liutites back down as he attempted to right himself. The warriors gathered themselves, rolling or falling to their stomachs, and gave pursuit.

Temalus stood shakily, having taken the brunt of Saeson's bull-rush, and looked at his brother, Liutites. Neither said a word when the Overlord approached. Antaean looked them both over then turned away. "Have the passages to lower reaches sealed. We will starve them out."

"Lord Saeson will not escape us," General Liutites said with his beak held high. Temalus aped his movements but said nothing.

Overlord Antaean surveyed the carnage of dead Royal Emperors. He walked to a wounded guard and watched him gasp for air through gouts of blood oozing from the corners of his beak. Antaean cocked his head, watching the dying penguin. "He already has." He plunged his spear through the penguin's chest and watched him die, leaving the weapon buried in his chest as a reminder to all of the consequences of failure.

# CHAPTER 2

ONE YEAR LATER: General Liutites crept through the darkness in the lower reaches of Pack Ice Command, straining his eyes against the gloom. Approaching a sharp turn, he hesitated, and looking back the way he had come, he spotted Temalus silhouetted against the vague light floating down from the entrance behind them. Steeling his nerve, he inched around the corner then pulled back with a jerk. His eyes narrowed as he slowly peered around again.

"I see you," he said, glimpsing the white of Lord Saeson's chest hanging like a ghost at the end of a long corridor. He stared at Saeson, standing still as a stone, the white nearly melting into the ice walls, and remembered the last time he saw the Cu-kisc and the power he'd displayed. He edged back and leaned against the wall, closing his eyes. He scooted farther back, lowered to the floor, and slid back the way he had come, cringing at the sound of his own scuffling claws.

"He's there, brother. Hiding in the recess," Liutites said just above a whisper when he reached Temalus.

"Then the Overlord's plan didn't work," Temalus said. "He obviously hasn't starved to death."

"Obviously," Liutites spat.

"He could've easily killed us. Maybe he lacks the fortitude now that he's trapped."

"Do not mistake defense with cowardice, Temalus," Liutites said. "He's biding his time. Nothing more. The time will come when he will show himself once more." He snapped his head toward the sound of ice grinding somewhere deep within the bowels of the under reaches. "Let's go. The darkness is his realm, and we have what we were looking for."

The two Royal Emperors began their slow climb back up the sharp incline to the main levels of PIC. Claws dug into the icy walkway, straining to keep their heavy frames from sliding back toward their lurking enemy.

"If Aperion is truly gone, Saeson is the only barrier between the Misshapen and our father's ambition," Liutites said between heavy breaths.

"If the Overlord was wise, he would have brokered a peace between us and the Cu-kisc, not try to destroy them."

"Who has ever accused our father of being wise?"

"Certainly not I," Temalus said beneath a laugh. "Perhaps we should go back and kill Lord Saeson to show the Overlord that we could do what he could not. If he's weakened by hunger, with our combined strength we might actually be able to pull it off."

"You saw what he did to the warriors. I doubt we could. And if he called on his minions before we killed him, what then, brother? And if the Overlord is wrong about Aperion and he's alive? We'd be dead before we knew we were going to die." Liutites paused to catch his breath and raised a dubious eye toward his brother. "Besides, what about your ideas of peace?"

Temalus squawked a sharp laugh. "You're saying I can't pull off the born-killer act?"

"Not when you talk about peace with our enemies," Liutites said flatly.

"What does it matter? We'll never know peace with your father in command."

"He's your father, too. It's not in our nature to know peace. We are the Royal Emperors—the K'tha. We were created to rule, not peacefully coexist with the lesser clans." Liutites reached the landing and turned to watch his brother hop the last meter of the climb, showing off as he often did. "Save your strength for your match against Reticles. He has the Grip. Those of us hatched without it must rely on our wits, cunning, and strength, as they rely on their weapons."

"We've spent two days traversing these lower passages and you lecture me on saving my strength? I have to wonder if Reticles was given similar tasks days before our match." Temalus stared at a nearby Royal Emperor guard holding a long staff. "No matter. Their reliance on their tools makes their minds weak. Reticles will pose no problem."

"I hope so for your sake," Liutites said. His eyes followed Temalus' to the guard. "Close it."

The guard looked between Liutites to Temalus then inserted the butt of the staff into a hole in the wall with a cocky flair. A heavy ice door ground downward, sealing the passage.

Liutites eyed his brother. "Let's give our report and then I think you could do with another round of sparring."

"I thought you said I should save my strength."

"You seem to be intent on squandering it," Liutites said, nudging his brother with his wing. "You might as well waste it for a purpose."

Temalus clicked his beak at him. "As long as it's not with Diutes. He's such a poor loser."

"You'd prefer another horde of Adélie?"

Temalus snorted. "Fifty against one was not a fair fight."

"But it was entertaining."

"I'm glad you thought so...*brother*."

# CHAPTER 3

"If I were Overlord, I would see that all of the Cu-kisc were immediately exterminated, not simply sit back and wish they'd die," Lieutenant Diutes said, walking between his brothers, Liutites and Temalus, as the trio traveled through a wide passage.

The three entered the dimly lit main hall, shoving their way through a crowd of newly conscripted Chinstrap penguins. When one Chinstrap didn't move fast enough for his liking, Diutes reared back as if to slap the offender aside. Liutites quickly stepped between them, blocking Diutes' strike. "Save your aggression for their training. It's not wise to discipline them so early upon their arrival."

Diutes growled, watching the Chinstrap scurry away.

Temalus pushed his way between Diutes and Liutites, drawing insults from both. He ignored their protest. Instead of listening to another round of bickering between the two, he focused on the enormous ice stalactite hanging in the center of the main hall. The cobalt and azure blues of the monolith migrated to cerulean and cyan, frosted over with a light coat of periwinkle and white, all of which seemed to transfix Temalus. He stared at the tip that hung a meter above a smaller, but no less impressive, stalagmite protruding from a pond of clear ice. Liutites came beside him, followed by Diutes. "It's magnificent," Temalus said without looking at either.

Liutites looked the stalactite over. "You've seen it a thousand times."

"And it's no less spectacular."

"Not as spectacular as the designs of future *Overlord* Diutes," Liutites said with a hint of mischief.

Temalus' shoulders slumped. "Why must you ruin my brief moments of repose by mentioning him?"

"Because I'm trying to figure how he's going to kill the Cu-kisc, something that hasn't been done in our long history," Liutites said, turning to Diutes. "Maybe I can use this brilliant plan of his as my own to court favor with the Overlord."

Diutes narrowed his eyes. "It can be done."

Liutites laughed. "Truly? And what of the Misshapen, the byproducts of Overlord Antaean's breeding plan? They're both K'tha and Cu-kisc. Will you wipe them out, too? And the Kaurochs? You know of them, the enormous beasts digging out the new auditorium and light tunnels as we speak. Will you kill the workers, too?"

The escalating discussion pulled Temalus away from his wonderment of the stalactite, replacing it with amusement of the new spectacle.

"They are a means to an end, for the time being. If you lack the courage for the task, perhaps the Overlord should promote someone more suited." Diutes stood beak to beak with Liutites.

"Lord Saeson, alone and surrounded, escaped from forty trained warriors, killing half, then disappeared into the lower reaches. The Overlord himself trapped him and still couldn't contain him." Liutites sniffed his contempt at Diutes. "I don't lack the courage, I lack the stupidity. And you, Lieutenant Diutes, are as stupid as any I have seen. How you managed to scratch your way out the egg is a miracle of the Ancients."

Diutes glowered at Liutites, turned away, then spun back toward him, attempting to strike Liutites with his flipper.

Liutites blocked the strike with little effort and returned his own, catching Diutes on the beak and following up with another strike on the back of his head, which knocked Diutes to his stomach. The general stood over the dazed penguin, looking as if he would have liked to go for the kill.

Temalus once again stepped between his brothers, shaking his head at Liutites.

Liutites stared at Diutes until the fire in his eyes was replaced with a cold darkness. "That was for thinking you could. Try it again, and I won't be so merciful."

Diutes scrambled to his feet, his eyes shining with fear mixed with anger. When it appeared he was about to forego better judgement and attack again, a voice from the rear of the main hall interrupted the spat.

"General Liutites," a tall, lithe and frail looking penguin shouted. "Overlord Antaean demands your report."

Liutites sneered at Diutes, looking as if he would strike him again just for the pleasure of it.

"At once, General," the scrawny bird called again in a raspy voice.

"We shouldn't keep the Overlord waiting," Temalus said, leading Liutites away. He stole a glance at Diutes as he passed and leaned into him. "He could have killed you. Mind your temper, or it will be your end."

Diutes narrowed his eyes at Temalus. "I don't need your advice or protection. He'll regret this. Both of you will. Mark my words."

Temalus shook his head, nudged Diutes aside and hurried to rejoin Liutites. "You're right," he said when they were out of earshot of their brother. "Diutes is as stupid as any penguin I've seen or known."

"True, but his strength is his aggression. However, it is his weakness as well. I'm sure he'll either find a place or die trying."

"That may hold true for all of us hatched without the Grip."

Liutites nodded. "Perhaps, but we are the true form of our ancestors. As such, we will become the heirs to the legacy of our forefathers. They are merely aberrations, born with a defect that benefits them for the time we live in. They are weak swimmers, and a time will come when that will be their undoing."

"Is that a prophecy? I thought only females could be an Oracle. Is there something you're not telling me, brother? Or should I say sister?" Temalus joked earning a playful slap.

"No, to all your questions," Liutites said. His demeanor turned serious. "But men are coming here in greater numbers than ever before. And if history has taught us anything, where men are, penguins die."

"Then maybe we should turn our attention to ridding our territory of humans while we still can," Temalus said jokingly.

Liutites stopped and looked at Temalus, watching him in silence for a moment. When the Overlord's attendant clicked his beak for them to come, Liutites nodded. "More true than you know," he said and turned away, joining the other.

Temalus watched his brother walk away, wondering what he meant. If Liutites knew something he didn't, he was sure he would tell him when the time was right. He nodded, reassuring himself that nothing could come between them; not man, or Diutes, or their father, the Overlord. Their bond was secure and they would protect one another until death as brothers.

# CHAPTER 4

Liutites and Temalus were escorted through a wide corridor, crunching on fallen scraps of ice created by several Adélie penguins scratching designs into the walls. Mist hung near the ground as they drew closer to the Overlord's chamber. They passed under a broad arch into an enormous oval-shaped room with walls which seemed to be both blue and violet.

While Temalus marveled at the color and construction, Liutites stared at a single pedestal, which carried the skull of a Leopard Seal—Phocids as the penguins called them. He had heard the stories of how the Overlord had killed the beast himself, but the general was sure it had been scavenged from the corpse of a long-dead seal that had found itself too far from the sea. However Overlord Antaean had come across it, the display was impressive to most penguins, Liutites included.

"You may approach," the scrawny penguin announced, pulling both Liutites and Temalus from their examinations.

The pair walked in lockstep to the base of a large dais, stopped, and stood motionless, with their beaks held high in salute.

Overlord Antaean stepped from the darkness at the rear of the chamber. The long sealskin cloak draped over his hulking frame dragged on the ground behind him as he ambled toward them. "Your report," he said slowly, with a deep unnatural voice. His bearing had grown darker, more twisted, since the encounter with Lord Saeson. And as he continued to isolate himself, allowing visitors only on his orders, rumors began to make their way through command about the Overlord's sanity.

Liutites kept those rumors in the back of his mind, but when he lowered his beak to deliver his report, he spotted Mearna emerge from the shadows to stand beside Antaean, and his thoughts vanished along with his breath. He stared at her, lost in the carriage of the soft gold swath of color wrapping her face. Her eyes met his for the briefest of moments and he felt a subtle twitch of electricity jolt through his body. Mearna quickly averted her eyes. A whispered click from Temalus brought him back to reality. He looked at the Overlord, who returned a disinterested stare as Liutites struggled to regain his composure. "My lord, we sighted Lord Saeson twice during our survey of the lower reaches. He evaded us both times, leading me to believe that he moves through the middle levels with impunity."

"Two sightings does not indicate impunity, General," Antaean said while tugging the fringes of his cloak absently with his long beak.

"No, my lord, but we can assume he could've been elsewhere while we inspected other areas. The corridor system is vast and we were limited by the lack of light."

"I am aware of the layout of Pack Ice Command. Were there any indications that he might be attempting to dig through or around our safeguards?"

"No, my lord. Nor were there any signs of the Misshapen. All access to the lower reaches, save one, is now sealed." Liutites looked to Temalus for affirmation, who only nodded in agreement.

"And yet he lives. If he is truly trapped below, how does he eat?" Antaean sat back, waiting for an answer.

Liutites lowered his head, searching for an answer. "Perhaps he has resorted to cannibalism. That was true of his brother."

Antaean grumbled a condescending laugh. "Lord Saeson would sooner sacrifice his own body to the Misshapen than eat his *loves*."

Mearna shifted, stepped off the dais, and exited the chamber, stealing a coy glance at Liutites as she passed.

Liutites did his best to ignore the look, and tried to focus on Antaean, who stared silently at the ground. After nearly a minute of silence, Liutites clicked his beak.

The Overlord raised his head, eyes shifting between the brothers. "Lord Saeson's compassion is his weakness. He cares too much for the lesser clans. Exploit this weakness. Find him and kill him. And with his death, the Basileios will be no more."

Liutites shifted his weight. "My lord, Saeson knows our movements when we enter his realm better than we know his. The darkness is his ally and he will not come into the light."

"Did you hear nothing I said?" The Overlord rose to his full height. "I said exploit his weakness."

"Yes, my lord, but—"

Antaean waddled from the dais and casually strode around the general. "Liutites, how did we destroy the Skuas?"

Liutites thought for a moment. "By baiting them with Adélie chicks."

"Exactly, General."

"But we have no Adélie chicks here."

"True. But there are now many adult Chinstraps. Adélie too, for that matter, within our compound," Antaean said, his voice growing darker.

Liutites looked at Temalus, who kept his eyes locked on Antaean. "We should bait Saeson with Chinstraps? Won't they just run away?"

"Not if you wound them. Don't use too many. Their disappearances will arouse suspicion and I have use for them in dealing with the Phocids. One every other day will suffice. Do this for several days. Tell the sacrifices they are being punished or tell them nothing at all; they are merely bait. Lord Saeson won't be able to resist. And we will be waiting with a full regiment this time. With Saeson gone, his Misshapen will have no one caring for them and will die and our problem with the Basileios will go with him."

"What if Aperion is still alive? The Cu-kisc may yet rise again."

"Aperion is dead!" Antaean shouted. He faced Liutites as if challenging him to defy his declaration. When Liutites only nodded, he turned away, becoming almost thoughtful. "The females of their kind are dead. I saw to that some time ago. The Basileios will be dead. And soon the remnants of the Council of Thrace will be dead along with them. I will govern the clans, completing what our forbearers could not, the Royal Emperors will ascend to their rightful place as rulers of the Southern Realm and I will fulfill my destiny. Clayfus!" Antaean called to his aide. The gaunt penguin rushed to his side. "Issue an edict. The ancient language shall no longer be spoken. Any penguin caught speaking in the old tongue will be convicted of treason and summarily executed."

Liutites met Temalus' eyes; both were uncertain of Antaean's revelation.

"Go, now. See to it that the Basileios fade into memory. You are dismissed," Antaean barked.

# CHAPTER 5

"Well, that was interesting," Temalus said after they were clear of the main hall and free of any prying ears. "And what did he mean by *his destiny?*"

"I'm not certain. I'm guessing it has something to do with his meeting with the Oracle," Liutites said, scanning the surroundings. "But if we really do kill Lord Saeson... Fear of the Cu-kisc, I mean *Basileios*, is the only thing that has kept him in check this long. I fear the rumors are true. He is descending into madness."

"Are you suggesting that we should disobey his orders?"

"No." Liutites hesitated. "No. If we disobey we'll no doubt be executed. His plan is doomed to fail anyway. Lord Saeson is far too cunning to fall into such a trap. And he might even rally the lesser clans to his side."

Temalus motioned for them to keep walking. "What do you suggest?"

Liutites eyed him for a moment. "We do as instructed for now. The Chinstraps are so abundant, they're like vermin. They could do with a culling." He stopped walking again, and placed his flipper on his brother's shoulder. "I'm sure something else will present itself."

"I hope so. I grow weary of all this Saeson talk. It may be time we think about removing our father from the dais." When Liutites displayed no reaction, he clicked his beak at him. "No reply? I just said we should—"

Liutites waved his flipper at him, watching an unmistakable form lurking in a dark side passage. "I may have found another way."

Temalus followed Liutites' glassy stare and Mearna ducked out of sight.

"Go back to the quarters. Rest. Focus on your match with Reticles. I'm going to see if I can find out what this talk of destiny is. And maybe more."

"You be careful," Temalus said, keeping his eyes on where Mearna had been standing. "I doubt you can trust her."

"You worry about yourself, brother," Liutites said, a hint of mischief entering his voice. "I can handle this female."

"You'd better hope so," Temalus said, then walked away, shaking his head.

ʌʌʌ

Once Liutites was sure Temalus had gone, he began a cautious trek up the gradually sloping corridor to the darkness Mearna had disappeared into. When he reached the darkened side passage, he hesitated, made a motion to turn and leave, but stopped. He heaved a sigh and continued through the gloom. Rounding a slow curve, he spotted a pale yellow glow emanating from a chamber farther down the hall. He glanced back the way he had come, making sure he hadn't been followed, and continued toward the flickering light.

He arrived at the doorway, standing just out of reach of the light. Taking a deep breath, Liutites crossed the threshold into a chamber that was twice as long as it was wide and spotted Mearna, standing near the back wall. She stood silhouetted against the wavering light of a battery-operated lantern struggling to stay lit in its final moments of life.

"Liutites," Mearna said, her voice a mellifluous whisper carrying both curiosity and invitation across the quiet of the room. "I'm glad you came."

Liutites opened his beak to reply, but found his tongue too dry to speak. He swallowed, cleared his throat and searched for his voice. "Mearna, it's good to finally speak to you alone." He looked back at the doorway. "We *are* alone?" he asked, returning his attention to the prize he had watched from afar for so long.

Mearna cocked her head. "You wouldn't be here if we weren't," she answered with an amused tone.

Liutites berated himself for sounding suspicious. But they were Royal Emperors after all, and he trusted none but his brother.

"What brings you to my private wing of Pack Ice Command?"

Liutites straightened himself, thinking he had misinterpreted why she had been watching him. "Private wing?" he quickly recovered. "Privacy is a precious commodity in this compound. Especially now with so many new arrivals."

Mearna sniffed a laugh. "Being the matriarch of this clan has its privileges."

He agreed with a nod, though he had never thought of her as the matriarch. He wondered how many eggs she'd had during her tenure. Liutites' own mother had laid six, with only three surviving to maturity. But his mother had been nothing more than one of Antaean's breeders, who had died while he was away on his two-year trials at sea, but after laying the eggs carrying Diutes and Temalus. "Privileges such as light—a commodity almost as valuable as solitude."

"True," Mearna said, looking at the lantern. "But you haven't answered my question. Why have you come?"

Liutites watched her move against the light. "Curiosity. Questions. Among other reasons."

Mearna took a step closer. "Curiosity can be quelled. Questions can be answered. Other reasons… We'll have to see where that takes us."

"Yes, we will," Liutites said awkwardly, feeling an unfamiliar warmth beneath his thick coat of feathers.

"But let's start with your questions. Perhaps that will silence your curiosity as well." She took another step closer.

"Only partially." Liutites had to remind himself why he was there and resist her allure until he got answers. "Our eyes have met on several occasions. Why did you lead me here now?"

"Lead? You saw me and had the courage to follow." She turned away. "But," she looked back at him, "maybe I'm curious as well."

"That word again. Curiosity can be dangerous."

"We'll see," she said coyly.

Liutites resisted the urge to say something flirtatious. "What do you know about Antaean's claims of destiny?" he asked, killing any amorous tension between them.

Mearna snorted and turned away. "Destiny. Your father claims he spoke with the Oracle, Lapasia, before she was carried away by the great wave."

"I thought the Oracle was a myth."

"No. She is real. Or was real. During one of their supposed encounters she said that he would be the leader prophesized long ago to unite the clans and lead us to a time of unity and peace not seen since before the Great Auk Wars."

"You sound doubtful."

"It is only his word against someone who is gone and likely dead. But training warriors and commanders doesn't seem like peaceful intentions, does it?"

"True. But without the Council, how else would we keep order?"

"Ah, yes. The Council of Thrace. Many members were wary of our return to strength. Antaean doesn't care for those who disagree with him."

"Sometimes the masses need strength of will over democratic deliberations."

"I don't disagree. And that's why the Council is nearly dead. They sealed their fate when they sat idly by when the humans first came this far south. Millions died as they discussed, argued, and deliberated over the best course of action. When the Order of Kings withdrew from the body, they were left with only a few contemptuous rebels struggling to hold on to the old ways. And the rebels will soon be gone as well."

"The old ways are dead. We are the future."

"Yes, Liutites. *We* are the future," Mearna said, once again moving closer to the general. "I can tell you this; the Overlord will soon be looking for a supreme commander. One who will lead the warriors against any ideas of insurrection the remnants of the Council inspire in the lesser clans. Perhaps a penguin who has the strength to command our forces to drive the humans out of the homeland."

Liutites stared at Mearna, puffing his chest. "Perhaps I'm that penguin."

"Perhaps you're more," Mearna said, her voice returning to a whisper.

*More?* thought Liutites. He wondered if he should be Overlord, not his maniacal father who claimed ancient mystics ordained that he should rule. He watched the flicker of the rapidly dying light, imagining himself on the dais. "Can you tell me Antaean's weaknesses?"

Mearna stepped close to Liutites, her beak nearly touching his. "I can. But do you really want to spend all of our fleeting moments alone together discussing the Overlord? Perhaps we can discuss your other reasons for following me here."

Liutites lowered his head, resting it against Mearna's. He watched the final glimmer of light fade to darkness. "Perhaps we can."

# CHAPTER 6

General Liutites crept back into his shared quarters before the predawn bustle of busy penguins filled the halls. He stumbled to his favorite resting spot, letting out a tired but satisfied sigh as he sat. A second later his eyes were closed. Another second after that, he heard his brother's voice.

"I don't see how cavorting with the Overlord's mate will help us in unseating him," said Temalus, lightly but with a touch of scorn.

Liutites rolled his head, loosening his tired muscles. "Actually, I learned more tonight than we have in the past several months of prying. But I need rest. We'll discuss it later."

"Later? There'll be a thousand penguins in every nook of this place later. And you did say you'll help me train for my match. So cough up what you learned. You can sleep later."

Liutites cracked his eyes open. He had forgotten about the training. As tired as he was, he would do everything he could to ensure his brother's victory, including dealing with the occasional bouts of lost sleep. "Right," he said, shaking the sleepiness from his head. "The Overlord is seeking a commander—a supreme commander, to be exact."

"Supreme commander? What's a supreme commander?"

"Whoever is chosen will be second in command only to the Overlord. He will have control over all of the warriors, generals included. And from

what I gathered, this supreme commander will lead us against the humans."
Saying the words filled Liutites with desire for the position.

"Against the humans? That's ridiculous. Why, that…it would be suicide.
I wasn't serious when I said it earlier. The humans have resources that we
can't even imagine. It'd be the death of us all. Who would be stupid enough
to take such a position?" Temalus asked. When the answer didn't come, he
sat back. "Not you?"

"Yes, Temalus. I'm stupid enough," Liutites said with a hint of humor.
"But before you pass any more judgement, hear me out. If I can become this
supreme commander, I will control the warriors and then we could take the
dais from our father. We would rule and command this burgeoning alliance
of clans. We could control the future of our kind. We will be remembered
for all time and take our place alongside the Ancients."

"Why would I care what a bunch of penguins think of me a hundred
lifetimes from now?"

"It's called a legacy."

"And why would Mearna want a new Overlord?"

Liutites ruffled his feathers and began to pace. "I believe she wants out
of her subservient role."

Temalus watched Liutites pace around in the gloom. "Don't we all?
Do you really think she'll be content with answering to us both? If she's
conspiring to remove Antaean, I doubt she'll be happy with having two
overlords."

"It doesn't matter." Liutites stopped pacing. His eyes darted between
his brother and the ground. "We'll keep her in check. She can have more
authority over the operations of PIC; that should pacify her. Need I remind
you she commands the rookeries? She determines the loyalty of the warriors.
Each new crèche will be loyal to us."

"Like we're loyal to Antaean? And when she decides it's time for a change
again, what then?"

Liutites opened his beak, but didn't say anything. Apparently he hadn't thought it through to that end. "Then we'll deal with that if it happens. For now, I think this is how we should move forward. The Overlord is too well protected for us to make any attempt to remove him. Currently, it's our best opportunity."

Temalus moved close to his brother, resting a flipper against his back. "You may be right. I just hope your emotions aren't clouding your judgement."

Liutites jerked his head back. "What do you mean?"

Temalus laughed. "If you don't know what I mean, then you're already too deep," he said, walking toward the entryway. "Come on. I need to train."

"I really don't know what you mean," Liutites said, following him out of the chamber.

"I'm sure you don't, brother. Hey, if this doesn't work out, we can always make an alliance with Lord Saeson."

"Now I know you're talking nonsense."

"Am I?"

# CHAPTER 7

"Good! Parry left, strike right, thrust with your beak. Go for the eyes and throat. It takes a precise stab to cause damage to the chest, so stick to the more vulnerable spots." Liutites circled Temalus, watching him spar with an unfortunate Chinstrap penguin.

"My opponent will be much larger, and he'll fight back much harder," Temalus said, stepping back from the fight.

Liutites looked at the Chinstrap and nodded. The Chinstrap took the cue and rushed in, slapping wildly and pecking at Temalus.

The much larger Royal Emperor, caught off guard, bore the unexpected but ineffectual assault, then countered with a series of quick slaps, knocking the Chinstrap off his feet. The incensed penguin quickly stood and attempted another attack. Temalus returned to a more controlled fighting style.

"Never underestimate your opponent. Chinstraps may be smaller, but you'll rarely encounter one by itself. This one seems to have some fight in him." Liutites laughed. "We might have to keep an eye on them."

Temalus feinted with his left, followed by another feint with his right and the Chinstrap took the opening, landing a solid beak jab to his chest. Temalus let out an oof, glared and knocked the Chinstrap unconscious with a hard strike with the back of his flipper.

Liutites gave him a reproaching glare. "Had that been a Royal Emperor you'd be dead. Always follow a feint with a strike. Never feint twice."

"I thought you said the chest wasn't vulnerable," Temalus said, taking a calming breath.

"No. I said the throat and eyes were *more* vulnerable. To deliver a killing blow to the breast, you have to be exact and strike here," he pressed his beak against Temalus' chest, "above the sternum, between the ribs, and downward, to pierce the heart. That kind of precision during the heat of battle can be difficult. It's a quick kill, but it's better to weaken and tire your opponent into exposing himself to such an attack. You can stab through the eye as well, and pierce the skull, but your victim will automatically recoil at such a strike, making it harder to complete the kill. You'll blind him, but you'll only kill him if he is pinned."

Temalus nodded while catching his breath. "I understand. I hope this is enough for my match tomorrow. Reticles will likely have a weapon. Antaean seems determined to be rid of those of us without the Grip."

"The principles are the same whether your opponent is armed or not. Dodge, parry, strike. Get in close and render the weapon useless. Remember what you learned and you'll do well."

Temalus nodded again and then motioned toward the unconscious Chinstrap. "Is he alive?"

Liutites examined the Chinstrap. "He's breathing." He walked to the doorway and looked either way along there corridor. "Grab a flipper and help me carry him."

"What are we doing with him?"

"Bait for Lord Saeson."

Temalus looked at the Chinstrap, seemed to hesitate for the briefest of moments, then took the flipper in his beak.

Liutites nodded his approval and followed suit.

# CHAPTER 8

Lieutenant Diutes skulked through the halls, throwing angry glares at any penguin who dared make eye contact, steaming over his brothers' continued disregard and mistreatment of him. He vowed to find a way to bring them down to size, but he needed allies. However, owing to his generally acerbic and petulant disposition, friends were hard to come by. There were plenty of other Royals who were not happy about Liutites achieving the rank of general before them. Biochilles, for one, had a particular dislike for the general, but he was too passive. Captain Astramachos had the venom, but was too easily provoked. None of the leadership trusted one another. Diutes knew he would have to do things on his own.

He continued into the main hall. His eyes were fixed on the ground, and he was still weighing his options when he bumped into a King penguin, nearly causing both of them to fall. "Watch where you're going," Diutes snapped.

The King penguin jerked his head toward Diutes. He stepped close. "That is Admiral to you…Lieutenant."

Diutes stared down at the smaller King, wanting to take his frustration out on something smaller. The King stood unflinching beneath his glare.

"If you're going to act, do it now. You won't get a second chance," the King admiral said.

Diutes raged inside. *How dare an inferior race act so boldly in the Royal Emperor command center?* His muscles tightened, ready to strike. As he reared back to wipe the King's insolence from his face, a large Royal Emperor stepped between them.

"Come now, Lieutenant Diutes. Accidents happen in such a busy place," the newcomer said. He guided Diutes aside with his powerful flipper with ease. He turned to the other. "Admiral Gregor, my apologies on behalf of this one. He apparently hasn't been educated in hospitality."

Admiral Gregor pulled his eyes from Diutes. "No harm done to anything other than pride." He turned to catch up with a much older King, stealing a glance back at Diutes.

"I could've handled that myself, Talus," Diutes barked at the Royal Emperor.

"Admiral Gregor is not to be trifled with. Had you survived the fight, and I say that with no particular confidence in that outcome, the Overlord would've had you executed." He turned Diutes' head, pointing to the Kings. "The old penguin you see there is King Elinthaw. And they have just agreed to join the alliance. It wouldn't bode well for you to attack them on their first day as allies."

"I didn't realize," Diutes said. Not only did he have no allies, but the Overlord was reaching accords with new clans almost daily.

"There are many things you haven't realized, Diutes. Now that I've saved your life, I'll be on my way." Talus spun away and began to disappear in the crowd.

He glared at the back of Talus' head, watching his long golden head plume bounce against his back, which somehow made him appear both carefree and arrogant. "If that rogue had shown any loyalty to the Overlord, he would be general and not Liutites," Diutes grumbled. He continued to stare, watching Talus' exaggerated head crest until he lost sight of it. An itch in the back of his mind formed. The itch became a notion, forming itself into a full-fledged idea. *Talus had no loyalty to anyone.*

Diutes called out to Talus, and hurried to catch him. He pushed aside other smaller penguins, and edged around those who couldn't be shoved. He found Talus waiting for him. "A moment of your time."

"You have already taken up several moments of my time, Lieutenant. The Ancients grant us only so much of that precious commodity before we are taken to the Great Sea."

Diutes studied Talus. He'd have to be careful. Despite the rogue's calm demeanor, Diutes knew he was as volatile as anyone he had seen, and he had the Grip to go with his abundant physical strength. "What do your Ancients think of this budding alliance?"

Talus looked over Diutes as if he were trying to gauge his motives. "I don't presume to know what the Ancients think. History will decide whether the Overlord's ideals are folly or wise. And he will be judged accordingly."

"I believe we are strong enough on our own. We don't need the lesser clans to accomplish what the Overlord has set out to do. We only need strong leadership."

"Spoken like someone devoid of individual thought. Is there something else you want from me or did you stop me just to spout your erroneous beliefs?"

It wasn't going as he'd hoped. All of the careful steps necessary for subterfuge were annoying and a waste of time. The thought of it made Diutes angry. Sneaking around made him no better than the Basileios hiding in the shadows below. Diutes met Talus' eyes, who looked like his patience was at an end. "I don't believe Liutites deserves his rank. I want to be rid of both him and Temalus and take the rank I rightfully deserve. I need help to achieve my goals." He looked around after speaking to make sure no one had been listening.

Talus laughed. "That's the first honest thing I've heard from another Royal Emperor in some time. But I know you, Diutes. You're as cunning as the ice we stand on, maybe even less so. No offense intended."

"You say I'm dumber than ice and expect me not to be insulted?" Diutes tried to quell his inner rage. He wanted to smack the beak from Talus' arrogant face, but he knew without a doubt the rogue would kill him without a second thought.

"Intelligence and cunning are two very different things. Unfortunately, the Ancients didn't see it fit to bless you with either."

Diutes tensed, ready to disregard better judgement and attack.

"But what they did give you is strength, and a strong will. Albeit misguided. Once your father secures his alliances, he will try to subjugate the lesser clans, as you call them, through fear and intimidation. I've seen this attitude in Liutites as well. True governance comes through the respect of the masses. If the populace loves you, they will follow you into the deepest desert. But respect goes both ways. If you don't return the respect and appreciate them for their unique contributions, they'll turn on you like a spring tide."

"What's a desert and what good is a horde of followers if they die in it?"

Talus studied Diutes, then shook his head and turned away. "I cannot help you with your brothers. The only way you can defeat them is with the aid of the Overlord."

"I doubt he would be willing. What you say is impossible."

Talus turned back to Diutes, raising his flippers wide, lifting his eyes toward the icy ceiling of the main hall. "All of this began with a single snowflake. Glaciers formed, lying silent and still until that one flake landed and pushed it past the balancing point, sending it forward, on a path of destruction, creating great rents in the land; all stemming from that one snowflake."

"I'm not a glacier."

Talus let out a long breath. "What is the one thing Liutites loves?"

Diutes blinked. "He doesn't love anything."

"Are you certain of that?"

"If it's anything, it would be Temalus. I've never heard him say a cruel word toward him."

"Very good. Now if you're capable, imagine what would happen to Liutites if Temalus were to die."

"Liutites would be devastated. I should kill Temalus?"

"No! No. Liutites would tear you apart, piece by piece. But, what if Liutites were to kill him?" Talus watched Diutes, waiting for a reaction.

Diutes shook his head. "No force in this world could make him do that."

"Do you believe that? Who in this world has the power of a glacier? One who, with a small nudge, could cause the destruction of both Liutites and Temalus?"

"The Overlord?" Diutes said.

"Yes," Talus snapped.

"But how could I convince him to destroy them?"

Talus eyed Diutes for a moment. "Be the snowflake." He turned away and disappeared into the crowd.

Diutes stared after him. "Be the snowflake?" He ambled away, trying to figure out just what Talus meant.

# CHAPTER 9

Talus walked alone through the roughly hewn corridors on the far end of Pack Ice Command, away from the bustle of the main hall and the Overlord's chambers. He preferred the solitude over the crowds. Having spent most of his life on the ice plains of Planarseae, Talus enjoyed the solitude. Other penguins, mostly outcasts from different clans and a few K'tha, had joined him on the plains. He didn't object. It was good to be in the company of like-minded penguins, those who didn't fit in with proper penguin culture, whether it be Chinstrap, Adélie, or any other; Talus was not a prejudiced penguin as so many of his kind were. The small band of outcasts had begun raiding human encampments, at first out of boredom or for entertainment. But as the Overlord's compound and armies grew, they supplied the Overlord with much needed resources, though Antaean was loath to admit his reliance on the rogue band, and few knew of this fact.

Talus surveyed the dimly lit corridor that had once served as the primary passage when the expansion of the natural ice caverns had begun by Antaean's forced laborers consisting of Adélie penguins and others. The abandoned section of PIC was rarely used after a more useful entrance had been constructed. But the Overlord's paranoia of Lord Saeson meant the halls were still patrolled by Royal Emperor guards, one of whom stood with a spear at the ready when he approached. Talus breathed deeply, longing to return to the frozen plains he called home. He would do that soon, but he had work to do first.

"What business do you have in the restricted areas?" the guard asked, seemingly surprised that anyone had entered the mostly forgotten passage.

Talus looked the guard over, guessing the poor fool must have done something to upset his commanding officer to pull such a lonely duty. "My business is my own," he said, squinting through the dim light at a closed door where the passage terminated.

"No one is allowed in without permission from the Overlord," the guard said, raising the spear tip at Talus.

Talus eyed the spear, then slowly let his gaze meet the other's. "I don't need permission. Open the door. I haven't the time to waste on debate."

"The passage is closed and you are not permitted." The guard brought the spear closer.

"Your devotion to duty is admirable, but let me ask you something and then you can decide if threatening me is really necessary." Talus spoke calmly, hoping to avoid unnecessary bloodshed. Not that he shied away from violence; it was what he lived for, his life's purpose in fact. But killing a guard relegated to a section as far away from the main halls of Pack Ice Command as one could get wasn't very sporting.

The guard cocked his head, waiting for whatever excuses Talus was ready to spout.

"You do know why the Overlord hasn't had this section sealed, don't you?" Talus lifted his flippers as if presenting the corridor. The guard squinted one eye, but didn't answer. "I thought not." He approached the guard with a conspiratorial look in his eyes. "It's because the Overlord wants the conflict—he *needs* it, like fish need the water, like wings need the air." He looked at his own wings modified through the ages for swimming. "Like most wings, anyway."

The guard looked at Talus, clearly not amused.

Talus shook his head. At first he had considered offering to take the guard with him when he left, to give him a chance to truly live as most Royal Emperors hadn't since their trials. But he could see that the guard had grown soft in mind *and* body patrolling Pack Ice Command with no other purpose than to do as told by his commander, who, in turn, had been trained to do as told by his commander, and so on, all the way up to the Overlord. "You see, the Overlord needs conflict to keep the masses in line, to give them something to fear, a reason to obey. Without that, you— they—would be free to live your lives with nothing to fear other than what nature provides. No fear, no threat, no control. Remember that."

The guard stared at Talus while fidgeting with the spear still held at the ready. He was obviously becoming bored with the lecture.

Talus saw his boredom and decided to skip the rest of his social-political lesson on fear control. "You see, eventually Lord Saeson will use this single point of entry to attempt another insurrection—you can only oppress a group for so long before they rise up against their oppressor. And when Lord Saeson does rise up, if you're still relegated to this duty, or," Talus gave the guard a cold, steely glare, "still alive, the Lord of the Misshapen will kill you. And the Overlord won't give two squirts of guano and a frozen rock about your death. In fact, he might even use your death as an excuse, a call to action, if you will. Rally the troops and all that. He knows this day is approaching and he is counting on it." Talus lifted his flippered wings imploringly. "Now ask yourself, do you really want to die for the Overlord?"

The guard stared blankly at Talus. "Go back the way you came," he said, unmoved by the rogue's speech. He rested the spear tip against Talus' chest.

Talus looked at the spear, pressed firmly enough against his chest to make an indention in his fatty layer of protection. "I really don't want to do this," he said with a sigh filled with honest regret. "It is such a waste." Before the guard could react, Talus swatted the spear tip aside, slapped the guard, then wrenched the weapon from his hand, and pointed it back at the guard. "Do you still want to stop me?"

The guard narrowed his eyes, appearing to calculate his next move. He reached with his rudimentary hands, attempting to repeat Talus' move. The rogue pulled away and stabbed the guard in the throat with little effort. "I said I didn't want to do this," he growled as the guard gasped for breath that wouldn't come. Talus pulled the spear away and watched the guard fall. He stabbed him once more in the chest, then again in the stomach, giving him the benefit of a quicker death. He left the weapon in his victim's body, and continued to watch until the death spasms ended. The Overlord's soldiers had indeed grown soft in the safe confines of Pack Ice Command.

Talus now had the problem of what to do with the body. Considering his options, he studied the door, then looked at the dead Royal Emperor. He shrugged, took the shaft in his grip and with the weapon still impaled in the body began pushing the body down the hall like a broom.

When he reached the doorway, he pulled the spear out and put the end in the keyhole. Waiting for the door to complete its slow grind open, he looked at the dead body. "If the Overlord had any sense he would seek to restore the Council instead of destroying it," Talus said without preamble.

"Antaean will never let go of his prejudices," a low voice said from the darkness beyond the doorway. The voice's owner strode forward and stared at the dead Royal Emperor. "Was it necessary to kill him?"

"Something about having a spear against my chest makes me want to kill the bearer." Talus lifted his head from the sight of his kill. "They will blame it on you and then no one will know about it. You're supposed to be starving to death, Lord Saeson." He patted the Cu-kisc on his bulbous stomach. "I'm surprised to find you this close to the upper levels. I usually have to wander blindly through the darkness to find you."

"I was hoping you were Liutites. I planned to kill him the next time he came in to my domain."

Talus nudged the body inside, pulled the spear butt from the keyhole and ducked inside the dark room. "Leave Liutites to his own devices. I have it on good account that he has no desire to seek you out, though his orders are contrary."

"On whose account is that?"

"While the Overlord seeks to subjugate the Chinstraps, I have made allies of some. And there are many Chinstrap ears within Pack Ice Command."

"You disappear for months and return with more devoted allies than Antaean could hope for." Lord Saeson hissed in amusement.

Talus waved his flipper in dismissal. "I simply know how the Overlord thinks and do the opposite. And speaking of Liutites, I've had the good fortune to run into his idiot brother, Diutes. If the oaf can stay on the path I've set him, Liutites' only focus will be killing the Overlord."

Lord Saeson stood silent for a moment. "You are the only K'tha I trust. Let's hope it will be as you say."

"It will. Diutes' jealously and ambition will be the catalyst for the Overlord's downfall. Provided, of course, he can follow the plan to its end." Talus looked around the darkness, unable to see. "If not, I can always say in public what should be said in private, our conversations notwithstanding. There are others with ears in PIC who would love to see the Overlord fall, as well." He grunted in annoyance. "Do you still have light available? The darkness is your ally, not mine."

"Of course." Lord Saeson clacked his beak and a faint yellow glow ignited nearby.

Talus' eyes were drawn to the light, where he could see the outline of a two-foot tall penguin holding a flash light in its broad, oddly curved beak. He looked the penguin over, noticing it had only nubs for flippers. "I've never seen this sort before."

"There are many so-called Misshapen you haven't seen. You've been away for some time."

"I should have liked to have been gone for much longer, but the rumors of Antaean's growing alliance drew me back," he said as Lord Saeson stepped into the light. His six-foot tall frame loomed over Talus.

"Antaean is attempting to draw me out. Walk with me." Lord Saeson lifted his long flipper, guiding Talus to a side passage.

"Of course he is. What's news about that?"

"Liutites and Temalus cast a wounded Chinstrap into my realm. I am sure it was at the Overlord's behest; he knows my compassion for outcasts."

"I find outcasts can become valuable allies," Talus said, casting an eye at Saeson. "And what became of the Chinstrap? Your brother didn't eat him, did he?" He looked at Lord Saeson from the corner of his eye. He knew the rumors of Aperion's cannibalism were true.

"Aperion has gone for now. He seeks the Oracle, whom he will not find. And once he returns, I fear he will be the more distressed." Saeson stopped and regarded Talus. "As for the Chinstrap, we led him to the pathways beneath the ice, but he chose to stay instead. Though I think he would be safer at sea. But I have another spy in my service."

"*If* he had survived the journey, you mean. The passage below the ice pack is arduous, even for the strongest swimmers. I've taken it myself on more than one occasion." Talus shivered, remembering the last time he had made that trek. He shook away the memory before he could linger on it. "You should let me take the next. I'm sure there will be more."

"I doubt they would trust a Royal Emperor after being so mistreated," Lord Saeson said, then resumed walking.

"As I said, I've made allies of many. In fact, I've made friends of those who have suffered worse."

"You have no friends, Talus."

Talus barked a laugh. "Truly spoken, Lord Saeson. Let's call them associates then, for lack of a better word."

They walked through the darkened tunnel in silence for nearly a minute before Talus finally spoke, "Antaean is claiming Aperion is dead."

Lord Saeson let out a bellowing laugh. "I know. He finds hope in his own lies. Lies are the weapon of the weak. And another's belief in lies is our strength. Though I fear Aperion's mania is only growing worse. He will not be the ally I'd hoped for. I also fear that, at some point, he will have to be destroyed. But for now, he is the face of the Overlord's fear, and I am just his weak shadow."

"He sees your compassion for the Misshapen as a weakness—a sentiment I do not share."

"And that is why you are the only one of your kind I trust. Perhaps you should depose the Overlord. We could end this ancient feud once and for all. It would be a terrible waste of life if things are allowed to continue as they are." Lord Saeson stopped once again and stood before Talus, waiting for a reply, his face carrying a trace of hope.

"I have another calling." Talus turned away, staring at the darkness and into a future only he could see. "And I have no desire to give up my life of freedom in the plains of Planarseae. Besides, I fear that moment has passed us by. The prejudice against the Cu-Kisc is embedded in the minds of the K'tha. They and the recruits of the other clans are *educated* about your betrayal in the learning centers. They are indoctrinated into hate."

"Are you saying all is lost already?"

"No," Talus said immediately. "Not all. When you clutch a fish by the tail and hold it too tightly, it only serves to tire your beak. He has entered into an alliance with the Order of Kings, and I hear he is attempting to do so with the remaining clans as well. He will find that his beak will tire before long."

"Then we will not hope for peace between the K'tha and Cu-Kisc. I only hope we will not have to wait too long before his beak tires." Saeson stretched his long flipper in front of Talus. "This is where I must leave you. Beyond are secrets even my brother is not privy to."

"Very well. I will see myself out." Talus turned to go, but stopped. "Before I go, there is the reason for my visit. Bide your time, but be ready to act should the opportunity present itself. The time will come when you will be the last thing on the Overlord's mind."

"And what will preoccupy the Overlord so much that he will forget about us?"

Talus studied Lord Saeson for a moment, wondering how much he should tell him when even he didn't have all the facts. "Only rumors for the time being. I'll stay here long enough to find out if the rumors are true."

"Cryptic as always." Saeson studied Talus, dark eyes piercing the Royal Emperor's. "What drives you, Talus? Why would you go against your own kind for the Cu-kisc, for the Chinstraps, for any clan? You're risking your life, you know?"

"I serve only the Ancients. And the Ancients deemed that we are all equal in their sight. It is by their will that I live or die, not the Overlord's." Talus bowed his head to Saeson and walked away.

"So may it be for all of us," Lord Saeson said, watching him go.

# CHAPTER 10

Temalus awoke to find Liutites pacing around their quarters. His brother came to a sudden stop, preened a few loose feathers, then returned to pacing. "What are you doing? I'm trying to sleep."

Liutites pulled his beak away from plucking another loose feather. "Your match is today. You need to prepare yourself."

"I was…by sleeping and not worrying about it." Temalus stood upright and shook. Watching Liutites continue on his anxious path, he walked to him and fell in line behind him, mocking his nervous waddle. Liutites turned for another pass, with his eyes fixed on the floor, and bumped into his brother. "Is this how it's done?" Temalus asked, meeting Liutites' half surprised, half angry glare.

"Is this how what's done?" Liutites asked, then stepped around him.

"Walking in circles like a nervous hatchling." Temalus hurried in front of Liutites, raising his wings to stop him. "You're making me anxious. You need to stop."

Liutites relented and squatted beside Temalus. "I went to see Mearna while you slept."

Temalus stood and turned his back on his brother. "And you thought this was the best way to prepare for the match? I need you alert in my corner, not exhausted from a night of cavorting with the Overlord's female."

"I wasn't cavorting…much. However, I did learn something of use regarding the match. And I doubt you'll like it."

Temalus faced him. "I don't like any of this. We both know Antaean uses these matches to rid himself of those without the Grip. How often have we seen two combatants with the Grip face each other? Twice?"

Liutites agreed with a nod. "But that is irrelevant at the moment. I learned that Reticles will be using a short weapon—something more akin to a dagger. We will need to rethink our strategy."

"No. It's too late for that," Temalus said. "Like you taught me, the technique is the same whether you have a weapon or not."

"You won't be able to get close enough to deliver a disabling strike."

"Then I will disarm him and then kill him." Temalus let out a heavy breath. "How many matches have you won?"

Liutites peered up at him from studying the ground. "Thirty-two."

"Thirty-two. And how many has Reticles won?"

"Six," Liutites answered. "And you've won three. I don't see how our records matter."

"Because it is by your training that I've won three times. I trust what you have taught me and you should trust that you've taught me well enough. If I should fall then it is the will of the Ancients. Besides, I can't refuse the match. That would only lead to my execution, and no training on your part could help me with that." Temalus studied his brother with narrowed eyes. "This isn't what's got a stone in your gullet."

Liutites looked at him, then averted his eyes. "It is. But that's not all." He lifted himself from his squat and began pacing again before Temalus' clicking beak stopped him. "I also learned that our father has several candidates in mind for the position of supreme commander and I am not one of them. He's even considering Biochilles. Biochilles makes Diutes look intelligent by comparison."

Temalus laughed. "Diutes is incapable of looking intelligent compared to anything."

"We mock our brother, but he is one the few true K'tha left. And he's won more matches than Reticles." Liutites fixed an icy glare on Temalus. "Fortunately, I am the only one who knows of the rank. I need to become supreme commander. It is the only way we can garner enough support to overthrow our father and for one of us to become Overlord."

"Not one of us, brother. You can have it. I have no desire to be Overlord. And to be honest, I'm losing the desire to be part of this militaristic regime."

"Don't say that. We need to stand together."

Temalus regarded Liutites. His brother's ambition for power had seemed to increase ever since he fell in with the Overlord's consort, Mearna. It worried him, though he didn't dare say so. "To what end? Why are we building armies? To defend ourselves from the Cu-kisc? Lord Saeson wanted to broker a peace and the Overlord tried to kill him in return."

"Lower your voice," Liutites said, moving closer to Temalus. "The Overlord has spies, and your words could be seen as treasonous."

"More treasonous than forced combat, making us kill one another for sport?"

"Yes." Liutites turned away then back to his brother. "I don't like it any more than you. But—"

Temalus snorted a laugh. "Don't lie to me. You relish in the glory of combat. I've seen the fury in your eyes—the pleasure you take in besting your opponent. It is where you outshine even the Overlord himself. In every opponent you defeat you see our father's face. His disregard, his insults, his slights, his punishments—they are the fuel for your every victory. And every victory forces him to see what you are capable of. It's why the warriors and his elite fear you. They fear what your fury would do to them if it were directed toward them, or toward the Overlord. It's why you've risen to the rank of general where no other without the Grip has been able to. I have no doubt that one way or another you'll become supreme commander. And when that time comes it may be best for us to part ways."

"Don't say that. We do this together or not at all." Liutites came closer, resting his head against Temalus'. "When we overthrow Antaean, you'll have the peace you desire."

"No. No, we won't. You said yourself that we were destined to rule." Liutites made a motion to protest, but Temalus stopped him. "I harbor no ill will against you for it. But the truth is once you achieve your place of power, there will be others who will be jealous of it. And they will use your love for me, your desire to protect me, against you. I'll be a hindrance."

Liutites shook his head. "No. You have never been a hindrance. We are brothers to the end."

"Of course we are. But I don't have the same fight within me that you do." Temalus stepped away and took a deep breath. "After I defeat Reticles we need to plan for how to depose the Overlord. And I am with you to that end." He tapped his flipper against Liutites' and walked away.

"Where are you going?" Liutites asked, following after him.

"To the food troughs. I'm hungry and it wouldn't do for me to be weak with hunger during combat." He looked at his brother earnestly. "Are you coming? I could use the company."

"Of course I am. I'll be with you in feast or famine. I will be by your side always," Liutites said and fell in step with him.

"Except when you're with Mearna," Temalus said under his breath.

Liutites angled his head toward his brother. "Is that jealousy?"

"Jealousy?" Temalus said a little too loudly. "No, it's wariness—concern, but not jealousy."

"Save your worry for those who need it, brother."

Temalus stopped and watched Liutites walk ahead. "I am, my brother. I am," he said, then followed after him.

# CHAPTER 11

Day broke over the ice compound known to all penguins as Pack Ice Command, or PIC, as some called it when brevity was called upon. The massive symbol of Royal Emperor authority loomed over the rolling and sometimes jagged ice fields, which stretched as far as any eye could see, until the ice floes crumbled into the Southern Ocean. The strong Antarctic winds blew a maelstrom of icy dust across the plains, heralding the approaching fall and an end to the brief Antarctic summer, howling with a primordial rage that warned all who lived there that winter was coming and only the strong would endure its wrath.

Temalus and Liutites braced themselves against the onslaught of the portending gale and casually strode toward a large, shallow, bowl-shaped depression, thirty meters wide, lying in the ice field, where the first spectators had gathered in anticipation of the morbid spectacle of combat to the death. The crowd, mostly consisting of Royal Emperors, with a smattering of Chinstrap and Adélie penguins, jostled and squabbled over the best places to view the impending blood sport. Temalus stopped and surveyed the masses. "Our society has reached its nadir," he said with a touch of gloom and remorse for what they were becoming.

Liutites clicked his beak in amusement. "This is the beginning, Temalus. We will grow from this point forward. We will see to that."

Temalus shook his head. "This is a distraction from what's really going on for the simple-minded masses. Even as we speak the Overlord has emissaries meeting with the Gentoo and Rockhoppers asking, or more likely coercing them to join his alliance. And I hear he has sent a squad to dissolve what remains of the Council of Thrace."

"The Council of Thrace has outlived its usefulness."

"Meaning they should have allowed a Royal Emperor on the council," Temalus said absently, watching more spectators file out of the wide entrance of Pack Ice Command. "For all the difference that would have made."

"You should focus on your match, not politics."

Temalus snapped his head toward Liutites. "I am focused. This match is politics. It's our father's way of controlling the masses and ridding his realm of those he deems unworthy. It's in our very language. We call the Chinstraps and others *lesser* clans, as if they have less of a right to live than us, that they're beneath us in some way."

"It has always been that way—since time immemorial, since before the Great Auk War." Liutites studied his brother's eyes. "What's bothering you? Your attitude shifted rather quickly. Nerves? I too get a feeling of uncertainty before a bout. There's no shame in that."

"I've already told you. We are lesser penguins in Antaean's eyes."

"Then we shall prove him wrong," Liutites said as his gaze fell to Reticles making his appearance surrounded by a throng of young Royal Emperors chattering enthusiastic support.

"You already have. But it will take a beak in his heart for him to believe it. And what if the so-called *lesser* clans should want to prove the Overlord wrong? Ever think about that?" Temalus looked away from his opponent and spotted a familiar Royal Emperor approaching them. "Talus."

Liutites puffed his chest when Talus approached the pair, noticing the spear in his grip. "Talus, I hadn't realized you returned from your life of isolation in Planarseae. Have you come to watch the show or pass judgement on those who do?"

"I am far from isolated on the plains of Planarseae," Talus said, then turned his attention to Temalus. "And I defer judgment to the Ancients. Only they can truly judge our actions."

Temalus stared at Talus, words forming in his beak he decided best left unspoken.

"And yes, I've come to see the *show*, as you call it. And maybe do a little eavesdropping while I'm at it," he said to Liutites, then turned his attention back to Temalus, regarding him intensely. "You'd be surprised at what you learn by listening and not spouting the Overlord's rhetoric. As far as the *show*, in spite of my own disposition, I find it rather barbaric and an incredible waste of life." He turned away and eyed Reticles making his way into the arena. "But so goes life under the Overlord's rule."

"A rogue such as you has no right to judge those who live by the rule of law," Liutites said, puffing his chest once again.

"Again, it's not judgment. It's just a matter of opinion," he said without looking at the general. After a few moments of silence, he turned back to Temalus. "You should take care when expressing your opinion in the open air. Most are too busy in their minds to notice anything beyond their beaks, but not all. Me, I don't care one way or another. But that may not be true for the next pair of ears your words fall on."

"We will take your advice under consideration," Liutites said rather snidely.

Talus jerked his head in amusement at Liutites' tone. "It is not advice for you, Liutites, but for your idealistic brother. There are too few like him." He regarded Temalus once more then looked back to Liutites. "If I were to give you advice, I would say you should heed your brother's words more so than your desire for power and your father's acceptance."

Liutites clacked his beak in anger and looked ready to strike the rogue.

Talus threw up his flippers in mock defense. "But once again, that is just a matter of opinion from an outsider's observations—a rogue," he said with a hint of mirth.

Liutites glared at Talus in response.

"Every action toward change begins with a difference of opinion," Temalus said, keeping a keen eye on Talus, trying to gauge his reaction.

Talus looked at him with one eye narrowed. "Perhaps," he said, revealing nothing. "But I will take my leave and let you prepare. I'm sure your brother will appreciate that." He bowed his head toward Temalus. "May the spirits of the Ancients be at your side." He turned sharply and joined the increasing crowd.

"You don't like him," Temalus said, watching Talus leave.

"What's to like? He's arrogant, rude, and self-important, all while he's proved himself disloyal and self-serving," Liutites huffed.

Temalus looked at his brother from the corner of his eye. "Sounds like someone else I know."

Liutites shifted his weight. "Are you suggesting we are alike, little brother?" he asked. If anyone else had compared Talus to him they would have met the tip of Liutites' beak.

"No," Temalus said, shaking his head. "He lives his life the way he chooses, free of all of this nonsense." He waved his flippers toward the crowded arena.

"And yet here he is," Liutites said, leaning close to Temalus. "Make no mistake, he may spout his deference to the Ancients, but I can guarantee he has an agenda. There's something he wants. He sows discord to his own ends."

"Probably. He is a Royal Emperor after all." He looked toward the entrance to Pack Ice Command and saw Overlord Antaean strolling toward the arena surrounded by his entourage of sixteen elite guards, trailed by Mearna and the ever present attendant, Clayfus. He nodded toward the group. "Here comes your father and your girlfriend. We should head down."

Liutites followed his nod and growled. "What's gotten into you today?" he asked, leading the way.

"What do you mean? I always get like this when I'm forced to fight for my life and kill someone I have no particular problem with," Temalus said with strained flippancy. He mustered his resolve, and followed General Liutites to the killing floor.

# CHAPTER 12

Temalus and Liutites carefully made their way down the long gradual slope to the arena floor, doing their best to keep their footing on the slippery ice; it wouldn't do to take an embarrassing spill moments before the match. Temalus watched the Overlord take his position on the small, outdoor dais opposite from him across the arena, adjusting his stupid seal-skin cape and ridiculous necklace. He resisted the urge to shake his head in disgust at his father's excess and pomp. He pulled his eyes away; the more he looked at him, the more his contempt grew. Instead, he kept his eyes focused on the ice beneath his feet as he made the short walk to the south side of the arena. When he reached his position, Temalus turned and faced the north, rolling his head, loosening his tight, stressed muscles.

Liutites gave Temalus a reassuring nod as both waited for Reticles to start down the same path. Temalus snorted in disbelief when he saw his opponent making his way down draped in a seal-skin wrap similar to the Overlord's, led by Leotholis, a young Royal Emperor who'd returned from the Trials only a year prior. "Playing up to Antaean, are they?" Temalus muttered to Liutites.

"Let them play their games. You just stay focused on what I've taught you," Liutites said, glaring across the ice at Leotholis, who returned a narrow-eyed glare of his own. A low rumbling came from the back of

Liutites' throat.

Temalus looked at his brother. "Is Leotholis trying to intimidate you?" he said, his voice carrying a hint of amusement.

"I believe he is. I will have a discussion with him after you kill Reticles. Make it quick."

"I'll do my best," Temalus said, noticing the violence in Liutites' voice. He stepped forward. "Let's get this over with."

Liutites put his flipper in front Temalus. "We have to wait for Clayfus to make his pronouncement."

Temalus clacked his beak indicating his displeasure and stared across the arena at Reticles, who returned the stare beneath a mop of yellow-gold head plumage. Something in the way his opponent looked at him felt odd. "He's up to something. They seem a little too confident."

"Mind games. Nothing more. Stick to the plan and you'll do fine." Liutites looked to the Overlord, tapping his foot impatiently. "Draw him to you. Force him to make the first move then counter."

"I know, I know," he said, feeling his adrenalin build in anticipation of the battle before him. It wasn't a feeling he relished like his brother did, but he would embrace the bloodlust of his kind to get through the Overlord's spectacle. He was about to comment further when Clayfus' raspy voice cut through the chatter of antsy spectators, calling for attention. A hush fell over the crowd.

"Penguins of the Southern Realm," Clayfus announced, his thin flippers spread wide. "Two combatants have entered the arena, chosen by his eminence, Overlord Antaean, Protector of the Realm. They, at the will of the Ancients, shall engage in competition for the right to advance in standing with the Overlord. The victor shall stand as a testament to the strength of our kind; the defeated shall join the spirits of our forbearers in the Great Sea, from where no penguin returns."

"Did you hear that?" Temalus whispered. "Maybe he'll make me supreme commander."

"Shut up," Liutites whispered back. "You need to take this seriously. I don't want to lose you."

"I don't want to lose me either," Temalus quipped as Clayfus continued to ramble about Antaean's right to rule. "They make it sound like this is the will of the Ancients. I doubt the benevolent penguins of the past would look upon this favorably."

"In the south, cornered by General Liutites, Temalus, captain in service to the Overlord," Clayfus continued, "prepared to live or die for the honor of the Overlord."

Liutites shot Temalus a look, warning him not to make any more remarks. Temalus kept his beak shut and eyes trained on his father. From the corner of his vision he saw Liutites' gaze shift slightly when Mearna stepped closer to Antaean. "You need to stay focused as well, brother." Liutites grumbled that he was focused.

"In the north, cornered by Colonel Leotholis, Reticles, captain in service to the Overlord, prepared to live or die for the honor of the Overlord." Clayfus brought his flippers down, slapping them against his side. "Champions, step forward, make yourselves known or forfeit your life and your honor."

Temalus inhaled deeply and took three steps onto the arena floor. Watching his opponent do the same, he jerked in surprise when Leotholis pulled the seal-skin wrap from Reticles' shoulders revealing he held two weapons: the short spear he had been warned about, and what appeared to be a club. Temalus twisted his head toward Liutites, looking at him in question.

Liutites shook his head and stepped forward angrily. "My lord," he said, not waiting to be called on as etiquette dictated. "What few rules we have regarding combat clearly states a champion may only carry one weapon. Reticles is in obvious violation of such edict. I formally protest as is my right."

The Overlord rose without speaking to Liutites. "Leotholis, answer the accusation," he said in a booming voice.

Leotholis stepped forward as well, casting a smug look toward Liutites. "My lord," he said, raising his beak in salute. "Reticles' spear broke in half during training. As such, it is still one weapon in two parts. As you can clearly see." He motioned to Reticles, who raised both pieces, showing the frayed ends of both of them.

Antaean lowered back to his resting position. "It will be allowed. Let the combat begin."

Liutites stiffened and looked as if he was about to protest further when Temalus stopped him. "Let them play their games, remember? It will only hamper him. And you should question your sources," he said, glaring up at Mearna, who stood stoically at Antaean's side.

"I will," Liutites said, matching Temalus' glare toward Mearna. "Are you certain it will hamper him?" he asked doubtfully.

Temalus shook his head. "No. But do I have a choice?" He faced Reticles as he waddled across the ice toward him, head bobbing with each step, weapons ready.

"Kill him," Liutites said, drawing out the words, the venom in his voice as crisp as the Antarctic wind.

Temalus firmed his beak and, as planned, waited for Reticles to come close and make the first move.

# CHAPTER 13

Reticles crossed the arena with confidence and violence burning in his eyes, while Temalus waited, inhaling and exhaling in even breaths, focused and calm. Liutites barked instructions as the bleating calls of the crowd rose to a steady din, overtaking the howl of the Antarctic wind. Temalus closed his eyes, drew a deep breath, and took a step forward, ignoring the protests of his brother.

His opponent, seeing Temalus move closer, raised both weapons from his side, waving and brandishing them wildly in an effort to intimidate him. Temalus took another step, his countenance showing his approval of Reticles' energy-wasting display. Reticles rumbled a guttural clicking noise and increased his pace. Temalus stood in place, watching and waiting. He narrowed his gaze when he saw Reticles increase his pace, seeing his clawed feet struggle to maintain their grip on the slippery ice. When three meters separated the combatants, Temalus saw Reticles tighten his rudimentary grip around the short spear. He braced himself for what was to come. With the gap sufficiently narrowed between them, Temalus took another step beneath the increasing objections of Liutites, and dove forward, propelling himself on his stomach with powerful feet directly at Reticles. He barreled into his legs, knocking the surprised penguin over like a ball striking a bowling pin, a lesson he had painfully learned from Lord Saeson.

Temalus felt the weight of Reticles' body land on him briefly then tumble over. He drove his beak into the ice, stopping his slide, then quickly got to his feet. Spinning back, he saw his opponent lying belly down on the ice with one weapon, the club, resting several feet away, but the short spear still firmly in his grasp. Temalus hurried back as best as he could in hopes of ending the fight quickly under Liutites' encouragement and the braying calls of penguin cheers.

The slick ice slowed his movements, and not wanting to match his adversary on the ground, he reduced his gait to a slow waddle. Reticles stood before he got to him, ending any chance of an easy victory.

"Nice trick," Reticles said, glancing toward his other weapon lying uselessly on the ground. "Something your brother taught you?"

Temalus cocked his head. "No, I just took advantage of an unprepared fool."

Reticles snorted a laugh. "You had your opportunity. You won't get a second." He closed the distance between them, flailing his weapon wildly, causing Temalus to shuffle back to avoid a random stab.

Temalus watched the motion of flippers, noticing the pattern of left, right, left, right swings. He stood his ground patiently until Reticles was upon him, then, timing his movements, brought his left flipper up to block the spear while receiving an ineffectual slap against his shoulder. Reticles didn't have the presence of mind to switch tactics, and Temalus jabbed his long beak at his throat, narrowly missing a disabling blow but still managing a glancing stab on the side of his neck. Reticles reared back and lashed out weakly with his short spear, which Temalus deflected easily.

Seeing his opponent on his heels, Temalus feinted left, then struck with his right flipper, followed by attempting a stab with his beak. Reticles was ready. Blocking the jab with his own beak, he brought the spear-head across and landed a poke against Temalus' meaty flipper. Temalus winced and rammed his beak against the other, meeting his breast plate, and doing little more than raising a dot of blood.

The combatants broke apart, both watching each other with beaks wide, spouting heavy breaths. Temalus ignored the pain of his wound. It did little more than sting, but he knew it could have been worse had the blow met his ribs. He watched Reticles carefully as he circled, waiting for the moment to strike. Temalus listened to Liutites' barks of approval and reminders of their sparring matches. He let his brother's voice fade into the sound of the excited squawks of the crowd, focused on his breathing, and waited for the next assault.

He didn't have to wait long. Temalus made ready, standing loose and relaxed. Reticles moved in, feinted with his open flipper, and then again with the spear. Temalus took the opening before the next left came and met his foe in the meaty part of the chest with a hard stab of his beak, immediately drawing more than a dot of blood. Reticles howled with rage and slapped him with enough strength to force him off-balance. Temalus spun to his left and saw the spear rising to meet him. Jerking his head back mid-fall, he felt the sharp tip graze his lower beak. He hit the ice on his side, rolled to his stomach, and kicked away, sliding across the ice before Reticles could deliver a more lethal strike.

Temalus stole a glimpse of Liutites, who urged him to his feet before Reticles could reach him. He looked back and spotted his enemy coming at him with as much vigor as he dared. Temalus dug his beak into the ice, brought his feet up, and pushed himself upright. Facing Reticles, he scratched his claws on the slick ground for traction, and braced himself for what he was about to do.

Reticles lunged into him bodily and Temalus dug his claws deeper into the ground and leaned against him, focusing his attention on the spear. He tucked his beak against his chest and weathered the open-flipper slaps while blocking each attempted jab of the weapon. He heard his rival growl through the impotence of his ineffectual assault, then felt a searing burn when Reticles plunged his beak into his shoulder. He grimaced through the pain, never taking his eye off the spear and felt another stab in his shoulder. He felt the hot flow of blood rising from the open wound as

Reticles continued to stab with his beak. Temalus heard Liutites yelling at him, telling him to break away, but he ignored the advice.

Temalus began to weaken beneath the continuous assault, shrinking with each peck and jab Reticles delivered. He had to withstand the attack a little longer to do what he hoped would end the match. The crowd roared at the sight of claret stains against the white ice, calling and squawking in a fevered bloodlust, swelling to a deafening crescendo. Through the clamor, Temalus heard one voice, but it wasn't who he expected. He blocked another swipe of the spear and heard the voice again. It was Talus, telling him that Reticles had tired and now was the time. He shrugged off another peck against his open wound and when Reticles lashed out with the short spear once more, Temalus was ready. He lifted his head and took the spear shaft in his beak, ripping it from Reticles' tired grip. He looked in Reticles' surprised eyes, and holding the weapon sideways, swung his head, driving it into Reticles' throat.

Reticles stumbled back, eyes wide in horror and disbelief, waving his flipper impotently at the spear tip lodged in his neck. Temalus took a single step, and beneath the thunderous calls and eyes of the onlookers, drove his beak into his opponent's chest, piercing his heart. Reticles looked at him once more with eyes filled with a final plea for life and fell dead at his feet.

The cheers died with Reticles and the sound of the Antarctic wind returned to its rightful dominance over the landscape. Liutites rushed to Temalus' side and Leotholis hurried to Reticles' corpse. Liutites said nothing as he stood beside his brother and both turned to face the Overlord, who stood at the edge of the dais, watching with eager delight. After examining Reticles for signs of life and finding none, Leotholis matched the others' stance.

"Leotholis," the Overlord bellowed, "has your champion passed to the Great Sea?"

Leotholis raised his beak high. "He has, my lord. At the will of the Ancients."

Antaean fixed his dark gaze on Temalus and Liutites. "Then, by my authority, I proclaim Temalus the victor, and as such, he shall be promoted to the rank of commandant," he said with all of the pomposity that made Temalus revile his father. He spread his flippers wide and announced the end of the day's combat. The crowd once again erupted into a tumult of cheers and cries.

Liutites fixed a sinister glare at Leotholis. "I will see you in my quarters later." The other looked as though he was going to protest, but seemed to think better of it and nodded and shuffled away instead.

Temalus studied the corpse of Reticles, his eyes following the flow of blood terminating in a frozen puddle. He shut his eyes at the sight of his work. He took no pride in the ritualized murder of a fellow penguin. He vowed never to take part in the Overlord's spectacle again, even if it cost him his life. There was only one penguin he wanted to see die, whether it be by his own beak or the beak of another, and that was his father.

He felt Liutites' gaze on him and met it with glassy, tired eyes. They stood in silence for a moment regarding one another. Temalus glanced at the dais, empty of the Overlord and his entourage. A chill cut through his layers of feathers and blubber, bringing with it an impending sense of doom. He twisted his head toward Liutites. "We need to end this. Sooner rather than later, or it will be the death of us all."

# CHAPTER 14

Liutites left Temalus in the infirmary, after staying long enough to watch a female Royal Emperor dress his wounds with a paste of ground sea stars and guano. He walked through a wide corridor of polished walls glimmering white and blue in the last traces of the waning day, beaming in from a newly constructed bank of skylights. Deciding to make Leotholis wait for a while longer, he stopped for a bite in the mess hall. Stepping through the crowd to the nearest feeding trough, filled with freshly caught squid and ice-fish, he noticed a group of four Royal Emperors gathered in the corner engaged in raucous conversation. Curious to hear what the masses thought of Temalus' victory, he edged closer, snagging bits of food while eavesdropping on their conversation.

"It doesn't matter," one of the four said. "His victory only postponed the inevitable. Those without the Grip will soon become extinct."

"It doesn't seem that way to me. The match was one of the shortest we've seen. Temalus made Reticles look like a fool," another said.

"Now he's a dead fool," said the third. "And General Liutites has made quick work of everybody he's been matched against."

Liutites puffed his chest at hearing his praises. At least his subordinates understood his dominance in the arena and knew his strength couldn't be matched, even by those with the Grip. He continued to listen.

"Liutites?" the first one said. "He's strong, no doubt. But his arrogance makes him weak. The guards don't respect him. I know I don't. How about you, Leotholis? Are you really going to go listen to his silly rant about the disrespect you showed him in the arena today?"

"Liutites is my commander. I shouldn't have acted with such hubris. I will take whatever reprimand he sees fit," Leotholis said, sounding despondent. "My overconfidence cost Reticles his life. And you, Heltius, should take my example."

The other let out a derisive snort. "What's gotten into you? Are you afraid of—" His voice trailed away at seeing General Liutites standing outside their circle.

"Don't let me interrupt, Heltius. You were asking Leotholis if he was afraid of something. What would that be?" Liutites stepped closer, black eyes burning with such violence the others couldn't help but take a step back.

"I…I was just. . . I didn't know," Heltius stammered, trying to find his earlier conviction.

Liutites glanced at Leotholis and the other two. "Do you share his opinions?" Each shook their heads adamantly. He let his hateful gaze fall back on Heltius. "It seems you are alone in your opinion of me. And to show that I am not without a sense of fair play, I will allow you the first strike."

Heltius looked at the others. "I don't understand. I wasn't—"

"Do you forfeit the opportunity I have given you?" Liutites interrupted.

"Do you mean to challenge me here in the commissary?" Heltius asked, his voice betraying his fear and uncertainty.

Liutites spat a laugh. "A challenge implies a difficult undertaking. You will be dead before you give me such."

Heltius' eyes widened then narrowed at the realization that he was about to fight the general. "One strike is all I need." He lunged forward, swinging wildly at the general.

Liutites blocked the slap easily and returned his own, nearly knocking

Heltius off his feet. He struck again, sending him spinning against the trough. Heltius righted himself and came at Liutites. "You should have fled while you had the chance," Liutites said with such sadistic venom it stopped Heltius in his steps. Liutites struck again with his left flipper, then with his right. He moved in and continued to slap the other repeatedly, beating Heltius without mercy.

Heltius tried to free himself of the onslaught, only managing to back against the wall. He lashed out with a feeble stab that failed to break Liutites' skin. Liutites howled with rage and began beating Heltius more, slapping him with ferocity. Heltius tried to protect himself, ducking his beak against his chest. The general struck him with the back of one flipper, followed by a quick strike of the other, which sent Heltius to the floor.

Seeing his victim try to scoot away on his stomach, Liutites fell against Heltius, driving his beak into the soft flesh of his neck. Heltius cried out in pain, and Liutites stabbed again. He stabbed deeply, tearing away chinks of flesh with each peck and spitting it aside. Heltius begged for help from his companions, who backed away.

Liutites stabbed and tore at Heltius over and over until the blood flowed freely, gushing over the icy floor. With a final effort, Heltius twisted, trying to free himself of the murderous general. Liutites took the opportunity of the exposed throat and plunged his beak deep, tearing away his windpipe. He didn't stop. As Heltius gurgled through his final breaths, Liutites continued tearing away ragged flesh until he hit the exposed neck bone. He stabbed twice more and finally relented. He stood and examined his work, shook his head, sending droplets of blood over the bodies of the onlookers, then faced Leotholis. "Is there anything you want to say to me?" he asked, panting through his breath, almost hoping for the other to say something not to his liking.

Leotholis shook his head and immediately raised his beak in salute. "No, sir. Other than I apologize for my earlier behavior. I was caught up in the ecstasy of combat. Please, sir, accept my apology and my loyalty." He lowered his beak and spread his wings wide.

Liutites' gaze fell on the others, who all repeated Leotholis' actions. General Liutites nodded his approval, snatched a fish from the trough, and strode across the commissary as all the penguins in the room saluted him. All, that is, except one. Talus stood, casually leaning against the doorway. Liutites ignored him as he approached.

"Impressive," Talus said when the general didn't so much as glance at him.

General Liutites made a meager acknowledgement of the rogue's statement. Heltius' congealed blood on his beak strung out in sickly strands when he parted his beak to clack it at Talus in a penguin sign of disrespect.

Talus ignored the insult and continued. "You have earned their fear and commanded their respect. A difficult proposition; I commend you, General."

"Save your commendations for those who care of your opinion," Liutites said as he passed, not giving him a second glance.

Talus snorted a laugh which Liutites ignored as well.

# CHAPTER 15

Commandant Temalus thanked the caregivers and stepped into the corridor. He thought about going to his quarters and taking a much deserved rest, but hunger gnawed at him, so instead, he made his way to the commissary. Stepping into the vast room, he was pushed aside by two Misshapen dragging a ravaged corpse through the entryway. He looked at the exposed neck vertebra and felt his ravenous appetite disappear. But he knew sustenance would aid in his recovery and made his way to the food troughs.

Taking his first bite of a meal, he felt more than heard Talus come to his side. "Does the sight of butchering fellow penguins whet your appetite?" Temalus asked without looking up from his well-deserved meal.

"On the contrary," Talus said, nabbing a squid that had somehow survived transport from the sea to the trough alive. "I find the fiasco barbaric, as you know."

"So do I," Temalus said and speared an ice fish from the trough. "I regret taking Reticles' life. But, had I refused, I'd be dead instead of him. A small consolation for committing murder."

Talus regarded Temalus for a moment. "I see myself in you…in a way. You have feeling beyond those who surround you. I respect you more than the Overlord, your brother, or any other in the hierarchy here at Pack Ice Command. You carry a depth in your being that would be better served beyond the constraints of this place—beyond the reach of the Overlord."

Temalus threw his catch down his throat and cast his eyes toward Talus. "If only I could escape this."

"You could, you know," Talus said, stepping close, looking earnestly at Temalus. "I enjoy freedom on the ice plains of Planarseae. It is as life should be—to live it as you wish, free of the demands of others."

"And yet you come here annually."

Talus laughed. "I come here from time to time, that's true. I come here to see if there is any hope in our kind. And as of yet, I've found none. Your father will be the death of us all. Not just the Royal Emperors, but all penguins." He angled his head at Temalus. "If there were more like you— those who can see the folly of subjecting our brothers, whether they be K'tha, Cu-kisc, Gentoo or any clan—then maybe we'd survive in a world that is leaving us behind."

Temalus took another morsel and regarded Talus as he swallowed, then leaned close to the other. "There are those who would take your words as treasonous." Temalus pulled back and studied Talus' unreadable expression. "But I am not one of them. I hold no allegiance to my father's ideals. There are far better uses of our talents than to suppress those who are deemed weaker than ourselves. The sooner Antaean finds his way to the Great Sea, the better."

The rogue nodded. "If you would let go of your prejudices, there may be a way."

"Are you speaking of Lord Saeson?"

"The Cu-kisc have no desire for domination. They only want freedom. Lord Saeson will stop at nothing to achieve that end."

Temalus looked at Talus furtively. "And what of Aperion?"

Talus blew a sniff at the name. "Aperion will be controlled before long. While it is true that he desires to rule, Lord Saeson will bring his brother under control or kill him outright. It's unfortunate; Aperion could be a powerful ally, but he may prove too volatile to be an asset."

"Do you truly trust Lord Saeson? I saw what he is capable of."

"I don't trust anyone," Talus said with a trace of mirth. "But I believe he may be our best hope of ending Antaean's rule before it's too late."

Temalus was about to ask Talus what he meant by *too late*, but saw Diutes enter the room and abruptly ended any talk of overthrowing Antaean.

Talus spotted Diutes as well and changed the subject. "I liked your strategy. You let your opponent think he had weakened you and used that to your advantage. I'll have to remember that should the occasion ever present itself."

"He had weakened me. I got lucky," Temalus said, falling into the new subject with ease.

"Luck?" Talus scoffed. "The Ancients guide our actions and the results of them."

"Are you saying that what we think of as freewill are the whims of long dead penguins? That we're not responsible for our actions?" Temalus noticed Diutes shove a Chinstrap aside and tilt his head, trying to overhear their conversation.

"It's nothing of the sort." Talus stole a peek at Diutes and snickered. "Your brother is as subtle as a beached whale."

"I wouldn't go so far as to say even that." Temalus leaned over the trough and looked down the line at Diutes. "You could hear our conversation much better if you came to join us."

Diutes snapped his head stiff. "I care very little of your conversations, Temalus."

Talus gave him a doubtful look. "Please, join us, Lieutenant Diutes. Many voices can make a discussion much more interesting." He waved his flipper with invitation. Temalus questioned Talus with a look. "You'll be surprised what you can learn by simply listening," the rogue said and patted Temalus with reassurance.

"I didn't realize you were friends with my brother," Diutes said, giving Temalus a stern look.

Talus turned to Temalus. "Aside from knowledge of one another, we've only recently become acquainted. Are we friends, Temalus?"

Temalus studied the other for a moment, wondering what his motives were. From what he knew of the rogue, he wasn't one to make friends easily and generally looked down his beak at others. He worried that he may have said too much already. But if Talus truly could aid him and Liutites in ridding them of Antaean, then he would see where this new found relationship would take him. But he would have to swim carefully through a dangerous current. "Perhaps. Friendships develop over time, and only time will tell us."

"Truly spoken," Talus said, regarding him with eyes that belied intrigue and respect. He turned his attention to Diutes. "Now, Diutes, we were discussing the role the Ancients play in our lives, whether the legends are merely moral allegory or they actively participate in our daily lives. What say you?"

Diutes jerked his back. "The Ancients? The Ancients are dead. The only lesson they teach is that we all die." Talus laughed and Diutes bristled under the laughter.

Temalus looked at his brother wondering if his views had been brought on by Antaean's disregard as well. He had never taken the time to really get to know him, but Diutes had always been so caustic, and Temalus had followed Liutites' lead when interacting with him. He decided to at least try to see what made Diutes... well, Diutes. "That's a rather dismal outlook, don't you think?"

"Do you really think that if there were an afterlife, a spirit would give one guano heap about what happens to the living? Death holds its own concerns." Diutes eyed Temalus for a moment then looked at Talus.

Talus looked between the two. "I can't speak for the Ancients, you, Temalus, or anybody but myself, whether I'm hunting, being hunted, or simply roaming the plains; I see the work of the Ancients all around me. The landscape is moved by forces greater than ourselves, the seasons change, the moon and sun travel the sky, and do so whether we want them to or not, yet every season holds its own rewards. Huhellsus, the Shaper, blows the ice and reshapes the land; Calophus, the Trickster, undermines our greatest ambitions to ensure we do not become too proud; and, as you know, Diutes, the Great Sea reclaims us when our time ends. Are these the Ancients? I will never be able to say with certainty while I live. I may die and be proved a fool if death truly is the end. If it is, who would know I was a fool? Yet we believe that spring will return after the long dark of winter. We believe the sea will provide us with nourishment though it owes us nothing. While these are not great leaps of faith, we believe all of these things and more will come to pass without a single trace of doubt. And that is a testament of faith in itself."

"And what of purpose?" Temalus asked. "What is the purpose of suffering? Penguins lived for a thousand generations in relative peace until man arrived. A single seal can take a hundred lives, and an orca even more."

"When man arrived the clans were separated," Talus continued. "The Council of Thrace was a name, not a body. Each clan sat in their own complacency. The Kings died by the thousands, and no one acted. The Rockhoppers, the Emperors, the Chinstraps were killed for food for man and their beasts. No one acted. Farther north, eggs were taken by the millions—no one acted. The Council reformed and coincidentally the killing, the purge if you will, subsided. The Ancients rewarded us for our actions. The Phocids, the great seals, take what they need, as we take what we need. The strong survive, the weak are culled, and the strong beget the strong—that is the purpose."

"I've heard you kill for pleasure," Diutes said. "You kill without discretion. What is your purpose?"

Talus laughed. "Without discretion? The Ancients have blessed me with great strength and a mind for the fight. I make no apologies for who I am, and I never kill indiscriminately. If a seal attempts to make food of me, I'll destroy it. If a penguin attempts to disrespect me, I'll kill him without mercy. It is the same for a Petrel, Skua, or even a man. Threaten me, and I will take your life. I hold true to my nature. I am a hunter, a predator, I am K'tha, and that is my nature. Do I take pleasure in killing? Yes. When you are attuned to your nature, you are within the will of the Ancients. Do I seek confrontation? Only if it serves the ultimate purpose—to make me stronger."

Temalus nodded, finding a new respect for the rogue. He could be a powerful ally if he would just stick around and have a care in the day-to-day events at Pack Ice Command. "And what of your fellow K'tha, the Royal Emperors?"

Talus gave Temalus an amused look. "There is not a K'tha here who could or would challenge me. Life on the plains of Planarseae has made me strong and hard; life in Pack Ice Command has made the K'tha weak and soft."

"Are you calling me weak?" Diutes asked, puffing his chest.

"Yes," Talus replied, looking Diutes over. "You have strength of body, but not of mind. I could kill you as easily as I could kill a seal pup."

Diutes glared at Talus and looked as if he were about to challenge his assessment when Temalus spoke. "What of the Cu-kisc? Do you think you could end their threat?"

Talus blew a laugh through his beak. "The Cu-kisc aren't the threat. To be honest, I doubt I could defeat either Lord Saeson or Aperion. Like times of old, they are the strength of penguinkind."

Diutes laughed at his remark. "What of Theosidon? He defeated the Great Auks *and* ended the threat of the Cu-kisc a thousand generations ago. The Basileios are not the strength of penguinkind, the Royal Emperors are. They always have been and always will be."

"Are you so certain Theosidon was K'tha?"

"Are you saying he wasn't?" Diutes laughed. "This is where I leave you. You can listen to his delusions if you want, Temalus. I'm done."

"I apologize for threatening your beliefs...your faith," Talus said.

Diutes hesitated for a moment, then turned and left. Talus watched him go. "There's no hope in him."

"I've known that my whole life. Or at least suspected it," Temalus said with regret. "Now I know it with certainty."

"Don't hate him for it. We are what life makes us." Talus faced Temalus, looking at him sincerely. "There is hope in you. I see it. I would urge you to leave here—if not with me, then on your own—before it's too late."

"Too late for what?" Temalus eyed him suspiciously.

"For what? Not for what…for you."

"I'm sorry, Talus. I can't make changes by running away. I'll do what I can here." He looked at him for a moment. "My brother and I will be the change."

"The choice is yours to make." Talus looked at him with what could be seen as disappointment if not sadness on his face. "Liutites has a growing lust for power. If I've seen it, then I'm sure you have as well. How long do you think you can keep that buried within him? The desire for power is like an avalanche—it begins with a small trickle of snow, then soon becomes a raging torrent of destruction. It destroys everything in its path."

Doubt crossed Temalus' face. He had seen signs of it in Liutites, especially after he began cavorting with Mearna, and it had grown with the prize of supreme commander dangling in front of his beak. Still, Liutites was his brother and he would do what he could to save him from becoming the avalanche Talus spoke of. "He would never betray me," he said without conviction.

Talus nodded. "I believe you're correct. He never would…willingly." He straightened and met Temalus' eyes. "I'll be leaving PIC soon. Before I go, I will broker you a meeting with someone."

"Who?" Temalus asked, doing nothing to mask his suspicion.

"Someone who may change your mind. He is more reasonable than your previous meeting with him would suggest."

"You mean…" Temalus scanned the room, not wanting to say Lord

Saeson's name aloud again in case someone had taken an interest in their conversation.

Talus gave him a knowing look. "In the meantime," he said, raising his beak to Temalus. "Keep your beak sharp, know your brothers, and may the Ancients be at your side."

Temalus watched him leave without returning a word. *Know my brothers?* One of them was jealous, petty, desired power, was violent and firmly entrenched in the dogma of Royal Emperor superiority. The other wasn't jealous or petty, but everything else and twice as strong in him as the other. He knew his brothers. What he didn't know was whether he could save them.

# CHAPTER 16

A Royal Emperor messenger stood before the Overlord with his beak held high, waiting for the other to acknowledge his presence. Antaean looked at him, distracted by his presence for a moment, then turned his attention back to Mearna. "How long until the current brood hatches?"

"The egg tenders believe it is only a matter of hours." Mearna too glanced at the waiting messenger and turned her attention back to the Overlord. "These are the special breed, my lord. When they reach maturity, their coat will be pure black as you wished."

"You said that about the last clutch."

Mearna lowered her head briefly, as if swallowing her frustration. "Yes, there is always the chance of unexpected variations when breeding specific traits. However, this new group was bred from the successes of the previous two groups."

Antaean eyed her for a moment. "Is there anything else to report?"

"Two groups will be returning from the Trials within the week and will begin their training the day after arrival. The rookery is in order," Mearna said, sounding both formal and bored.

"Is there something else?" the Overlord asked again, keeping a steady gaze on her.

Mearna shifted under his examination then tightened her eyes defiantly.

"Should there be?"

After several heartbeats, Antaean looked away. "No. Inform me when the eggs begin to crack so that I may have them imprint upon me. That will be all." He barked for a guard and instructed him to double the post at the rookery as Mearna left.

Clayfus stepped from the shadows at the rear of the chamber after Mearna had gone. "Lord Antaean," he said, lowering his beak. "This messenger brings you information about the Council of Thrace."

"Did you allow him entry to my chambers?"

"Not precisely, my lord. He is new to his assignment, and perhaps a little eager."

Antaean looked over the messenger who stood with his beak held high as he had for the previous half hour. The messenger's beak trembled over a tired neck. "Who was his trainer?"

"Daekon, my lord," Clayfus answered, tilting his head, awaiting further instructions. He seemed to know what was coming.

"Have Daekon walk to the interior marker and back for not educating the messengers in proper etiquette. If he survives the march, he may keep his position." Antaean looked the messenger over with a satisfied countenance, knowing the trainer would not likely survive the grueling trek to the marker, the farthest inland a penguin could travel and still have the slimmest hope to survive the return trip. The path was littered with the mummified corpses of those who had failed. He felt it was a good lesson to teach the young messenger about failing to do a job properly. Antaean nodded to Clayfus, who in turn nodded to the messenger.

The Royal Emperor lowered his head in relief and worked his beak to ease his stiff muscles. "My lord, I have brought information about the Council of Thrace."

Antaean nodded for him to proceed.

"The warriors have disassembled the council."

"Details," the Overlord snapped. The Council of Thrace, the governing body overseeing the affairs of penguins since time immemorial had been a persistent stone in his gullet since the foundation of Pack Ice Command. With the council out of the way, he could bring the clans into his new alliance, and under his control. Though the message was good news, he was certain that the entirety of the message wouldn't be.

"The Rockhoppers, Gentoo, Blackfoot, Macaroni, and Snares have pledged to the alliance."

"And the others?" Antaean asked, eager to hear their ends.

"The Tawaki member was killed for refusing outright."

Antaean snorted. "Of course they would refuse. Cryftin instilled a rebellious attitude in them all," he said more to himself than Clayfus or the messenger.

"The other crested clans have deferred to their clan councils, but will likely join. The Humboldt and Galapagos were not present."

"The Humboldt and Galapagos clans are too few to matter, as are the Hoiho. What of the Magellanics?" Antaean asked, pacing at the foot of the dais. He turned to Clayfus. "The Magellanics are the largest clan north of the peninsula. We need them. They are key to my future plans." Clayfus nodded toward the messenger.

"Cuh-trük has taken the offer to T'Cuh-ka, the clan elder," the messenger continued when the Overlord returned his attention to him. "She assures us they will join, but only after seeing to the relocation of a particular nesting area bothered by human raiders."

"And the Emperors?" Antaean asked with a disinterested voice, awaiting the answer he already knew was coming.

"They refused, and as per your orders, their council members were allowed to leave unharmed."

The Overlord turned to Clayfus. "The Emperors are far too passive."

Clayfus lowered his head. "If pushed, they could pose a problem, my lord," he said in a whisper. "Their numbers alone could challenge your rule. And the reverence the lesser clans have always shown them—"

"Which is why I will let them be for now," the Overlord snapped. "The time will come when they will see the error of their ways." Antaean noticed the messenger still standing at attention. He dismissed him with a wave of his flipper and watched Clayfus escort him from the chamber.

Clayfus returned and stood before the Overlord, awaiting further orders. Antaean descended his dais and waddled to the pedestal holding the Leopard Seal skull. He stood in admiration of his past kill for several moments before bringing his attention back to the attendant. "It has been too long since I have drawn blood from the hunt," he said, to which Clayfus only returned a small nod. "I should have killed Saeson, but I have become too dependent on my guards. I am weakened by them."

"You are not weak, my lord," Clayfus said, not pulling his eyes from Antaean's.

"True, but my skill for the fight has deteriorated. I must amend that." He spread his flippers wide and flapped them several times. "If I were to be challenged for the dais in this state, I may lose."

Clayfus cocked his head. "Who would challenge you? Certainly not Talus. He is perhaps the strongest, but he has no desire for rule. Liutites?"

Antaean lifted his head toward the domed ceiling examining the translucent blue ice fade into white at the apex. "He alone has the lust for power. But he is not ready, and he knows it. But the day will come when he will do so." He pulled his gaze away from the ceiling.

"Then you must prepare for that eventuality, my lord." Clayfus lowered his beak against his chest.

"True, as do you."

"My loyalty is to Royal Emperor blood, my lord. I cannot intervene. I serve our lineage." Clayfus met Antaean's black eyes.

"And for now, you serve your Overlord as well." Antaean returned to studying the seal skull. "The skull of the Phocid serves to show not only my power over our enemies, but our domination of those who once hunted us…over nature."

"Which reminds me," Clayfus said, followed by a pair of clacks of his beak. Another equally gaunt penguin entered from the antechamber hidden in the shadows at the rear of the main room. The newcomer carried a wad of seal-leather in its beak, which it placed at Clayfus' feet and then scurried from the room.

Antaean watched curiously as Clayfus unwrapped the skins. "What do you have for me?"

"For all of us, my lord." Clayfus pulled a Petrel skull from the wad with his beak and carefully placed it on an empty pedestal adjacent to the other. He presented the trophy with a wave of his flipper and bowed. "A symbol of conquest over those who have fed on the young since our time began, my lord."

Antaean studied the skull. "So small for a creature that wreaked such havoc." He nodded his approval and returned to his dais, lost in thought.

Clayfus stood before the dais, waiting for further instructions. When none came, he cleared his throat. "Will there be anything else, my lord?"

The Overlord raised his head from his contemplation over the dangers of small things. "Yes, in fact. Summon two warriors for sparring. Then I want you to summon my commanders: General Liutites, Lieutenant-Generals Biochilles and Persus, Colonel Leotholis, Commandant Temalus, and Lieutenant Diutes and Captain Astramachos. It is time to unveil my plans."

"Will they bear witness to your sparring?"

Antaean considered letting them watch but thought better of it. Most had never seen him in combat. If they watched, they might find a way to exploit his technique if they gathered the fortitude to challenge him for the dais. "No. Have them wait in the hall. Let them listen."

Clayfus tilted his head slightly. "And what if, however unlikely, you should fall during your bout?"

Antaean regarded Clayfus for a moment. Anger flashed across his face, but was quickly replaced by a resigned calm. "In that event, I would no longer be Overlord and you should name my successor," he said with a confidence that told the other the outcome was not in doubt. The Overlord watched Clayfus exit the chamber then returned to studying his trophies. He stared at the skulls thoughtfully. "One day we shall have dominion over our world." He looked to a third pedestal free of any adornment and pondered what skull should fill the void.

# CHAPTER 17

Lieutenant Diutes approached his brothers in the corridor outside of the Overlord's chamber. "*Commandant* Temalus," he said, doing little to mask the contempt in his voice. "What responsibilities come with your new rank?"

Temalus sighed and turned from examining a recently completed relief sculpture of a Rockhopper penguin, cringing at his brother's condescending tone. As if Diutes needed another reason to expand his already over-inflated jealousy. "As of now, it appears to be a title only. But if I feel it becomes any concern of yours, I'll be sure to let you know…Lieutenant."

Diutes gave Temalus a scornful glare, then snorted. "I doubt it will ever be my concern."

"Then why bother asking?" Temalus shook his head then returned to studying the artwork created by Adélie penguins. He pushed past Diutes and walked farther down the hall, and stopped behind an Adélie standing on an ice scaffold who was adding the final touches on a King penguin relief. Temalus noticed that all of the sculptures were at eye level with most Royal Emperors. "I guess the art isn't for the masses," he muttered quietly to himself.

The Adélie turned at the sound of Temalus' voice. "I'm sorry, sir?"

Temalus shook his head. "Nothing. I just noticed that all of your work is placed higher than most penguins are tall. It won't be seen by many."

The Adélie regarded Temalus for a moment. "I doubt that many of us will ever enter this hall anyway," she said, then turned back to her work.

"It would be just as easy for us to look down at it," Temalus said absently.

"It's always easier for some to look down at things," the Adélie said without looking back. "Others are always forced to look up."

Temalus stared at the back of the artisan's black head, watching her worn beak chip away at the ice with the ease of a practiced artist. He stole a glance toward the other Royal Emperors down the hall, then leaned close to the Adélie. "You create spectacular work. I'm envious."

The Adélie peeked back at Temalus. "Don't be envious of what you could do yourself."

"I doubt I will ever have the opportunity in this…" Temalus waved his flippers toward the walls, but caught himself before he said anymore on the subject and began to walk away.

"The choice is yours," the Adélie said without pulling her beak away from the work.

Temalus jerked at the Adélie's words. He sniffed a laugh, thinking of Talus. Approaching Liutites, who stood as near to the entrance of the Overlord's chamber as Clayfus would allow, Temalus looked back at the artist once more.

Liutites raised a suspicious eye when Temalus arrived by his side. "What were you speaking to the Adélie about?"

"Art," Temalus said without elaborating.

Liutites stared at him for a moment then turned his attention to the sounds of fighting echoing from within the Overlord's chamber. After a moment of listening to the grunts and wails of combat, he returned his interest to Temalus. "You shouldn't socialize with the lesser clans. It wouldn't do for them to see us as equals or to show that you see them that way."

Temalus snorted derisively. "I don't see them as equals," he lied. The fact was, he did see the so-called lesser clans as equals, and was beginning to see them as more. The years of indoctrination had begun to fade away. Temalus wondered what had caused the change. Was it his talks with Talus? Was it the ruthlessness of being forced to kill for his father's entertainment? Or was it seeing Liutites' growing lust for power? He wasn't sure. It could have been a combination of all, or none of it. A small spark of empathy had risen in his heart, and there was no going back to the way things were.

Turning his ear toward the sounds of fighting, and listening to yet another penguin suffer for no other reason than to puff up the Overlord's ego, his eyes met Liutites' and in that moment, he knew what he had to do. He would help his brother wrest the dais from their father, then he would leave and hope Liutites would be a more benevolent ruler. He didn't know where he would go with any certainty. His newly hatched purpose was still too young to know such things. Perhaps he would join Talus on the plains, or perhaps not. Maybe his future lay along a different path. Temalus averted his gaze. There would be no more killing on his part at the Overlord's behest, and he would live his life as he chose.

"Sounds like the Overlord is doling out punishment to someone," Biochilles said, interrupting Temalus' thoughts.

Liutites choked on a laugh before Temalus could reply. "I'm sure it isn't punishment. It's merely a display designed to intimidate us. Why else would he have us wait outside? Isn't that right, Clayfus?"

"The Overlord has motives I am not privy to, General Liutites." Clayfus stared unflinching at Liutites as the howl of a dying penguin echoed from the chamber. "If you are intimidated, the onus is yours alone."

Liutites leaned close to Clayfus. "I am not intimidated," he said in a low, threatening voice.

Clayfus tilted his head with a shrug. "By me, I am certain you are not." He lifted his beak to the sound of spears cracking together, followed by a loud grunt. Silence fell over the hall and Clayfus excused himself.

Temalus shook his head at Liutites. "Does it really matter why the Overlord is doing whatever he's doing in there? Everything he does is done solely to bolster his own power and pride or to keep others under his foot."

"As it should be," Colonel Leotholis chimed in from behind the two. "He is our Overlord. And he has led us into a greater era. He has accomplished what even the great councils of the past could not achieve. Dissention is the great enemy to our society. A show of authority or power, however the means, is necessary…from time to time." Leotholis bowed his head to Liutites.

Liutites shot Temalus a warning glare, telling him to say no more. Temalus ignored the hint. But seeing Leotholis' new found respect and loyalty to Liutites, inspired by their earlier encounter, he changed his tone for fear of being seen as disloyal. "You are correct, Colonel. What I was saying is that we should—"

"What you were saying doesn't matter," Diutes broke in. "You are all cowards. The Overlord knows of and expects disloyalty in his commanders. He cannot rule forever. One of us will become the next Overlord so why fear saying it out loud when it's what we all want?"

"Do you think *you* will be the next Overlord, Diutes?" Biochilles scoffed.

"If the opportunity presents itself." Diutes stepped toward the other. He stopped and looked back at Liutites. "Though some seem to think they already have the title in their beak."

Liutites stared at Diutes for a moment, letting silence hang between them. "Mind your tone, Lieutenant."

Diutes jerked in response. "General, we are all just penguins talking here—casual conversation among equals." He took a step back in case Liutites lashed out.

"Don't fool yourself into thinking you are my equal." Liutites fixed Diutes with an angry glare, causing the lieutenant to take another step back.

Seeing the tension rise, Temalus stepped between the two, as he so often had. "I wonder what's taking them so long. It sounds like the fight, or whatever it was, is over."

Diutes looked at Temalus and turned his attention away from Liutites. "What about you, Persus? Always the silent fool. You haven't had much to say."

Temalus shook his head at Diutes, wondering why he always felt the need to antagonize others. If he would try to forge alliances, he might actually raise his station at Pack Ice Command. But that was Diutes' nature, and he knew there was nothing he could do to change him. Temalus decided he wouldn't waste his time trying.

Persus fixed his eyes on Temalus for a second then looked at Diutes. "It is sometimes better to be silent and thought a fool than to open one's beak and prove it," Persus said, drawing a laugh from the others.

With the insult lost on him, Diutes laughed as well. "Come now, you don't want to become Overlord?"

Persus shook his head. "I have no desire to be Overlord. Supreme commander would be fine with me."

Temalus snapped his head toward Liutites, who remained oddly impassive to Persus' remark. He briefly wondered how Persus had learned about the title when so few knew of it. But then again, many Royal Emperors had their means of finding out information. Sometimes the best way to let a secret be known was to say there was one. It was a wonder the whole of Pack Ice Command didn't know about it. Temalus was about to make a further comment on the subject when Clayfus returned.

"If you are done bickering amongst yourselves, the Overlord will see you now," the scrawny aide said, then motioned for them to enter.

# CHAPTER 18

General Liutites led the procession to the foot of the Overlord's dais and stood waiting with his beak raised. The others stood in a line beside the general, carrying the same salute. Temalus followed suit but not before looking at the bodies of two dead Royal Emperor warriors lying beside one another; one with a broken spear lodged in his chest, the other with bloody holes where its eyes had once been. Temalus scanned the floor quickly, making sure not to step on the missing eyes. He briefly wondered if the Overlord had eaten them. Who knew the depths of his father's insanity?

The Overlord stepped forward and nodded almost imperceptibly. The line of commanders lowered their beaks in response. Clayfus went to Antaean's side and Mearna came out from the dark recesses behind the dais, followed by two elite guards. After a brief pause, the Overlord took another step closer. He motioned with his flipper and two guards at the entrance saw to closing the door. When the slow grinding of ice ceased, Overlord Antaean began. "This day marks the beginning of a new era in penguin history. The Council of Thrace is no more and the Penguin Defense Alliance, under my rule, shall govern the affairs for all of penguinkind."

The announcement caused a stir among the commanders. Temalus exchanged looks with Liutites then turned his attention back to the Overlord. The words, however grand they may have seemed, stirred a sour feeling to rise in Temalus' gut. The sensation gave way to a sense of dread. He wasn't sure why. Perhaps he saw it as the end of civility as far as he had known it.

"What I'm about to say must be guarded with the greatest confidentiality for the time being," the Overlord continued. He eyed each of the penguins carefully, warning them with a simple ocular gesture, making certain they understood the seriousness of his words. "The time has come for us to retake the homeland. For far too long man has had free reign in our world. In days of old, the men came and killed penguins by the millions. They performed atrocities against our forbearers that only the most depraved minds could invent. And now they come by the hundreds—by the thousands. They build their structures and they stay, taking residence in our homeland. More and more come every season. How long until they decide we are in their way?"

Temalus shifted slightly and peeked at Liutites. He looked beyond the Overlord and saw Mearna staring at Liutites. She glanced at Temalus and quickly averted her eyes, looking straight ahead, no longer staring at his brother. *She will try to drive a wedge between us*, Temalus thought. A tightening in his chest prodded his thoughts to Talus' words. He should leave before it's too late. Temalus returned his attention to the Overlord's speech, listening half-heartedly to what he already suspected was to come.

"And it is with history in mind that I have decided on a course of action," Antaean said, his voice growing louder. "We will strike at them before they grow in numbers and strength."

The line of commanders stood silent, each lost in their own thoughts over the implications of the Overlord's designs. The penguins hadn't engaged in warfare since ancient times during the Great Auk Wars. Fighting seals, other penguins, or birds of prey was one thing, fighting man with his machinery was another.

After several moments of silence, Leotholis raised his head to the Overlord. "My lord, do we have the numbers for such an undertaking? I've heard rumors that men dominate the rest of the known world and their numbers are uncountable, not to mention the power of their machines."

"They are not rumors, Colonel Leotholis. Their numbers are equal to the krill in the sea," Antaean answered.

"Then how do you propose we fight such an enemy, my lord?" Captain Astramachos asked. "We, the K'tha—I mean the Royal Emperors—number only in the thousands."

"I'm glad you asked, Captain Astramachos. Our new alliance will bring a swift end to the conflict. The Chinstraps number in the millions, the Adélie, the Kings, the Gentoo and others, they will do the bulk of the fighting."

"My lord," Lieutenant-General Persus interjected. "The lesser clans are weak and unmotivated to fight. They are not warriors. It will be slaughter."

The Overlord hissed a disturbing laugh. "You are correct. But when the time comes, I assure you that they will fight. Their commanders will be indoctrinated into the Royal creed and they will pass on that knowledge. It is already true for the Chinstraps and the Kings."

"But my lord, they will still be ill-equipped to fight such a foe," Leotholis countered. "If they should fail…"

"True, Lieutenant-General. But they will be the face of the enemy. If they should fail, man will see them as such. And with the lesser clans gone, we will dominate the Southern Realm, free of competition. The Royal Emperors will win whatever the outcome."

Temalus fought back his shock. The Overlord's war would bring about the extinction of every other penguin clan on Earth. And did he really think the humans would stop their killing at the other clans? He resisted blurting out his feelings on the Overlord's plans. All it would do is get him killed. Temalus hoped he hid the hatred for his father burning in his eyes. There was no doubt left. They had to kill the Overlord before they all died. When he felt he could no longer hide his frustration, Liutites spoke up, much to Temalus' relief.

"My lord, where do we, your commanders, fit in with your designs?" Liutites asked while stealing a glance at Temalus, seeming to sense that his brother was about to say something ill-advised.

The Overlord watched Liutites for several heartbeats before replying. "As you know, I have already begun construction on several fortifications encircling the homeland. What you should know, as well, is these forward command posts will be the base of operations for the duration of the conflict. Each outpost will be under the command of a Royal Emperor general. From there, pertinent information will be relayed to and from Pack Ice Command. Forces will be directed to the respective regions as deemed necessary."

"And will you be the director of such activities?" Liutites asked.

Temalus noticed Liutites' claws scratching at the ice. *Here it comes.* Liutites was about to ask, or demand to be commander of the Penguin Defense Alliance. Though he wanted to stop him, to speak to him and make him see the folly of the Overlord's plans, he knew there was nothing he could say to stop it and his brother would give himself over to his lust for power.

"I will appoint a supreme commander to oversee the operation. Someone who I deem fit to carry the responsibility." Antaean met Liutites' eyes, seeming to know his desire for the position.

Temalus watched his brother. The Overlord had him now. But he didn't abandon hope in saving Liutites. There was still the possibility that his brother would want to overthrow the Overlord before the war began. Temalus looked at Mearna, noticing a glint of satisfaction in her eyes. He wondered if perhaps the Overlord had conspired with her to plant the idea in Liutites' mind. There was no way to know.

"Then, my lord, I would like to be considered for the rank of supreme commander," Liutites said, standing firm and proud before the Overlord and especially Mearna.

"I will take it under consideration, General Liutites," the Overlord said.

He looked to others in line. "Is anyone else interested in the position?"

Temalus looked at Diutes, who had remained conspicuously silent through the proceedings. He was surprised when the lieutenant didn't step forward. Temalus guessed he had his own ideas for power and glory. In fact he could read it in his eyes.

"I would like to be considered," Persus said, raising his beak to the Overlord, but not before taking a quick glance at Liutites.

Antaean looked over the line of officers. "Is there anyone else?" When nobody spoke up, he lifted his staff and ground the butt against the ice. "Very well. Persus and Liutites will meet in combat to determine who attains the position of supreme commander. Be ready in the morning."

"That isn't much time to prepare, my lord," Persus said. He looked to Liutites for support. Liutites ignored the statement, and kept his eye on Mearna.

"As a commander, you should be prepared at all times," the Overlord barked. "Do you withdraw you request?"

"No, my lord. I am prepared," Persus answered, taking a step back at the Overlord's sharp reprimand.

Antaean narrowed his eyes at Persus. "Good," he said in a voice oozing with the anticipation of carnage on his behalf. The Overlord stepped closer and met each of the officers' stoic expressions. "You will be responsible for finding warriors under your command to fill needed positions. I need commanders for the outposts, regimental officers—those who are most equipped for leadership."

Liutites raised his beak. "My lord, do you have any officers in mind to command the outposts?"

"Perhaps, General. Would you like to recommend someone?"

"Yes, my lord." Liutites took a deep breath. "I recommend Commandant Temalus."

The Overlord stared at Liutites for a few moments in tense silence. His eyes fell on Diutes, who gave Liutites a look of detest and betrayal. Antaean clicked in amusement. "Very well. Commandant Temalus, when Forward Command One is complete, you will be promoted to the rank of general and command the first outpost."

Temalus looked sharply at Liutites, then to the Overlord. He then met Diutes' angry glare, and reluctantly raised his beak. "I will fulfill my duties to the best of my ability, my lord." His gaze fell back on Liutites for a moment and he wondered what his brother could have been thinking. He looked at Diutes and felt the rift between them grow wider; it was almost palpable—a living, breathing creature, a manifestation of hatred. The thought of it made him shiver, and he knew, with certainty, that it was time to leave Pack Ice Command and leave Liutites to his fate.

The Overlord returned to his position on the center of the dais and handed Clayfus his staff. "Our meeting is done. I do not need to remind you that what we have discussed does not leave these walls. In a year's time I will make the announcement to the alliance, and the penguins will rise and retake their rightful place as lords of the Southern Realm."

Temalus watched Mearna and Liutites exchange furtive glances, then followed the others from the Overlord's chamber. Once outside, he tried to stop Diutes and tell him he didn't want command of any outpost, but Diutes ignored him, brushed him aside, and stomped angrily down the hall. Temalus let Liutites pass without saying a word, then looked to the Adélie artificer putting the final touches on her work. He stood behind her, watching flakes of ice fall to the wayside. "The choice is mine," he said quietly. "And I have made it." He turned and walked away, and the Adélie watched him go.

# CHAPTER 19

Liutites stormed into Mearna's private chamber. "How did Persus know about the position of supreme commander?" he demanded.

"Liutites," she said in her most placating voice. "As you know, the secrets of one can be the gossip of many within these walls."

"I don't care about the many. You told me this was privileged information. That no one knew. And now it seems half the compound already knew."

Mearna watched Liutites for several heartbeats. "Whether or not Persus knew beforehand matters little. Once the Overlord made the announcement, he would have wanted the title. I simply told you before anyone else knew."

"Did you tell him?" Liutites asked, his voice filled with accusation. He moved closer to Mearna.

Mearna matched his steps, moving closer as well. "You don't achieve rank around here without having spies. You of all penguins should know that." Her eyes matched the cold surrounding them. "Do you fear Persus? Did you come to my chambers, throwing your allegations of treachery at me, because you're afraid of him?" Liutites' eyes flashed with rage, but Mearna stood her ground.

A moment later Liutites' expression softened. "No," he said, turning away. "The position should be mine without debate. I don't fear Persus. In fact, he's one of the few with the Grip that I respect. He's intelligent and a good leader. It will be a waste to kill him."

Mearna circled Liutites. "Do you think he has mutual respect for you?"

"Does it matter?" Liutites snapped. "The Overlord's word is law. I will do what I must."

The two stood in silence until Mearna turned away. "You got Temalus promoted. I'm sure that didn't sit well with Diutes."

Liutites didn't speak at first. He did what he did to protect Temalus, knowing full well the back-stabbing that was to come as the Royal Emperor junior officers vied to achieve their rank. "Diutes will have his own command in due time. As of now, he is unfit. Perhaps he always will be. But I have no doubt he will somehow rise above the others. And I won't allow him to challenge Temalus for the command. There are a dozen outposts. He can have one of the others."

"You slighted him in front of the others *and* the Overlord. I doubt he will let it rest. He might be dangerous." Mearna walked to the back of her chamber and turned off of her lanterns with her beak.

Liutites watched her walk then slowly followed. "Diutes lacks any degree of cunning. He knows if he tried to move against Temalus I would kill him without a second thought, if Temalus didn't do it first."

Mearna met Liutites and began guiding him toward an antechamber at the rear of her room. "Temalus doesn't have the fire you have. He's intelligent and compassionate. Intelligence could serve him well, but his compassion could be used against him."

"Did he show Reticles compassion?" Liutites countered.

"Did he have a choice?" Mearna quickly replied.

"Do any of us?" Liutites turned away and stared at the doorway. He needed to speak with Temalus. There had been a change in his brother's demeanor. He had sensed it and wanted to find out why.

Mearna stood between Liutites and the doorway. "We all have choices, Liutites. The trick is knowing what to do with the ones we are given." She gave him a coy look. "Like your choice to be here with me."

Liutites looked at Mearna, then back to the doorway. He made a motion toward the antechamber. The thought of Temalus' safety fought with Mearna's allure. Liutites turned away and marched to the exit.

"Where are you going?" Mearna asked, not masking her annoyance.

"I have to see Temalus," Liutites said walking with his head down, lost in thought.

Mearna rushed to get in front of him. "Your brother can take care of himself. You can't protect him forever."

Liutites stopped and faced Mearna. "Who said anything about protecting him?"

"It's in your eyes. He is your weakness. Your brother is holding you back."

Liutites leaned close to Mearna, his countenance turning fierce and determined. "Nothing and no one will hold me back." He turned sharply and left Mearna alone in the darkness.

# CHAPTER 20

General Liutites found Temalus walking alone near a passage leading to the lower levels. He watched him for a moment before calling to him. Temalus jerked to a stop at hearing his name called. "Why are you down here alone?" Liutites asked when he approached.

Temalus took a deep breath. "Because I *wanted* to be alone," he answered. His tone was unusually terse.

Liutites hesitated before speaking. It was obvious that his brother wasn't in the mood for company. "I can go if you want me to." Thoughts of Mearna filled his head. Thoughts of what could have been instead of trekking through the cold empty halls made him regret his choice until those thoughts fell on her words. Temalus was not holding him back. He felt a twinge of anger well up. *What did she know?* Mearna was a hanger-on. She would clutch his tail-feathers until he became Overlord so she could keep her place of power. Liutites would allow it as long as she remained useful. And there was no doubt that she was useful. She controlled the rookeries, and there was no way around that.

"No...it's fine. You can stay," Temalus said, snapping Liutites out of his wandering thoughts. "What brings you here? You weren't very talkative after our meeting with your father."

"Our father, you mean," Liutites said, trying to find the humor he shared with Temalus, but his reply came across as strained and angry. He looked down the hall to see if anyone was near.

"Try as I may, I can't seem to forget that fact." Temalus tilted his head, waiting for Liutites to answer his question. When the answer didn't come, he asked again. "Why are you here? Was Mearna busy conspiring with someone else?"

Liutites snapped his head toward Temalus. "Conspiring? I'm certain she may have ulterior motives, but for the moment, those motives serve me, as well."

Temalus turned away and stared down the corridor to where he had been heading. "Why did you put me in command of the outpost?" he asked without looking back.

"To protect you," Liutites answered without hesitation.

"Protect me?" Temalus snapped back, turning to face his brother. "By putting me on the front lines of the Overlord's ridiculous plan? How can we hope—" He looked down the hall as if expecting someone to be listening and lowered his voice. "How can we depose the Overlord if I'm stuck in an outpost miles away from here?"

"There is still time. Forward Command One won't be completed anytime soon. And if it is, it is the closest to Pack Ice Command. With me as supreme commander, I will have the messengers to use as I see fit."

"If the messengers are loyal to you." Temalus hesitated. "And *if* you are supreme commander."

"Are you saying Persus can defeat me?" Liutites asked, trying to maintain his calm. He had heard enough from Mearna and was loath to hear anything similar from the one penguin he was closest to.

"No, no." Temalus shook his head adamantly. "I have no doubt you can defeat Persus, though his death will be a great loss to us all. All I'm saying is what if the Overlord doesn't promote you? How do you think it would look if his second in command is a true K'tha—one without the Grip. That flies in the face of his ideals of Royal Emperor superiority."

"When I defeat Persus there will be none who would dare challenge me…none who could."

Temalus shook his head and took a few steps away before turning back to face Liutites. "This war against the humans is folly. You know that. Whatever small victories we achieve will be returned to us tenfold by the humans. It will be the death of us all. And not just the other clans. Man will come and they will destroy us. And what will this all be for? Legacy? There will be no legacy, no glory, no history if we're all dead."

Liutites inhaled and held the breath for several moments before letting it out in a long, tired hiss. "And what do you propose we do? The Overlord's word is law, and the tides are already in motion."

"We need to act sooner rather than later. Once I'm stationed at Forward Command, there will be little I can do to help."

Liutites shook his head. "As I already said, the outpost isn't ready yet. But I doubt I can convince Mearna to help us just yet. As of right now, it will take more than just the two of us. With the Overlord's plans revealed, there will be those who will try to stop us."

"You don't need her. I don't trust her, and you shouldn't, either. She's too close to the Overlord, and like you said, she has ulterior motives." Temalus cocked his head, his eyes following the length of the corridor.

Liutites followed his gaze. "What? Is there someone there?"

Temalus watched the walls at the end of the corridor for several breaths before shaking his head. "I believe we can get help. But you would have to trust me, and most importantly, you have to let go of your prejudices."

"I don't have prejudices without good reason." Liutites averted his eyes.

"Are you certain of that?"

Liutites stared at his brother. He didn't like the way things were going any more than him, but any feelings of superiority over other clans, in his opinion, were well founded. Why else would the other clans join them so easily? What other reason would the Basileios have to hide in the shadows if it weren't for fear of the Royal Emperor's dominance? As he continued to read Temalus' expression, realization dawned. "Are you saying we should seek the aide of Lord Saeson?"

Temalus said nothing as he continued to meet Liutites' eyes.

"No," Liutites said, shaking his head. "I want to usurp the Overlord as much as anyone, but I will not consider an alliance with our enemy."

"It's the only way, brother. The Overlord is too well entrenched in his power. And you do not have the loyalty of the warrior caste yet." Temalus leaned in, looking at Liutites even as his brother tried to turn away.

"Who filled your head with these ideas?" Liutites asked, even though he was sure who was responsible. He had seen the way Talus had spoken to Temalus, seen the way he inflated his brother's pride.

"My ideas are my own," Temalus barked. He let out a tired sigh. "I can't do this for much longer. You…you were made for this." He waved his flippers to walls of Pack Ice Command. "I'm leaving this place. Whether it is after you become Overlord or before is up to you."

"Where will you go? With Talus? Will you live your life as a rogue, fighting for every scrap of food, praying to the Ancients for protection from the Orca?"

"No, I will not go with Talus. He seeks conflict, and that's a life I do not want. And that's why I'm leaving. I don't want conspiracy, back-stabbing, and war. There are others who want the same as I do. But they are too afraid to make that change."

"I will not make an alliance with the Cu-kisc to make that change." Liutites snorted while shaking his head.

"It is the only way. I have no doubt that this war will be the end of us, and I think you know it, too. You worry about legacy. What better legacy to last through the ages than making peace with an ancient enemy? What better legacy than saving, not only the K'tha, but all penguins? You would be revered through the ages. Just let go of your ambition and work to make it better. If not for your legacy, then for me."

Liutites stared into Temalus' pleading eyes. There had to be another way to defeat their father. He would die before lowering himself to seek the aid of the Cu-kisc. But the more Liutites considered his brother's words, the more he realized he didn't know why he hated the Cu-kisc. It was something all Royal Emperors had been taught since they were hatched. And Temalus... did he really believe they could broker a peace between the two clans? If Temalus was wrong and the Cu-kisc betrayed them, Liutites knew his legacy would be that of the fool who led his enemy to victory over his own kind. But he couldn't betray Temalus. Liutites had promised to be with him always. And in that promise he felt a spark of hope. "Are you certain the Lord Saeson will join us?"

"I'm not certain of anything."

"I take it you were headed this way to meet with him?" Liutites asked. He paced from one side of the corridor to the other, his mind poring over the possibilities.

"Yes," Temalus answered plainly.

Liutites stopped pacing and squared himself toward Temalus. "Do what you can. But I am not committing myself to this end just yet. This time tomorrow I will be supreme commander and I will have control of the warriors. Give me two days. If all goes well, I will challenge Antaean for the dais and avoid all of this."

"And if it doesn't go well?" Temalus stood with his chest puffed, the hope as plain in his eyes as the white of his feathers.

"Then we'll do it your way." After a moment of quiet, Liutites nodded to him. "Go. Plant the seed. Tell no one, and for your sake, do not get caught."

Temalus nodded, turned away, and hurried along the corridor to the underworld of Pack Ice Command. Liutites watched him go then turned back the way he had come. Lost in his thoughts, Liutites didn't notice Diutes hiding in the shadows of an alcove as he passed.

# CHAPTER 21

Diutes scurried through the halls of Pack Ice Command mulling over the exchange between Liutites and Temalus. His mind twisted in knots as he tried to puzzle out what to do with the information. His first instinct was to go straight to the Overlord and tell all he had learned. But what would that get him? A promotion maybe, command of an outpost, perhaps, but little else. What Diutes wanted was to see Liutites, and especially Temalus, punished. Temalus had always acted altruistic, like he cared little for power. But he had shown otherwise. Hadn't he killed Reticles without a second thought or remorse? And with Liutites' aid he had been given command of Forward Command One. And now the two of them were conspiring to overthrow Antaean, and worse, do so with the help of Lord Saeson.

"I should have Forward Command One," Diutes muttered to himself, his thoughts falling back on his lust for power over conspiracy. As he traveled along the corridors with no destination in mind, lost in his silent fuming, Diutes blundered into a pair of Gentoo, nearly knocking one to the ground. "Watch where you're going," Diutes snapped, ready to strike the offending Gentoo.

"Watch where we're going?" one of the Gentoo snapped back. "If you were watching where you were going we wouldn't have to watch where we're going."

Diutes sneered at the impudent Gentoo and nearly lashed out until he spotted a dozen more headed toward him. Unsure how the Overlord would take to him reprimanding a member of his fledgling alliance with the Gentoo, he restrained his impulses. He looked at the gathering Gentoo, then down at the nuisance standing before him with its beak held high in defiance. Diutes clenched his beak, resisting his violent urges even more. Pack Ice Command seemed to be filling with more and more of the *lesser* clans every day. "This place has become infested," he grumbled to himself.

"Infested?" the Gentoo asked. "Infested by what?"

Diutes turned away, not wanting to give the annoying Gentoo any more of his time. He took a step, but spun back toward the Gentoo, who was watching him with an amused glint in his eyes. "Infested by you," Lieutenant Diutes barked.

"Bah! One Gentoo does not make an infestation. There are more Royal Emperors in this command center than Gentoo. Who is the infestation?"

Diutes quivered with a building rage. "Not one Gentoo, idiot. All of you. Gentoo, Chinstraps, Adélie." He watched the other penguin, who seemed to be taking delight in his anger, and thought of what the Overlord had said. The lesser clans would be the face of the enemy to the humans. *They'll be dead soon enough.* He had other problems to deal with.

"You may outnumber us here," the Gentoo said, waving his flippers at the walls. "But out there," he motioned with his head, "our numbers are like the snowflakes that fall in winter."

*Snowflakes?* The word struck a chord in Diutes' mind. He couldn't quite place it; it was on the edge of a memory lost in the haze of anger with his brothers. Diutes stared at the Gentoo for another moment. "Just watch it," he said, then walked away.

"Hah!" the Gentoo blurted. "Watch what? Should I watch where I'm going or watch it?"

Diutes ignored the Gentoo's babbling and continued on his way. "Snowflake," he said quietly as he tried to figure out the significance of the word, his brain aching with unaccustomed intense thought. After several more minutes of deliberations, his eyes flashed wide at remembering his conversation with Talus. The rogue had told him to be the snowflake—that a snowflake could move a glacier. Diutes struggled with the metaphor as he continued his aimless walking. A glacier was a powerful force that appeared unmovable, this much he knew. Talus had told him to be the single snowflake that set the glacier moving. If he was the snowflake, then what was his glacier? Diutes pondered on until he understood. Liutites and Temalus were the glacier. But how could he move them? His mind swirled, dizzy with thought.

Diutes found an isolated nook and squatted down to think and reason out how he could achieve removing both of his brothers. If he moved against one brother, the other would come to his aid. Maybe Liutites would lose in combat to Persus. Persus was strong and intelligent, and he had the Grip. But Diutes knew better. Liutites had never come close to losing a match. In fact his matches rarely lasted longer than a few minutes before he killed his opponents. What if he could get the Overlord to match his brothers against each other? But there were rules in place. Not many, but the Overlord had dictated that no siblings should meet each other in combat unless by direct challenge. Diutes sat and turned the questions over in his head repeatedly. The answer seemed to be there, at the tip of his beak, dangling like a fish waiting to be consumed.

Diutes knew that by this time tomorrow, Liutites would be supreme commander and both of his brothers would be untouchable. But he also knew the pair were scheming to betray them all. *Be the snowflake.* The words ran through his head once again. But how could he? How could he nudge the glacier forward? "Unless…" Diutes whispered. "Unless I'm thinking of the wrong glacier." He stood with a jerk.

Surveying the halls to make certain Liutites was nowhere near, Diutes firmed his resolve and marched toward the Overlord's chamber. It was time to move the glacier.

# CHAPTER 22

Temalus stood outside the doorway leading to the lower reaches, keeping a cautious eye on the length of the hall behind him. There would be no going back once he entered Lord Saeson's domain. He wished Talus would show up and guide him to the Lord of the Misshapen, if not for direction then at least for protection, but it was too late for that. It was his own choice, and he would undertake this endeavor on his own. He knew that if Talus had misjudged Lord Saeson's desire for peace, or his ability to see reason, or if the Cu-kisc were simply the murderous lot Overlord Antaean had made them out to be, he'd be dead and any hope he held of saving Liutites or the future of penguinkind would die with him.

Temalus studied the door. He examined the keyhole, but without a staff or the ability to use one there was no way to open it. With no other recourse, and certain his time was limited, he stuck his beak in the hole, pressed it against what he hoped was the trigger mechanism, then stood back and waited. Nothing happened. Grunting in frustration, Temalus examined the door, paying close attention to the seams where the door met the frame. He dragged his beak along the joints, hoping to find some way to trigger the door open. There was no way in.

Pacing in circles, Temalus decided to try the only option left. He knocked with his beak. No reply came. Maybe he had to give whoever was on the other side time. After only a few moments, and with his patience and nerves frazzled and wearing thin, he knocked again, tapping his beak against the hard ice in several different places. Minutes passed with no sign of acknowledgement. Temalus knew Talus had to have entered here; there were no other passages that weren't permanently sealed shut. "Maybe there's a code, or word I have to say to let them know to open," he said, trying to puzzle out a solution to his conundrum. Discouraged but not defeated, Temalus decided he would have to seek out Talus for help.

He began walking back up the slow sloping corridor, lost in his thoughts, when he spotted a lone Chinstrap hurrying in his direction. The Chinstrap stopped when he saw Temalus, eyes wide with doubt and fear. Temalus scanned the corridor for another penguin, but no one else was there. He stopped and stared at the Chinstrap and the Chinstrap stared back. They stood locked in their staredown for several heartbeats before the Chinstrap turned and began hurrying back the way it had come.

"Stop," Temalus called, wincing at the loudness of his voice. It wouldn't do to attract attention. He hurried to catch up to the other, if for no other reason than to ensure no one would find out he was in a restricted area alone. When the Chinstrap ignored his command, he called out again. "I said stop. You're not in trouble."

The Chinstrap stole a glance back at Temalus, but continued away. Temalus uttered a curse. Chinstraps were quicker than Royal Emperors on foot, but he knew they couldn't match his speed tobogganing. Temalus dove to the icy floor, kicked hard, and began belly-sliding after his prey. Seconds later, he caught up with his quarry.

The Chinstrap, seeming to sense his pursuer, did his best to run. But Temalus wasn't having it. Digging his claws into the ice, he propelled himself harder, reached up with his beak, and knocked the Chinstrap's feet out from under him. The Chinstrap tumbled to the ground and Temalus quickly got to his feet and stood over the escapee. "I said you're not in trouble," Temalus said between breaths.

The Chinstrap stared up at him, saying nothing.

"What are you doing down here?" Temalus asked, doing his best not to sound overly threatening.

The Chinstrap cautiously stood and shook his head.

"I asked you a question. Can you not speak?" Temalus said. He tried to mask his irritation, but realized he was failing miserably.

The Chinstrap backed away, remaining silent.

Temalus took a deep breath. "Listen, I'm not going to hurt you, and you're not in any trouble. I promise."

The Chinstrap looked around the corridor, then narrowed his eyes in suspicion toward the much larger Royal Emperor.

Temalus' body sagged in frustration. The way the Chinstraps had been treated as subordinates, and even abused—he had even done so himself—he couldn't blame him for not trusting him. "I give you my word. I promise nothing will come of this."

The Chinstrap took a few more steps back. "The word of a Royal Emperor means very little."

Temalus let out a long breath. Of course the Chinstrap wouldn't believe him. But he had spoken, and that was progress. "I know. I know more than most. But my word is all I have to give you. You'll just have to trust me."

"Trust you?" the Chinstrap snapped. "You and your brother threw me into the under realm. Probably thought Aperion would eat me. And you expect me to trust you?"

Temalus threw his flippers up in frustration. "We sparred, didn't we?"

"If you want to call it that…yes. And then you tried to dispose of me."

"No," Temalus said. "I mean yes, but not in the way you think. It was the Overlord. We knew Lord Saeson would protect you, and you were supposed to be bait. I'm sorry. Truly. But I'm not going to do that again. I'm trying to make a change…for the better. For all of us."

The Chinstrap cocked his head. "I doubt that very much." Temalus opened his beak to counter, but the Chinstrap interrupted. "What would you do if I walked away? Would you try to stop me?"

"No. The choice is yours. You'd probably give me a sharp jab in my gut again, like you did during our sparring," Temalus said, trying to lighten the mood.

"And I was given a long nap in return."

Temalus shrugged. "You can go. No one will know. And I will find another way to speak with Lord Saeson."

The Chinstrap a motion to leave, but stopped. "Lord Saeson? What does he have to do with your supposed plans for a *better world*?"

"Nothing at the moment. But that could change."

"Why do you think I could help you, and if I could, that I even would?"

"I'm assuming Lord Saeson let you go. And I'm assuming you were going to see him, probably after running some sort of errand for him, likely delivering a message. There's no other reason for you to be here. And I assume Lord Saeson had something to do with the missing guard. There used to be guards patrolling this corridor." Temalus watched the Chinstrap. "Or are my assumptions incorrect?"

The Chinstrap seemed to turn the words over in his mind. "You're mostly correct. Though Lord Saeson had nothing to do with the guard's disappearance. Talus killed the guard when he tried to stop him."

"Doesn't surprise me." Temalus swallowed a deep breath. "Listen, I haven't much time. I can search for Talus or you can take me to Lord Saeson and save me some time. Either way, I'm going to see him. Again, the choice is yours."

"Why should I trust you?"

That was the question. Why should the Chinstrap, or even Lord Saeson, trust him? Temalus had spent much of the past year on the hunt for the Lord of the Misshapen, and the K'tha had mistreated the Chinstraps and other clans, albeit in secret. It was even apparent in their words—lesser clans. There was a great chance that even if he managed to get an audience with Lord Saeson he would be killed. "We both know each other's secret. I won't tell yours if you won't tell mine."

"The word of a Chinstrap doesn't hold much water with Royal Emperors. Besides that, you never told me your secret, other than you want to see Lord Saeson."

Temalus looked up the corridor then back to the Chinstrap. "All right." He leaned down, placing his beak close to the Chinstrap's ear, who stiffened, as if waiting for an attack. "I'm going to kill the Overlord and I need Lord Saeson's help.

The Chinstrap blinked several times while looking in Temalus' eyes. "That's a much bigger secret. Why would you want to do that?"

"Get me an audience with Lord Saeson and you'll find out. I might need your help with this plan, too." Temalus rose up and stared at the Chinstrap, waiting for a reply.

After a few moments, the Chinstrap nodded. "If this is a trick, Lord Saeson will kill you."

"I don't doubt that," Temalus said. "Does this mean you'll help?"

The Chinstrap looked furtively up and down the corridor. His shoulders drooped. "Follow me."

# CHAPTER 23

Lieutenant Diutes walked alone through the main hall, ignoring the crowds of busy penguins along with the crystalline stalactite that had always mesmerized Temalus so. The scenery and bustling bodies were background noise to his focused mind. He ignored a procession of King penguins, and walked through their line, drawing a rebuke from the one known as Admiral Gregor, which he ignored as well. Diutes continued forward, eyes down, with single-minded purpose until a familiar voice tore him from his thoughts of seeing to his brothers' ends.

"You seem to enjoy antagonizing the Kings," Talus said, his voice sounding half-amused.

Diutes jerked, noticing the rogue standing directly in front of him. He looked around and saw the angry glare of the Kings as they watched him. Diutes snorted. He couldn't care less about offending the pompous King penguins. "They should mind where they walk. Pack Ice Command doesn't belong to them."

Talus clicked a laugh. "Pack Ice Command belongs to everyone at the moment."

Diutes stared at Talus. The last thing he needed right then was to be drawn into another long conversation about ancient spirits or listen to the rogue's convoluted philosophies. He had work to do. "If you'll excuse me," Diutes said and tried to step around Talus.

"You seem distracted, Diutes. Your usual cross disposition is somewhat subdued."

"I'm far from distracted. Again, if you'll excuse me…"

"And where are you headed with such determination?" Talus asked. He seemed to be enjoying delaying Diutes' task.

"If it was any of your concern, and it's not, I'm going to see the Overlord." Diutes fought against his impatience. He had to stay focused. His plan swam in his mind and he feared the idea would flutter away like a determined squid if he didn't keep his mind on his mission.

"Ah," Talus said. "I just came from there. He's not seeing anyone at the moment. Clayfus, however weak he may appear, can be quite unmovable."

"He'll see me. You can count on that."

Talus regarded Diutes for a moment. "Anything I can help with? Sometimes two beaks are better than one when seeking the Overlord's time."

"You've done enough already." To his credit, Diutes remained remarkably calm. He knew it was Talus' guidance that had brought him to this and so afforded him some lenience. But now that he had his plan formed, he no longer needed the other's help.

"I have?" Talus said, sounding genuinely surprised. "And how have I done that?"

Diutes eyed Talus. "Let's just say that I am becoming the snowflake."

Talus jerked almost imperceptibly. He studied Diutes for several heartbeats while nodding to himself. "Well then. By all means. Flutter away, little snowflake." Talus stepped aside, waving his flipper as if allowing him to pass.

Diutes walked past the rogue, happy for the conversation to have been so short-lived. He took several steps before looking back. Something in Talus' reaction had struck him as odd. He scanned the crowd, but Talus had already gone, disappearing into the throng like a ghost.

Diutes shrugged off Talus' reaction and continued toward the Overlord's chamber. He passed the Adélie sculptor, glancing at the artist as she chipped fine details into the relief of a Gentoo. Diutes entertained the idea of adding a few chips of his own as he thought of his earlier encounter with the insubordinate Gentoo. The Adélie paid him no mind as he passed.

When Diutes arrived, he was surprised to find the door closed. And even more surprised to find Clayfus standing there with two elite guards on either side of him, with spears at the ready. "Open the door. I need to speak with the Overlord," Diutes demanded.

"The Overlord is otherwise occupied. Come back tomorrow," Clayfus said with a dismissive voice.

Diutes' eyes shifted between the guards then fell on Clayfus. He briefly considered striking the scrawny aide for his insolence. Who did this penguin think he was? Everyone knew Clayfus was nothing more than a sycophant, a weak servant clinging to the tail-feathers of the Overlord for survival. He'd be dead already if not for his position. But Diutes thought better of it. He had to convince his father of the threat, and beating up his slave wasn't a good way to begin. "It is urgent. I must see him at once."

"Perhaps you misunderstood, Lieutenant Diutes. I said the Overlord is busy." Clayfus raised his flipper and the guards stepped toward Diutes.

Diutes looked between the guards with their spears trained on him. "Don't try to threaten me. I've killed those with the Grip more than once in the arena and I won't hesitate to do it again." Diutes silently hoped his boast wouldn't be called out. While he had killed his competitors in single combat, he had never taken on two at once.

Clayfus stared at Diutes for a moment with a hint of interest. The aide raised a thin flipper at the guards, indicating to them to stand down. "While it would be a fascinating sight, there is no need for violence…at the moment. Tell me what your urgent message is and I'll see that the Overlord receives it once he is free."

Diutes felt himself shaking his head before he realized he was refusing. "I must tell him myself." There was no way Diutes would let the information be delivered by someone else. It was his chance, perhaps his only chance, to kill two birds with one stone and finally be free from the shadow of his brothers.

"Then come another time," Clayfus said plainly, then turned away and nodded to the guards. The guards brought their spears up once more and stepped toward Diutes.

"The Overlord's life is in danger," Diutes blurted. His statement got Clayfus' attention. "Please."

Clayfus faced him once again, and again the guards lowered their weapons, though only slightly this time. "Go on," the aide said in a greedy voice.

There was no way around it, he had to tell him something more. Diutes wracked his brain trying to figure out what to tell him without revealing too much. He stared at Clayfus, whose expression was quickly turning from one of interest to that of doubt. Diutes looked around, his eyes falling on the disinterested artist, then back at the barrier that was Clayfus. He was sure that Clayfus, like everybody, thought he was a dim-witted brute. Though he couldn't match others in intellect, he wasn't as stupid as they thought. But he would play the part. "It's difficult to say, so I want to say it only once to make sure I get it right."

Clayfus sighed with annoyance. "Then give me the gist, and I will see if the Overlord will give you audience."

Diutes did his best to mask his satisfaction. "It's Liutites and Temalus. What they're planning can have detrimental outcomes for us all. Not just the Overlord. It involves Lord Saeson."

Clayfus narrowed his eyes and took a deep breath, as if trying to determine if what he was told warranted disrupting the Overlord from his business. After nearly a minute of internal deliberations, he nodded and turned to one of the guards. "Make sure the lieutenant waits down the hall. You," he said to the other. "Open the door."

Satisfied, Diutes let himself be guided toward the main hall. He stood and surveyed the commotion of penguins going about their day, seeing to the mundane tasks of operating the large compound. His eyes fell on the stalactite and he thought of Temalus. "The snowflake has fallen, and you will no longer be any trouble to me," Diutes said with a click of his beak. His eyes widened, wondering if he had said that out loud.

# CHAPTER 24

Diutes fantasized of seeing his brothers fall from grace. And with them out of the way, he saw himself as commander of Forward Command One, and he would become a hero after defeating an army of men who had come to stop the penguin uprising. Diutes followed this fantasy to its logical conclusion and he saw himself as Overlord, with Clayfus groveling at his feet, begging for forgiveness and scraps of food. Diutes would sire the next generation of warriors, who would all want nothing more than to emulate their father. Overlord Diutes would then lead his devoted warriors into the under realm of Pack Ice Command and eradicate Lord Saeson and his band of freaks once and for all. He wouldn't have to suffer a Gentoo and all would be right under his rule. A jab in the ribs from the guard's spear jerked Lieutenant Diutes from his musings.

"The Overlord will see you," the guard said.

Diutes looked around then narrowed his eyes at the back of the guard leading the way. *That guard will be fed to the Phocids one day…* He walked behind his escort, passing the Adélie, who again ignored him. All would stop and salute Diutes when he became Overlord. His eyes surveyed what would one day be his as he crossed the threshold into Antaean's chamber. He looked at the trophy skulls and pictured the heads of Liutites, Temalus, and Lord Saeson adorning the pedestals.

Diutes looked to the dais and spotted his father standing with his head cocked and impatient. As he approached the dais, he heard what sounded like the scurrying of tiny feet coming from somewhere in the shadows. He dismissed it, certain that he would learn all of the Overlord's secrets when he ascended the dais. But today, Diutes stood before his father with his beak raised high.

"Clayfus said you had a warning," Overlord Antaean said, dismissing Diutes' salute with a wave.

Diutes lowered his beak. "Yes, my lord."

Antaean clicked his beak impatiently. "Get on with it, then. Let's hear this warning." His eyes shifted toward Clayfus, who stood nearby.

"Yes, my lord. General Liutites and Commandant Temalus have entered into a conspiracy to overthrow you," Diutes said, attempting to use his words wisely.

Overlord Antaean puffed his chest and looked from Clayfus to Diutes. "Half of the officers under my command have aspirations to *overthrow* me. Tell me something a common Gentoo doesn't know."

Diutes bristled at being compared to a Gentoo. He added Antaean's skull to his vision of trophies. "Forgive me, my lord. You already know they are working together?"

"Of course I know. It is in our nature to desire power. General Liutites desires the dais, as do you. Perhaps one day, when I am old and feeble, one of you may achieve it. But for now, I assure you I am quite safe. I am aware of their plans."

Diutes wondered how much the Overlord actually knew. His response had seemed rather generic—everybody *wants to be Overlord*. "I apologize, my lord. Then you already know that they are seeking the aid of Lord Saeson to see this plan to its end." A subtle twitch in the Overlord's countenance told Diutes his father hadn't known that part of the conspiracy.

A moment of silence passed between them as Antaean appeared to be contemplating how to proceed. The Overlord looked at one of his guards. The guard went to the door and closed it. After the slow grind of the closing door ceased, the Overlord stepped from his dais. He paused for another moment, looking at Clayfus, he then met Diutes' eyes. "How do you know this?"

A wave of doubt washed over Diutes. Had the Overlord known? Was this information he wanted kept secret and would he kill to keep it that way? Diutes looked at the guards. They stood motionless and at the far end of the chamber. "I overheard them, my lord."

"Dispense with the honorifics and tell me," the Overlord barked.

Diutes was more than happy not have to use *my lord* after every sentence. "After our meeting, I followed Temalus. He was headed to the lower reaches. I heard Liutites coming and hid in an alcove."

"Why were you following him? Did he indicate he was going to see Lord Saeson?"

"No," Diutes hesitated. "I was going to confront him. Maybe even kill him. I want Forward Command One." Diutes surprised himself that he had revealed his ambition. The fish was out the water now, no going back. "Like I said, Liutites came and I hid. They talked about the folly of your plans to go to war against the humans. And they talked of overthrowing you, as you already knew. Then Temalus suggested to seek the aid of Lord Saeson. He said something about killing you with Saeson's help and Liutites would be Overlord. It was hard to hear because they were speaking softly. Liutites didn't seem thrilled with the plan and he said so. But he also said that once he becomes supreme commander, he would have the resources to take the dais. They agreed to wait two days—until after Liutites' bout with Persus. I'm not sure how Temalus knows Saeson will help. Perhaps they've been allies all along and that's why Lord Saeson hasn't been captured."

"Is that all?" the Overlord asked.

Wasn't that enough? Diutes thought it would provoke a stronger reaction in his father. "That's all. Temalus continued on his way and Liutites left. I hid until it was clear, then came here."

"Have you told anyone else?" Antaean asked. There was something in his demeanor that held the promise of violence.

Diutes picked up on the promise. If Diutes told the Overlord he hadn't, he was certain his secret would die with him then and there. "If I don't return, Liutites will know you know," he lied. Diutes was a mindless brute, but not so mindless as to be completely honest.

The Overlord snorted his disbelief at Diutes' lie. He paced in front of the dais until Clayfus interrupted his thoughts. "Will you kill Liutites and Temalus?"

Diutes was near giddy at being privy to the conversation and watched with rapt attention.

Antaean stared at Clayfus for a moment or two. "Unfortunately Liutites is the best candidate for supreme commander, and our plans are too far along to wait for another. Temalus, however… He is dispensable." After another pause, Antaean nodded to himself, seeming to devise a plan. "We will carry on as if we know nothing of their treachery. When the time is right, I will have Temalus killed. From what Diutes said, it appears Liutites has no love for Lord Saeson. With Temalus dead, their alliance will cease to be."

This wasn't good enough for Diutes. He wouldn't allow it. He couldn't let them off so easily. The pair had combined to make his life miserable. They had kept him at bay, never letting him in their little plans and secrets. Liutites and Temalus had always dismissed Diutes as someone who was beneath them, never smart enough or strong enough to be included. Seeing Temalus die was all fine and great, and Liutites would be devastated, but Diutes wanted more. He wanted to destroy them. They were the reason he couldn't achieve his much deserved greatness. "No," Diutes blurted out.

The Overlord and Clayfus looked at him. "Do you disagree with the Overlord?" Clayfus asked. There was threat in his voice that seemed amplified by Antaean's silence.

Diutes swallowed hard. It wasn't wise to openly disagree with the Overlord. "No. I don't. But we could do better."

"We?" the Overlord asked. It was clear that Diutes wasn't part of this clutch either.

Diutes clawed at his thoughts, trying to come up with something better—something that would ruin Liutites if he were to survive. "If Liutites kills Persus and becomes supreme commander he might find a way to save Temalus, and Lord Saeson will still be a threat."

"What do you suggest, Lieutenant Diutes?" Clayfus asked for the Overlord.

Diutes paced in circles, trying to organize his thoughts. He raised a flipper. "If..." He paused. "If you deny Liutites the rank of supreme commander after he defeats Persus, that will push him over the edge. He will attempt to overthrow you and seek out the alliance with Lord Saeson. But he needs Temalus to do so."

"Isn't that what you were trying to prevent?" Clayfus asked in a condescending tone. He looked at the Overlord with his shoulders twitching with laughter.

"Shut up. I'm thinking," Diutes snapped, not caring if he upset the scrawny aide. The plan had been there before, swirling in head like a shrimp caught in an eddy, but now the eddy had stilled, and the plan came to him. "Make Liutites fight Temalus for the rank. He won't have a choice but to do it or he'd be put to do death. Once they find out about the impending match, the two of them will push forward their plans to seek Lord Saeson's help. And then you can nab three fish with one bite. Have your warriors ready for Saeson and stop him. Liutites will be forced to kill Temalus and if you choose to let Liutites live and be supreme commander, he will be devastated and completely subservient to you. He'll see that there will be no way to betray you." Diutes looked at the pair, breathing heavily, and eager to hear their approval.

Clayfus looked at the Overlord, then to Diutes. "There is the edict that siblings shall not be selected for combat unless one is challenged by the other."

Diutes shook his head. "The rules have changed a hundred times. Change them…my lord."

"Your plan does carry weight," the Overlord said. "And what do you hope to gain from this?"

"Respect," Diutes said quickly. "And a promotion…to general. And command of Forward Command One."

"The plan is crude, but with some tweaking it can be done, my lord," Clayfus said.

Diutes continued to listen. There was something in Clayfus' tone that seemed like he wasn't keen on the idea. The thought vanished when the Overlord stirred.

The Overlord walked close to Diutes. "I never knew you had the capability to be so deceitful. You will be general and have Forward Command One. But if I find there is any duplicity in your words, I will feed you to the Phocids myself."

"I understand, my lord," Diutes said. "All I've said is true."

"You should hope so." Antaean looked across the chamber. "Guards!"

Diutes watched as the guards hurried to the Overlord.

"You have heard all that was said. See that it goes no farther than this room," Antaean spoke with a low voice. The guards saluted, took their spears, and plunged them into each other's chest.

Diutes jerked back, shocked by the display of absolute loyalty. He watched them as they fell with no traces of remorse or regret in their dying eyes. Clayfus pulled a spear from one of the bodies and motioned for Diutes to follow. The Overlord's attendant thrust the butt of the spear in a keyhole and the door opened. Diutes looked back in time to see two Misshapen come from the shadows and begin dragging the corpses away. He turned away, satisfied that his brothers will finally get their comeuppance.

# CHAPTER 25

Mearna peered around the edge of the entryway of her quarters, making sure no ears were about. Certain there were none, she guided the Adélie to the back of the room. "What did you hear?"

"Diutes told Clayfus that he uncovered a plot involving Liutites, Temalus, and Lord Saeson. They are conspiring to overthrow the Overlord and form an alliance," the Adélie said at once.

"You're sure?" Mearna asked. She clicked her beak nervously. "The walls are thick."

"Yes. The voices resonate perfectly through the reliefs when I place my beak against them. They're not just art." The Adélie puffed her chest with pride.

"What else did he say? What is the Overlord going to do with this information?"

The Adélie recounted the events and told Mearna everything she had heard. When she finished her report, the Adélie spy waited for further instructions.

"You did well, Kima. Keep up your good work." Mearna circled the smaller penguin, lost in thought. Liutites was a fool, but a necessary fool. His impatience could cost him his chance to become supreme commander. But from what she understood, it was a foregone conclusion. However, there were always unforeseen events that had a bad habit of springing up like an Orca through thin ice, ready to disrupt the most carefully laid plans. "Events are unfolding quicker than I'd like. But not all is lost. Go now. And report anything else you hear."

"I will, M'lady. Our work on the reliefs is nearly finished and I fear I won't be able to listen much longer. But as you know, there are other ways."

"Let's hope so. The information you've provided has been invaluable." Mearna paused for a second. "Go. Hide in the shadows down the hall. Liutites is coming."

Kima nodded and hurried from Mearna's quarters, doing as instructed. Moments later Liutites appeared in the doorway.

Mearna instantly sensed Liutites' volatile mood. She let go a long cleansing breath and went to him. "Liutites," she said in her most placating voice. "I wasn't expecting you."

Liutites didn't say anything. Rather than greeting her, as he always had, he walked to the back of her quarters. He stood there silently, staring down at a flickering lantern, never looking back at her.

Mearna cautiously followed and stood next to him, staring at the light as well. She let the silence hang for a minute before making a subtle low-pitch noise. Liutites raised his eyes toward her. "What's troubling you?" she asked, keeping herself on guard. If Liutites was really considering an alliance with the Cu-kisc, then anything was possible, including more violent outbursts. She knew what he had done to Heltius in the commissary, and she kept that in mind, even though she doubted he would act in such a way toward her. Still, it was best to be cautious.

"I have something to tell you, but it stays between us," Liutites said, his voice sounding tired and worried, with a touch of doubt.

Mearna nodded and leaned her beak against his. "You know I tell no one of our secrets." She pulled back to look in his eyes. A flash of doubt crossed Liutites' face, which surprised Mearna. She guessed Temalus had been trying to turn him against her. But that would change. Mearna's eyes narrowed in a smile. "I have something to tell you as well. But it can wait. I'm sure whatever you have to tell me is much more pressing."

Liutites gave her a sideways glance. He opened his beak to speak, but stopped, as if the words were caught in his throat. Mearna walked behind him and ran her beak along his spine affectionately. Liutites stiffened, then spun to face her. "I'm going to depose the Overlord…soon."

Mearna eyed him carefully. She needed him to overthrow Antaean, but not yet. It wasn't time, and she wasn't ready to unveil the plans she held in secret. She had to find a way to delay him, or make him reconsider. But Mearna knew she had to tread carefully. "How will you do it? You don't have the support of the warrior caste yet. And you'll need them if you hope to have a successful coup."

"After tomorrow I will be supreme commander. When that happens, I will have the warriors at my disposal."

"Their loyalty might not be so easily swayed. It could take time for them to see you as their commander over Antaean."

Liutites shook his head. "Most of them have already been under my command for some time. They see that I'm not one to sit on a throne and bark orders—I actually do my part." He fixed his steely gaze on her. "And you did say they'd be loyal to me."

"It takes time, Liutites. You forget that most warriors imprinted on the Overlord upon their hatching. I think you expect too much of them. Give them time to truly see you as their commander. Give *yourself* time, plan carefully, and move when all of the pieces are in place. Rushing into this could only serve to get you killed. And then what? Where would your brother be without you? Where would I?"

Mearna turned away. Where *would* she be if Liutites got himself killed? Still stuck in the subservient role to Antaean and still his consort for years to come. She wouldn't have that. There would be other males to take Liutites' place, Talus for one, if he cared enough, but he was too strong willed and she was certain he didn't trust her. But Liutites could be manipulated. And he alone had shown the strength and desire necessary to take down the Overlord. As much as she loathed to admit it, she needed a strong male to rid herself of Antaean. And once that was done, she would rid herself of him, too. But for now, she still needed him.

"Temalus has his own plans," Liutites said. "He'll help me, but after that, he will follow Talus' lead and leave here. At times, I can't say I blame him. I almost envy him."

"Don't say that. You will make a magnificent overlord," Mearna warbled softly in Liutites' ear.

"First I must become supreme commander."

"Are you so sure Antaean will keep his word? He has been known to change his mind when it suits his own purposes. Especially if he suspects you might attempt a coup."

"He wouldn't dare."

"Wouldn't he?" Mearna smiled inwardly at seeing the seed of doubt take root in his mind.

"No. He wouldn't. The path to the dais travels through the supreme commander."

"Perhaps. Before that, you have to get past Persus." An idea sparked in Mearna's mind. If it worked, Liutites would be disqualified, temporarily, but he wouldn't be executed. Her Adélie spy had said Liutites would become supreme commander; he just didn't know it yet. "As valuable as he is, you must kill him."

"We've been through this. I know I have to kill him."

"When you go to the arena, kill Persus immediately. Don't give him the chance to defeat you, however unlikely that may be. The Overlord will see your strength of will—that you will stop at nothing to become supreme commander—and it will be yours." Mearna waited for the inevitable protest and was surprised when it didn't come. "Leave nothing to chance."

Liutites agreed. "The Overlord has his spies. If he somehow gets wind of our plans, I'll have to act fast. I have to protect Temalus."

"True. But Temalus can take care of himself, you know." Mearna fought back her irritation. Everything concerned Temalus with Liutites. It was time for her to make Liutites shift his priorities. What Liutites didn't know could kill him. In fact, it eventually would. Mearna had her own designs to become Overlord. The warriors Liutites so concerned himself with would never be loyal to him. When the latest group of warriors returned from their trials at sea, Liutites would find that they had imprinted on Mearna; they would be absolutely loyal to her, and they would carve her path to the dais. But first to ensure Liutites' loyalty. "Liutites, there's something I need to tell you."

"And there's something else I need to tell you," Liutites said before Mearna could speak. "If I don't move against my father tomorrow, Temalus will do something much worse."

Mearna feigned surprise. She wanted to tell him the news that would all but guarantee Liutites' complete loyalty, but she wanted to hear this conspiracy from Liutites' own beak. It was the only way she could be certain it was true. "What is it?" she asked in a gentle, unhurried voice.

Liutites gave the doorway a furtive glance then leaned close the Mearna and whispered. "Temalus plans to enter into an alliance."

Mearna played the part of ignorance and matched Liutites' conspiratorial tone. "With whom?"

Liutites stared into Mearna's eyes, letting the silence hang for several breaths. "Talus. If I don't act soon, he will have Talus kill the Overlord."

Mearna jerked her head back in surprise. This couldn't be. Her spies had always brought her accurate information. There had to be a mistake. "Are you certain?" she asked, doing her best to mask her shock. Someone would pay for this failure.

"Yes," Liutites continued. "He told me of their plans while we were in the lower passages."

"I don't understand. Why would he do such a thing? Would he really betray you?" Mearna no longer tried to hide her surprise. She turned over all that she had been told by Kima the Adélie in her mind. What had she missed? The more she thought about it, the more it made sense. It was that idiot Diutes. He had gotten the facts wrong. Of course Temalus wouldn't ally himself with Lord Saeson. He along with Liutites had spent much of the last year trying to capture him.

Liutites eyed her carefully. "You saw Temalus speaking with Talus before his match with Reticles. Talus planted the seeds on that day. And Temalus... He is doing it to protect me and himself. He doesn't believe I can defeat the Overlord. And I too have my doubts. But it has to be done."

"But Talus? He's a rogue. He's never shown interest in the dais."

"Talus knows of the plans to drive the humans out. He also knows that a war would end his life of freedom. If Talus becomes Overlord, there will be no conflict with man. He will disband the alliance and there will be no need for an Overlord, no need for a supreme commander, no need for any of this. He sows disorder. And Temalus, in his mind, would have saved me."

Mearna shook her head. She would have her warriors and her freedom, but she wouldn't have the dais. And the other Royal Emperors, the warriors, the guards, probably even Clayfus wouldn't acknowledge her claim as Overlord. She would be left with nothing but a plot of ice, raising chicks until the end of her days. Liutites was her ticket to absolute power. "Then after Talus becomes Overlord, kill him. Take control before he destroys everything we've worked for. You would become Overlord."

Liutites stared at the ground, shaking his head. "I can't. As much as I hate to admit it, I can't defeat Talus. He has spent years on the ice, killing for survival. I may match him in strength, but his skills in combat far surpass my own." Liutites met her eyes. "Now you see why I have to act soon? Even if Talus fails, Temalus will die for his part."

Mearna fought back her rage. Temalus would ruin everything. And Talus. The rogue had to go. The more she considered his words, the more she saw Liutites was right. She could put up with being at his side for a year.

He may even postpone the foolishness of war against man. She would tell Antaean of Talus' designs. That would put an end to that. Temalus would be neutralized, but would still be a problem. That could be taken care of later. Mearna still had one more stone to lie at Liutites' feet. She hoped it would be enough for him to question his loyalty to his brother. "Then you must do what you can to ensure victory. It is of the utmost importance."

"I will," Liutites said, then turned to leave.

"More than you know, Liutites. It's what I wanted to tell you."

Liutites faced her. "What is it?"

"I am with egg."

Liutites jerked his head. "Are you certain?"

Mearna's eyes softened. "Without a doubt."

"Are you certain it's mine?" Liutites asked. His eyes searched her face for a sign of deceit.

Mearna's head lolled sideways. "You know that it is." If she truly cared, Liutites' words would have hurt. But she didn't care. Liutites was an end to a means, nothing more.

"Then I will make certain I am Overlord," Liutites said. He spun on his feet and left Mearna alone.

Mearna watched him leave, satisfied that she had him in her beak. And she would hold him there until she had her warriors and he was no longer useful. But now she had to be rid of Talus.

# CHAPTER 26

Overlord Antaean watched Mearna in silence and she returned his unblinking stare. When she had told the Overlord of Talus' plans, carefully omitting her source, it seemed somewhat farfetched when put into words. Why *would* Talus, a penguin who enjoyed his freedom on the ice plains, want to chance losing that freedom? Would he really want to prevent a war? Talus was a penguin who thrived in conflict—lived for the fight. It didn't matter anymore. The stone had been cast, she had informed Antaean, and now Liutites' ambitions were in motion.

The Overlord looked to Clayfus, than back at Mearna. "Take a detachment of twenty warriors and capture Talus. Whether Diutes was wrong, or if you prove to be, his impunity has gone on long enough."

Mearna twisted her head around, looking for whoever Antaean was speaking to until realizing he was talking to her. "Me? You want me to capture him?"

"Should I send someone else? Liutites and Persus are preparing for their match, Temalus is assisting Liutites, Diutes would bungle the whole affair, and my other commanders are too preoccupied for such trivial matters." The Overlord turned to Clayfus and began discussing a different subject.

"Antaean, surely there's someone better trained—"

"You will address me properly in this chamber or you will find the limits of your privileges," the Overlord snapped.

Mearna glared at Antaean. She briefly considered aiding Talus in his quest after the rebuke, but thought better of it. If she wanted the mantle of Overlord, Liutites was her best bet. "I apologize, *my lord*. But my abilities in such matters are limited."

"You are proficient enough," Antaean said with a dismissive tone.

Mearna stared at the Overlord. Something in the other's demeanor told her he had suspicions of her long-term goals. But then again, the Overlord was suspicious of everyone. She decided to appeal one more time to avoid confronting Talus. "Is there no other commander who could assist me?"

The Overlord snorted and narrowed his eyes, clearly annoyed. "You will see this task to its end. If I have to do it myself, I will see that both Talus and you are fed to the Phocids. Now go. If Talus resists, as I'm sure he will, kill him only as a last resort. You are dismissed." Antaean ground his staff into the ice, indicating there would be no further discussion.

Mearna gave Antaean a final glance, then spun toward the exit. She left and headed for the warriors' quarters. As she passed through the main hall, Mearna spotted Diutes near the ice stalactite, talking to a Royal Emperor sergeant. She watched him, feeling a sense of loathing roil in her gut. If that bumbling idiot had gotten the correct information, she wouldn't have to face down the most formidable penguin in Pack Ice Command save the Overlord and Lord Saeson. Mearna considered going to him and telling him just how she felt about his erroneous report, but thought better of it. Females didn't have a place of authority in Royal Emperor society. But that would change soon enough. And when it did, she wouldn't have to suffer the likes of Diutes any longer.

Mearna would see to her appointed task. She decided her best course of action would be to send the warriors after Talus ahead of her while she stayed safely in the background. Mearna knew Talus was dangerous. She wouldn't take a single detachment to get the job done. She'd take twice that many. And if Talus got past them… Mearna would help him kill the Overlord.

# CHAPTER 27

Talus paced the dark recesses of a long forgotten alcove waiting for a Chinstrap messenger who he knew could be trusted. Trust was a precious commodity in Pack Ice Command and Talus gave it to very few. He had earned Temalus' trust and he would do his part to show it was well placed. Talus didn't berate himself for planting the idea to betray Liutites and Temalus in Diutes' head. Who would have known that the brutish oaf could have actually formulated a plan from his cryptic remarks? And wallowing in regret of one's actions did nothing to change the present. Perhaps it was the will of the Ancients that pressed Diutes into action. If it had been, then perhaps the Ancients had called on Talus to protect Temalus.

The minutes passed as slowly as a winter night and Talus meditated on what his best course of action would be. He cared little for Liutites. In fact, he didn't care at all for the general. As far as Talus was concerned, Liutites' purpose would be best served from the Great Sea. In his opinion nearly all modern K'tha would be better in the beyond. While he had to admit that a war with the humans would provide many great hunts, it was a war Talus knew they couldn't win. Men were too well equipped, even if they were out of their element in this frozen realm. For now, though, he had to get Temalus out of Pack Ice Command. If Diutes had convinced that inflated gas bladder Antaean to harm Temalus—the only K'tha he held any faith in—he had to help him. There were ways out of PIC that were unguarded. The Overlord, in his overconfidence, thought he was secure in his fortress, that none could leave without him knowing. But he was very wrong. Aperion had done it, as had had Talus on many occasions.

A scratch of a beak against the outer wall pulled Talus from his thoughts. "Here I am," he said in quiet voice.

"I am here," came a quiet response. Talus had made sure to have a certain safe phrase to avoid any unwanted interlopers. The response was correct.

"Come in. We haven't much time," Talus said, his voice unusually tense. "What news do you have?"

"Many things," the Chinstrap said, glancing behind him. He told Talus about Diutes and his scheming, and about Liutites' and Temalus' plans to overthrow Antaean.

"And you're certain Mearna doesn't know the Adélie is working with you?"

The Chinstrap tilted his head. "There are many beaks and twice as many ears in Pack Ice Command. I'm sure she knows secrets are passed around, and even counts on it at times, but as long as it doesn't interfere with her *so-called* resistance she's building, we'll keep our heads."

Talus snorted. "Resistance? Is that what she's calling it?" He took a frustrated breath. "Do not trust her. In many ways, she's worse than the Overlord. Mearna isn't an altruistic freedom-fighter. She has her eye on the dais."

The Chinstrap waved his comments away. "I don't trust her. But we will use her until the time is right. And to prove your point, we got word that she intends to have you arrested for treason."

"What?" Talus said, sounding half-amused and half-angry. "Treason? She should talk. Where did she come up with such an idea?"

"We're not sure. But she has already spoken with the Overlord, and whether he believes it or not, it's a good excuse to have you expelled for good, or even executed."

Talus laughed. "Like he could do either. Or even would. But I've lingered here too long as it is." He stooped to face the Chinstrap. "You've done well. You are always welcome to join me on the plains of Planarseae."

The Chinstrap shook his head. "When I do leave here, it will be to go home to the archipelagoes where my mate waits for me. But the Overlord draws more recruits day by day, and there is work to be done still."

"Very well." Talus tilted his head. His eyes narrowed toward the doorway. "Have you seen Temalus?"

"He went to see Lord Saeson." The Chinstrap looked at the doorway as well.

"Perfect. I can see him on my way out." Talus looked to the Chinstrap. "Go. And may the Ancients be at your side."

"And yours as well," the Chinstrap said and hurried away.

# CHAPTER 28

Temalus stood outside the door leading to Lord Saeson's domain, waiting for the Chinstrap's return from within. He stared at the plain white walls, pondering his future. Once he entered, there would be no turning back. The possibilities of what would come were limited. Lord Saeson could kill him at first sight—which was a very real and most likely possibility. Or the Lord of the Misshapen could hear him out, and maybe even agree to help. Temalus could save Liutites and hopefully prevent the Overlord's war, and perhaps broker a peace between the K'tha and Cu-kisc. Or, and it was the possibility that Temalus almost dreaded the most, Saeson would imprison him in the under realm of Pack Ice Command.

Temalus shuddered at the thought. To be stuck in darkness until the end of his days, without ever seeing the light of day, or feeling the freedom of swimming through the cold sea again filled him with an oppressive dread. The final possibility, and least likely, was that Lord Saeson would simply deny his request and send him on his way. If that happened, he would have no choice but to leave PIC and leave Liutites to his quest for power. There would be nothing he could do to stop him.

Time passed much too slowly. How long had the Chinstrap been gone? Temalus scratched at the ice impatiently. Could it be that another possibility was showing itself? Maybe Lord Saeson wouldn't see him at all.

Temalus doubted it. At the very least, Saeson would want to capture him and be relieved of one of his tormentors. With his patience at an end, Temalus pressed his beak against the keyhole and tried to mimic the sounds the Chinstrap had made to gain entry. He had watched the Chinstrap carefully as he placed his beak in the hole and had memorized each chirp and whistle the Chinstrap made. He stood back and waited. Nothing happened. The Chinstraps calls were likely at a different frequency, one he couldn't duplicate. Or maybe whoever was on the other side knew better, and wouldn't open the door to a counterfeiter.

Temalus had no choice but to wait. The minutes passed with such infuriating slowness, it was as if the Ancients were mocking his impatience and grinding time itself to a halt. Time continued to scratch away at what remained of Temalus' veneer of graceful tolerance until, finally, the door began its slow grind. Relieved, but uncertain, Temalus stepped away and braced himself. Whatever happened would happen.

When the door opened to its fullest, Temalus was surprised that the Chinstrap wasn't there, and even more surprised by the two Misshapen penguins standing on the edge of the darkness. Both had long, spiraling beaks, like the tusks of a narwhal, a legendary creature of the mythic north, and each stood four feet tall, with broad, jointed flippers terminating in knobs of flesh where the tips would be. One made a low honking sound and then motioned at Temalus with its elongated beak. Taking the cue, Temalus stepped inside. The door immediately closed behind him, leaving him in darkness. There was no going back.

Temalus listened to sounds of scurrying claws against ice, moving around him. He stood still, taking in every sound. He had been in this area before on one of his many surveys and searches for Lord Saeson or Aperion—before it had been supposedly sealed off. And he was familiar with the layout. He knew the tunnel led to his right, and that there was a long slope leading to yet another doorway.

"This way," a voice called from somewhere deeper along the passageway.

Temalus took a step, feeling the walkway's gradual incline. He dragged his trailing foot forward, his claws etching the ice for a grip. A sudden jab in his back from the beak of one the Misshapen behind him stole his precarious balance. The impact of his chest meeting the ice nearly stole his breath, which was followed by a wild, uncontrolled slide down the slope. With no way to stop his slide, Temalus tucked his head and hoped he wouldn't break his neck at the end of his ride. He slammed into the wall at the bottom much sooner than he expected, and let out an undignified grunt along with a few coarse phrases directed at no one in particular.

A light flicked to life and shined in Temalus' eyes as he lay there, surveying his body for injury. "This way," a voice behind the light said.

Temalus dug his beak into the ice floor, boosted himself to his feet, and shook away the pain from his sudden stop. He jerked at the sound of both Misshapen sliding to a stop behind him, still on their feet. "I could have made it without the nudge," Temalus said and followed the guiding light. The Misshapen honked in reply.

His guide waddled ahead of him, not bothering to wait. Temalus looked at his back, noticing the familiar shape of a Royal Emperor. "Who are you?" he asked, surprised to find another Royal Emperor.

The other turned slightly, holding the battery-operated lantern in his grip and briefly shining it in Temalus' eyes. "One of your father's outcasts," he said, not masking the venom in his voice.

"Most are outcasts, according to my father," Temalus said absently.

The guide raised his other flipper, showing that he was missing a large chunk of it. "Some more so than others."

Temalus looked at the flipper, obviously bitten by either an Orca or a Phocid. He averted his eyes, not from the gruesomeness of the injury, but for the shame of having been part of his father's institution of cruelty. "I'm sorry. It doesn't have to be this way. There's no need for the injured to be banished. Or outcast, as you say. We have the capability to take care of the infirm, not cull those who are perceived as weak."

"The sick and injured weaken us. Therefore they shall be cast away. If one survives his weakness, he may return to share his strength of will with his offspring. If he dies, then it is as it should be," the guide said. "Isn't that what Antaean taught us since we hatched?"

"Nearly word for word, I believe. It's been a while since I've bothered to recite the creed." Temalus felt a touch of pity for the Royal. He had been outcast because of his injury. What made it worse was that it probably happened in service to the Overlord. It probably even happened when returning from the Trials, when the Phocids awaited their arrival. Whatever the reason, Temalus felt a certain comfort in the familiar presence of another K'tha, even if the other hated him for his relationship to Antaean. "How long have you been down here?" he asked, hoping to change the subject.

"Does it matter?" the escort said. "Day and night are the same in the darkness. I know the seasons by the cracking of the ice."

"The cracking of the ice?"

The chaperon let out sigh, clearly annoyed. "When the summer brings the thaw, and the floes melt, the ice snaps. And it repeats when the winter comes. Have you been so involved in your service to the Overlord that you've forgotten the rhythms of nature?"

"Apparently, I have," Temalus answered, trying to keep his own annoyance from showing. He tried to keep in mind that this K'tha likely carried a fair amount of resentment for being stuck below for however long he had been. The escort hadn't answered his question, and Temalus thought it best to drop the subject. "Do you have a name?"

The guide stopped and turned to Temalus. "I do," he said, then turned away. "Wait here." He set the light down and left Temalus with the two Misshapen.

"Guess he's not going to answer that question either," Temalus said to the two penguins. Neither replied. He looked back the way they came; his gaze followed the gradual slope of the long corridor where the light succumbed to the darkness. Temalus waited in silence, listening for the tell-tale sign of another door opening. No sound came, and his mind began to wander. A slight breeze flowed through the passage, carrying with it the smell of seawater. So that was how they survived down here. There was an alternate route to the sea. The gatherers in PIC had routes to the sea below the ice, but those were unknown by most. Temalus wondered if anyone else knew of the alternate routes. Surely Talus did. The rogue seemed to know more about Pack Ice Command than anybody, the Overlord included. But if anybody else knew, they weren't doing anything about it. Temalus wondered if Antaean's plan to starve the Misshapen had been sincere.

The scratching footfalls of the returning Royal Emperor pulled Temalus' attention from his thoughts. "Lord Saeson will see you. Be respectful if you want to survive. Follow me," the escort of untold name said.

"What about the light?" Temalus had no desire to enter Lord Season's chamber blind.

"Leave it. Someone will come for it shortly."

Temalus walked behind his guide, noticing the two Misshapen hadn't followed. He looked back at the light and caught sight of something that sent a ripple of fear through his body. A Misshapen penguin with a long beak carrying what he was sure were rows of needle-like teeth, stepped into the light and flicked it off with what looked like a starfish of a hand. Temalus hurried to catch his escort, nearly bumping into him in the dark.

A pale light that scarcely illuminated the path ahead flowed from a wide entryway. When they reached the broad opening, the Royal Emperor stopped and motioned with his damaged flipper. "Enter," he said, then quickly walked away, disappearing into the darkness.

Temalus shook off the feeling that he had been guided by a spirit returned from the Great Sea to lead him to Cuasan the Taker, the lord of the Underworld, to answer for his earthly deeds. Steeling his nerve, Temalus stepped into a vast cavern devoid of any adornments. The room was as wide as it was long, with a low ceiling carrying a bounty of stalactites. The floor was smooth and clean. Absent were any signs of corresponding stalagmites, as if it had been meticulously maintained to remove any tripping hazards in the darkness. His eyes fell to the center of the room where the unmistakable form of Lord Saeson stood. The wane light emanating from an unseen source gave the Lord of the Misshapen the aura of a specter, a shadow in the gloom waiting to take Temalus to the nether realm. Unsure of what to do, Temalus took another cautious step inside.

"Temalus, son of Antaean," Lord Saeson spoke, his low voice reverberating off the ice walls. Silence crept over the space as the echoes died, giving Temalus pause.

"Lord Saeson," Temalus said. A gnawing feeling of dread mixed with a growing sense of uncertainty flowed through his gut. "Thank you for granting me audience. I have come—"

"I know why you have come here," Saeson roared back. He moved toward Temalus. Steady purposeful strides carried him across the floor, closing the gap between them much quicker than seemed possible for a penguin of his bulk.

Temalus stood his ground, fighting the instinct to back away, or turn and run. Lord Saeson stood before him and lowered his broad, deadly beak, the beak that had lopped the head off Royal Emperors with a single, easy bite, the beak that could disembowel a penguin with one smooth stroke. The impressive weapon hovered inches away from Temalus' own, less intimidating beak. Temalus met his gaze and the two stared silently at one another for several tense moments in the gloom.

"You have come here to plea for my aid," Lord Saeson said, his heavy breaths rustling Temalus' wiry feathered head crest. "You, with your brother Liutites, who pursued me, attempting to capture or kill me, or close me away to face certain death, have come to ask for my help. I should kill you for the pure audacity of your request."

"You are correct, Lord Saeson," Temalus said when he found his voice. He did his best to hide any sign of fear, a task he was failing miserably at. "I was a fool, a servant to my father. I was blind to the possibilities of peace between our kinds. But no more. I come here knowing my life is forfeit should you choose to take it. I hope that is not the case. I hope that the opportunity for an accord has not been squandered by the Overlord."

Lord Saeson snorted derisively, inching his beak closer until their tips nearly touched. "I would kill you." The Lord of the Misshapen paused. "If not for the word of Talus."

"Then I should thank him," Temalus said.

Saeson looked into Temalus' eyes a moment longer. He straightened and snorted a laugh. "Perhaps you should. He is the one K'tha I take at his word. If his judgement proves sound, you may be the second."

Temalus thought of the K'tha escort, but decided it would be prudent not to mention him. His body sagged with relief knowing he wouldn't die just yet. "Talus is a good penguin."

Lord Saeson shook his head. "Talus is neither good nor evil. He speaks the truth—a rare commodity with the K'tha. He is true to himself and true to his nature. Now speak, Temalus. What is your truth?"

The question caught Temalus unprepared. Of all the questions to begin an accord, why this? But he had to admit he didn't know the answer. What was his truth? If he couldn't look at himself honestly, what hope did he have to save Liutites from his ambition? And beyond that, how could he prevent the impending conflict? Was it his brother who he wanted to save? Did he want to save penguinkind from disaster, or was it his hatred for his father that drove him here? The years of being forced to kill for nothing more than what amounted to the Overlord's amusement had sickened his heart. The verbal and sometimes physical abuse had shaped him the way the sea erodes the shore, slowly and steadily taking chunks away, leaving jagged edges or strands of empty shore. But through it all Temalus still didn't hold to the same bloodlust as other Royal Emperors. Maybe it was an act of rebellion, known only to him. And maybe that made him an outcast. Or perhaps he wanted Liutites to be more like himself and watch as the Overlord's budding empire crumbled. And then Liutites, the one penguin he truly loved, would see the folly of such ambition, and they would be free of their father's shadow.

His eyes scanned the room, darting from one blank space to another, coursing wildly, following his thoughts as they raced from one possibility to the next, scrambled and confused, trying to find purchase on what his truth was. Temalus finally closed his eyes, searching further within. When he opened them, they fell on Lord Saeson. Maybe the truth was all of those things or none. But his heart told him the search for his truth began with one thing...Antaean's end.

"You know your truth?" Lord Saeson asked. His voice no longer carried any hint of threat, only curiosity.

"No," Temalus said with a slight shake of his head. "But I know how to find it. And I'll need your help."

Lord Saeson rose to his full height, turned away, and looked into the darker reaches of the chamber.

Temalus watched him and wondered what Saeson's eyes, accustomed to the dark, found in those far reaches. After a minute or more passed, Temalus sighed; the other's silence led him to believe he wouldn't help.

"We will aid you in your coup, but you and Liutites must be the ones to kill Antaean," Lord Saeson finally said. He faced Temalus once again. "But I don't believe Liutites will accept your plan."

"He will," Temalus blurted much too quickly. "I told him that I planned to meet with you."

"And he let you come...alone? Knowing you could have been killed." Lord Saeson narrowed one eye in suspicion.

Temalus opened his beak to respond, but the words caught in his throat. A sickly feeling of doubt rose in his gullet. Why would Liutites let him come alone? He shook the budding thoughts of betrayal away. "Liutites trusts my judgement."

"Do you trust his?"

That was a question Temalus could not answer with any certainty.

"He is possessed by a lust for power. That much I know. After Antaean is dead…" His eyes fell to the floor. Would it change anything? He had to believe it would. "After the Overlord is dead, he will be free, and his lust for power will die with our father."

Lord Saeson continued to look at Temalus with doubt. But a new expression appeared in his eyes. A look of pity. "I once thought that way of my brother, Aperion. I was wrong. And you must face the possibility of that truth. That some of us cannot be changed by love or any other force. That some cannot be saved."

Temalus nodded. He hoped he wasn't lying to himself. "If that is true, then I'll leave Pack Ice Command and leave my brother to his fate. But I have to try."

Lord Saeson stared at Temalus. "So you must."

# CHAPTER 29

Talus stood in the intersection of corridors, one of which led to the remaining passage to the lower reaches. He had taken a circuitous route through the maze of passageways, sometimes doubling back, hoping to throw off anyone who dared to track him. The Overlord had spies, Mearna had spies, and Lord Saeson had spies. It seemed that everyone had spies, himself included. Some spies even did their work for more than one. Kima, the Adélie artist worked for both him and Mearna, though Mearna didn't know of the arrangement. The ventilation shafts, which were found in nearly every part of Pack Ice Command, often doubled as listening posts for both Lord Saeson's and Antaean's networks of agents. However, unknown to most, to root one out, all you had to do was find a shaft with no airflow. Chances were, you had a set of curious ears following you.

There were no such ears where Talus stood at that moment. The air flowed uninhibited from the nearest shaft. But he knew that if Diutes had told the Overlord of Temalus' plans, as Kima had said, one would expect that the Overlord would have the location under surveillance. His expectations were met when, after standing for only a few minutes, he noticed the same Royal Emperor guard pass by three times. "Subtle as a seal in a rookery," he muttered.

Talus pondered his best course of action. He didn't want to kill the guard—not out of moral reasons or regard for the Overlord's drone; there were just too many penguins milling about for it not to go unnoticed. He could go back the way he had come, double-back, and try to slip past the guard. But he was running out of time. He had to get word to Temalus and then escape himself.

Adding to his troubles was the fact that Mearna had pegged him as the leader of a coup and informed Antaean. It was preposterous, and he was sure the Overlord knew that as well. Talus doubted that the Overlord would actually have him executed for such nonsense. He was too valuable to Antaean. He did the jobs that other Royal Emperors wouldn't, or more accurately, couldn't do. The lanterns and other trinkets and supplies were pilfered from human camps by Talus and his small band of nomads on the ice plains. Then there was the occasional assassination of dissidents in the early days of Antaean's burgeoning empire. No, the Overlord needed him. Then again, Talus didn't put it past Antaean's growing mania to think he was untouchable. He would warn Temalus and then disappear into the vast landscape until the winds of Huhellsus blew this inconvenience away.

Talus decided it was best to simply be bold and walk past the guard, and let the Ancients guide his path. If the guard had to die, then so be it. He stepped forward and watched the guard disappear into an adjoining corridor. Time to go. He walked forward but stopped when he spotted his Chinstrap informant round the corner ahead of him. The Chinstrap looked both ways, saw Talus, and then rushed to him. "Judging by the rapidity of your movements, you don't bring good news."

"She's coming for you," the Chinstrap said between breaths.

"She?" Talus asked. No females carried rank in Royal Emperor command, so it could only mean Mearna.

"Mearna. The Overlord has given her a regiment and they're nearly upon you."

This was a surprise. Talus wondered why the Overlord would break with custom and send Mearna, a female, to carry out his commands. Perhaps it was a test of her loyalty, or perhaps Antaean thought Talus would kill her and get rid of a problem he couldn't. He decided he wouldn't disappoint the Overlord on the latter. Talus watched the corridor ahead him. The guard had returned and stood at the intersection of passageways. Talus' intended path lay behind the guard. He had no choice but to go through the unfortunate guard. "Thank you once again," he said to the Chinstrap. "Now go. Things are about to become extremely bloody."

The Chinstrap went back the way he came and Talus went his own way, casually walking toward his escape route, gripping his spear firm, but keeping his flippers loose, prepared for the fight. As expected, the dutiful guard crossed his own spear in front of Talus. Talus looked at him from the corner of his eye. "You may want to move that."

"Where are you going?" the guard asked, not taking Talus' advice.

"Wherever I choose," Talus said, turning his head, meeting the other face to face.

"The Overlord has decreed that none shall enter this passage. What business do you have in the lower reaches?" The Guard turned his spear so that the tip was aimed at Talus' chest.

*This again?* Talus thought. "These confrontations are becoming an exercise in redundancy." He narrowed his eyes, ready to strike, when the voice of the Chinstrap rang out. Talus spun around in time to see his messenger lanced through the chest by the spear of a Royal Emperor warrior.

"I tried to stop them," the Chinstrap said through his dying breath.

Talus watched the Chinstrap penguin slide off the spear tip and fall to the floor, dead. "You did well," Talus said quietly. "Go, swim with Ancients in the Great Sea." He raised his head and glared at the Chinstrap's killer.

"Talus," a familiar voice called out.

Talus turned and looked down the opposing hall. A phalanx of warriors parted way to reveal Mearna. "Mearna," Talus answered. "I'm surprised to find you had the courage to come and face me yourself. Your place is among the shadows—scheming, and pitting penguins against each other for your own gain, a shadowy version of your master, Antaean."

Mearna stayed in place, not reacting to Talus' allegations. "You are under arrest for treason. Lay down your weapon and come quietly."

Talus scoffed at her demands. "Treason? You are one to speak of treason. Mearna, you must know me well enough to know that I will never lay down my weapon or, how did you put it? Come quietly. Whatever misguided information brought you here will prove you the fool when I kill you. Or worse, when the Overlord receives your battered body and you no longer prove useful to him as a breeder. That is, if I should spare your life." He knew Mearna hated her subservient role, and he hoped to enrage her enough to acting irrationally. He was surprised to see her remain in control.

"This is your last chance, Talus. Surrender and face the charges," Mearna continued, appearing confident in her odds.

Talus quickly studied his surroundings. Regardless of how many soldiers Mearna had brought, no more than six could face him at any given time, owing to the narrowness of the corridors. He liked his odds. "Do what you must, Mearna," Talus shouted back. "But be prepared to flee or die when I finish with your warriors. This is your last chance," he added, mocking her words. He heard Mearna's orders to attack in reply.

The guard blocking Talus' escape stepped forward with his spear ready for battle.

Talus looked at the guard. "Are you certain you want to die this way?"

"I will do my duty," the guard answered.

Talus sighed regretfully. "Then you will carry that belief with you to the Great Sea." He lashed out before the guard could react, driving his spear through the guard's throat, then turned to face the advancing warriors. He ignored the guard choking on his gurgling final breaths as he pulled the spear free of his throat. The body fell to the side, the first of what he hoped would be many.

The first Royal Emperor warrior approached, cautiously at seeing the guard so quickly dispatched. Talus kept his head on a swivel, watching each warrior as they came at him from opposite ends of the corridor, hoping to box him in. A glint of joy sparked in Talus' eye. It was time to do what he loved most. It was time to kill. He rapped the first warrior across the beak with his spear tip, swung back, knocking away a half-hearted lunge of another. Bringing his attention back to the first, Talus batted away the warrior's spear, then drove his own into the soft flesh beneath the beak. He rammed the butt of his spear in the gut of another attacker, then twisted around, swinging his weapon, batting away three spears trained on him. Talus gave three rapid thrusts into the chests of the spears' owners, drawing splotches of blood. Not enough to kill them, but it would slow them down.

Two warriors came at Talus from the corridor behind, one tripping over the body of his fallen comrade. Talus dispatched the stumbling penguin quickly, then ducked under the swing of the other. He brought his spear back and stabbed the eye of the next attacker. The half-blind warrior cried out and dropped his weapon. Talus gave him a quick death and provided the next in line a similar favor.

Exhilaration coursed through Talus' body as his lust for the fight rose within him. It had been too long since he had used his skills in combat, and they returned to him like a long departed friend. Killing seals and the occasional inept guard was all well and good, but he hadn't been truly tested in recent memory. The exhilaration of dealing death coursed through him, and he called out in a primal rage as the bloodlust reached its crescendo, thrilling him to the point of unmatched ecstasy. The three injured warriors came at him once more and Talus responded as he had before, knocking away their weapons with a single swipe. He stabbed each of them in successive thrusts, this time going deep enough to kill.

Talus felt a burning pain in his back as a spear found its mark. Any deeper and it might have ended the fight. He retook control of his emotions, remembering a calm warrior was a deadly warrior. He twisted

away, swinging his spear around, and slammed it against the offending
spear-holder's beak. He felt a glint of satisfaction at seeing the warrior's
shattered beak dangle from his face. Talus moved closer and delivered a
fatal stab to the warrior's midsection.

Undaunted by their fallen comrades, more warriors rushed at Talus. He
made quick work of the first two, but as more came, he took a step back to
brace himself and stumbled over the body of one of his victims. His fall was
broken by the soft flesh of a dead penguin, but he watched with dismay as
his spear flew from his grip.

Seeing their opportunity, three warriors lunged with their spears,
stabbing at their vulnerable enemy. Talus rolled left and right, avoiding
their stabs, until one found the flesh of his shoulder. Talus howled with
rage, and swung with his other flipper, snapping the spear in half. The
surprised warrior hesitated, and Talus seized the moment. Groping blindly,
he found the weapon of a fallen warrior, and quickly parried two spear
thrusts away. He looked at the warrior who had stabbed him and buried
the spear tip deep into the soft flesh between the warrior's legs. He batted
away more attacks from his back, making weak jabs at their midsections,
giving them pause as they tried to figure out a way around his defenses.

Talus took advantage of their indecision and gave one of his tormentors
a more meaningful stab in the gut, taking him out of the equation. The
second warrior clicked his beak in anger and stabbed downward hoping
to end the fight. Talus reacted and swung his spear, and just managed to
deflect the blow. With his momentum carrying him forward, the warrior
lost his balance, falling on top of Talus. Their eyes met, and in in the next
instant, Talus pecked both of his opponent's eyes out. The warrior writhed
in pain, and Talus buried his beak in the warrior's throat, ending his life.

Shoving the dead penguin off him, Talus scrambled to his feet. He
wondered why the other warriors hadn't attacked. All they had to do
was attack en masse and he would have been defeated. He looked either
direction and saw that the remaining warriors were struggling to crawl over

the growing pile of dead penguins.

"The Ancients are at my side," he said with satisfaction, knowing his faith was not misplaced. But his opponents hindrances were also his own. Talus looked to the corridor leading to the lower reaches and considered making a break for freedom. But he knew they would follow. And when they did, he would be boxed in and likely killed before Lord Saeson answered his call for help, if the Lord of the Misshapen even would, given the circumstances.

Talus made his decision. He would make his way toward Mearna and kill her, then simply walk out of PIC. If anybody else tried to stop him, he would add their blood to his growing body count. Talus climbed over a pair of bodies in the passage leading to Mearna and met the first penguin in line with a solid spear thrust in the chest. More came and more died. He heard Mearna call for the warriors to move in closer, and all of the remaining Royal Emperors came at him.

The warriors attacked as one and Talus met each of them. Had the warrior penguins used this tactic in the beginning of the fray, instead of taking turns, they might have stood a chance. But Talus had thinned their numbers, and the rivers of blood and piled corpses had planted doubt and fear in their minds. Despite their misgivings, the warriors pressed the attack. Talus fought furiously, ignoring the occasional jabs, stabs, and slaps as his lust for dealing death never diminished. His blood rage buoyed his strength, and when the warriors' bodies moved close enough to render his weapon useless, he abandoned the spear and used his beak, the weapon the Ancients had provided him.

Talus tore and ripped at the flesh of his attackers, taking satisfaction with each body that fell by the wayside, until finally only two Royal Emperor warriors remained. Talus stole a glance down the hall and spotted Mearna backing away. He eyed his two remaining foes. "You have fought bravely. You have performed you duty with honor," he said through ragged breaths. Though his bloodlust had not diminished, the fatigue of battle had begun to wear on him. "You may continue this fight and join your comrades in the Great Sea, or I will allow you to leave and live to fight another day."

One of the two growled and charged forward. Talus met his charge, batted away the spear with his flipper, and plunged his beak into his chest. He kept it buried in the warrior's chest until he felt his opponent's heart twitch to a stop. Talus withdrew and stood panting. Looking at the other, he awaited his decision.

The Royal Emperor looked at Talus, then toward the corridor filled with the bodies of those who had tried to stop him and failed. "You fight with the power of the Ancients," the warrior said and laid his weapon at Talus' feet.

Talus nodded and placed his flipper against the warrior's side. "The Ancients guide your actions. There is no shame in admitting defeat. Go, and may the spirits of the Ancients swim at your side." The warrior turned and hurried down the corridor, knocking Mearna aside as he passed. Talus watched him go until his eyes fell on Mearna. He watched her stand stiff and indecisive. Talus had to laugh. He knew that Mearna knew that if she tried to run she would be caught and killed. What she didn't know was that her fate was already sealed. "Time to finish this," he said and walked toward her.

Talus, covered with the blood of his opponents and a healthy dose of his own as well, his gold head crest pinned beneath a layer of crimson gore, and a spear, tacky with blood, clutched in his grip, approached Mearna.

Mearna straightened herself, her eyes growing wide at the gruesome visage of Talus. "You are the incarnation of Elatha-Cadail," she said, her voice a mixture of awe and dread.

Talus balked at the notion. "You need to study the deities more thoroughly, crèche-keeper," he said, always eager to impart a lesson to the ignorant, regardless of circumstances. "Elatha-Cadail is the demon of nightmares and chaos. In this instance, you should liken me to Cuasan the Taker. But I assure you, I have no need to make bargains with the Lord of the Underworld or demons of legend to kill. It is what I do, and it is my purpose. And now, Mearna, I must fulfil my purpose." He raised the spear toward her throat.

"It was on the Overlord's command," Mearna said with the spear tip pressing against the soft flesh beneath her beak.

"Nothing happens in Pack Ice Command without the Overlord's orders. Do you believe I should spare you and kill him instead?" Talus dragged the tip down her chest and pressed it against the soft spot below her sternum. "He ordered me captured or killed. Tell me why he should do this so that you may go to the Great Sea clear of conscience."

Mearna looked at Talus in confusion. "Because you sought to overthrow him? For treason."

Talus laughed aloud. "Treason? Overthrowing the Overlord? If I wanted to do that, I would've done so long before now." He brought the spear back up, prodding her throat. He waved one flipper toward the slaughter. "But I guess killing... what was it? Thirty-nine of the Overlord's warriors and one guard would constitute treason. A self-fulfilling prophecy, one might say." He looked at her through narrowed eyes. "As would be killing the Overlord's consort."

Mearna shook her head. "No."

"No?" Talus said through a half-amused voice. "You sent forty warriors to kill me and you think I should spare you? That I *would* spare you?"

"Help me. You can kill the Overlord. Dispose of him for me. I grow weary of being under his control. I—"

"I know what you seek, Mearna. I know what you think and how you think. You fool the malcontents into thinking you're their champion, that your *Resistance* will lead an uprising and all will gain their freedom. I also know that you desire the dais. That you see yourself as Overlord. Save your pleas for Cuasan when he takes your soul to the endless dunes of Cayaske." Talus once again dragged the spear downward and pressed it against her stomach. Mearna instinctively tried to push it away.

Talus cocked his head and squinted. He leaned close to Mearna and made a series of low-pitched clicking sounds. Talus brought his head back with a jerk and looked at her in amusement. "Whose egg is it?"

Mearna said nothing, only lowering her head.

"Not the Overlord's or else he wouldn't have sent you." Talus eyed Mearna steadily. "Liutites. You're carrying Liutites' egg." He laughed loudly, a bold mocking laughter. Mearna raised her beak saying nothing. Talus stopped laughing and shook his head. "The Ancients indeed have a sense of humor. I will spare you. Not for your sake, but to let you live out the purgatory you find yourself in. My only regret is that I will not be here to see how this ends. Good luck, Mearna. Good luck and farewell. I hope to never see you again." Talus walked away, his laughter bouncing off the walls.

Mearna let out a long breath of relief and leaned against the wall, looking at Talus' carnage. "Liutites," she said with a growl, and left the scene.

# CHAPTER 30

Talus walked through the main hall, bringing a hush over the throngs of penguins as each stood and watched or stepped out of his path. It didn't take long for word of what the rogue had done to spread through the busy halls of Pack Ice Command. No warriors or guards came to arrest or to try to stop him. No words were spoken as he passed each penguin, looking in as many eyes as dared to meet his own. It was as silent as Pack Ice Command had ever been, and only the steady moan of the Antarctic wind risked breaking the silence.

Talus spotted Diutes lurking behind a trio of Royal Emperors. He considered killing the fool—no one would try to prevent it—but he decided to let fate have its way and let life play out as it may.

Walking up the wide sloping passage to the exit, Talus never looked back. He knew the faces of each penguin there and he would remember them all. He wondered how many would still be alive the next time he came to Pack Ice Command. If the Overlord had his way and a conflict with man began, he guessed not many of them, if any at all. It didn't matter to Talus. If he ever did come back, and if the command center still stood at that time, it would be with a greater purpose.

Talus stepped outside and stared across the vast Antarctic landscape, eager to be back home on the plains of Planarseae. The ever present and powerful polar wind buffeted his body as he ambled his way up a slow rise.

When Talus reached the top of the rise, he spotted a familiar dark form silhouetted against the bright southern sky. He knew at once that it was the Overlord.

Antaean stood with his back to Talus, staring at the same landscape, his seal-skin cloak snapping in the wind, and a long staff in his grip. "An impressive show of skill and strength," he said when Talus arrived.

"It is as the Ancients will it to be. I am only a vessel." Talus stood beside the Overlord, preening away flecks of frozen blood from his coat.

"The Ancients," Antaean said. "Is it the Ancients' will that I am Overlord, or my own?"

"The will of the Ancients is open to our own interpretation. I won't pretend to know what their will is for you, only what it means to me." After a long pause, Talus looked at Antaean. "Treason?"

Antaean waved his flipper dismissively. "I'm uncertain where she got her information, but it was a decent test of her loyalty. She proved herself well enough. Though she brought twice as many warriors as I allowed her. I'm surprised you let her live."

Talus laugh inwardly. *Loyalty? Mearna doesn't know the word.* "I'm surprised as well. But I'm sure you'll have a few more surprises before your time is done."

The Overlord turned his head toward Talus for a second, then looked back at the horizon. "You don't agree with my plans to drive the humans out," he said, changing the subject.

Talus repeated Antaean's actions by looking at him then turning away. "Whether I agree with them or not, it won't stop you from carrying them out. You will do as you wish. Some may disagree, some may even try to stop you, but as for me, I'll watch from a distance."

"Then you don't believe the Ancients have willed it to be?"

"If your intent was to simply drive the human presence out, maybe. But I know your motives, and those motives will undoubtedly lead to disaster."

"The Royal Emperors are the rightful heirs of this realm," Antaean said, raising his voice and puffing his chest. "Conquest is in our nature."

Talus continued to preen his feathers. "No one owns this world. And if there is anything our history has taught us, it is that conquest always leads to a fall. Conquer yourself—then you will know the will of the Ancients." He stopped preening and stared at the Overlord. "This is where I'll leave you, Antaean. I truly wish the Ancients to be at your side. But I fear that is not the case." Talus didn't salute or acknowledge Antaean, he simply walked away.

Antaean huffed loudly. "I could stop you."

"On an open field and with a hundred warriors to aid you, maybe," Talus said, continuing to walk at a languid pace, as if he had no care in the world.

Antaean watched him for another moment. "I may need your services again in the future."

"And if I feel the need to give them, I will," Talus said without looking back. "Until that day...give my regards to Mearna." He walked away, leaving the penguin alliance and Temalus to their fate.

# CHAPTER 31

Temalus skirted the edge of what remained of Talus' carnage, having to pause when a Misshapen servant crossed his path while dragging away the last Royal Emperor body. He had heard enough chatter to get the gist of what had taken place. Lord Season had gotten word and was reluctant to let Temalus go, not for fear of betrayal, but to protect Temalus and the hope their alliance would bring.

In the end, any caution was unwarranted, as the ensuing chaos of the slaughter garnered all of PIC's attention. After the Misshapen passed, he continued back to his quarters. At the end of his slow walk he stepped inside his shared space to find Liutites sitting silently, with his eyes closed. Noting that his brother's head wasn't tucked, therefore he was not asleep, Temalus crept closer and looked at Liutites with curiosity. *Since when had Liutites taken up meditation?*

Liutites' eyes blinked open. "Did Lord Saeson agree to your plans?"

Liutites' unusually harsh tone stirred a sense of caution in Temalus. It wasn't like his brother to speak to him so abruptly. "He did," Temalus said, circling him.

"Am I privy to these plans?"

His brother's continued harsh tone put Temalus ill at ease. "You are. But tell me first what's wrong."

Liutites grumbled beneath his breath. He stared at Temalus for several moments before speaking. "You need to leave."

"All right. I can come back later. You seem to have a lot on your mind," Temalus said with hesitation.

"No, Temalus. You need to leave Pack Ice Command. It's no longer safe for you here."

Temalus straightened. "I do plan on leaving, but not before the Overlord is gone."

"No. Go now. Join Talus before he's too far away from here. He will show you how to survive on the floes." Liutites stood and looked deep into his brother's eyes. "Your presence here will only get us both killed. I won't be able to protect you for much longer."

"Do you want to protect me?" Temalus asked. Lord Saeson's words hung in his mind. Liutites said nothing at first and it was all Temalus needed to hear to know the truth. His brother was consumed by his lust for power.

"Of course I do," Liutites eventually said. "That's why I need you to go. They, the Overlord and others, will use my love for you against me. Even when I become Overlord, usurpers will come and they will exploit that love."

"You speak as though it's a weakness."

"It is," Liutites said. The expression in his eyes said that it pained him to say it. "In Pack Ice Command, in this world our father has created, love is a weakness."

"No, Liutites. It's not. It is our strength. The desire to make the wrongs right, to create peace instead of war, for the sake of not only ourselves but for those we love, is our strength. It is the greatest strength we can hope to have."

Temalus stood firm before Liutites. He wouldn't give up yet. The only way to save his brother was to eliminate the Overlord. Not just his father, Overlord Antaean, but the need for all future overlords. With a peace between the K'tha and Cu-kisc, as well as ending the ludicrous idea of a war with the humans, there would be no need for an Overlord. The Council of Thrace could be reformed to govern the affairs of penguinkind. It was Temalus' only hope.

Temalus stared at Liutites, waiting for a reply, but was answered with silence. Nearly a minute passed with Liutites studying the ground, never lifting his eyes to Temalus. When the silence became too much to bear, Temalus tapped Liutites on the beak with his own. "Lord Saeson has agreed to help us. But he won't kill the Overlord. He knows, as well as you and I, that if he were to kill Antaean, there could be no peace. We have to do it."

Liutites raised his head. "Then what support will he provide? What does he hope to gain from your plans?"

"He will send the Misshapen. They won't attack, but they will keep Antaean's warriors occupied while we depose the Overlord. As far as what Saeson hopes to gain..." Temalus looked at Liutites before continuing. He felt that what he said next could determine not only *their* fates, but those of all K'tha, and possibly all penguins. "Lord Saeson wants freedom and equality for the Misshapen. The Misshapen *are* both K'tha and Cu-kisc." Temalus chose not tell Liutites the rest of his demands, one of those being that there should be no Overlord. If they were successful in usurping Antaean, they would dive into those waters then. Temalus met his brother's gaze. A feeling of unease washed over him—nothing he could put his beak on, but something told him that Liutites *knew* he wasn't being told the whole truth, but chose to let it be.

"The Cu-kisc will never keep their word. They are the same as us. They desire to rule...conquer, and they desire to see the Royal Emperors fall. This is an ancient feud, it is who we are, and it has been bred into us for generations."

"Are you so certain that what we've been taught is the truth? Even if it is, there is nothing stopping you...us, from making a change and ending that feud. The Overlord already uses the Misshapen as servants. Why can't we let them choose their own fate and maybe... Maybe we can work together." Temalus studied Liutites. When they had previously discussed seeking Lord Saeson's aid, Liutites hadn't been so opposed to the idea. Temalus wondered what had changed.

"By agreeing to send the Misshapen, it seems Lord Saeson has chosen their fates for them. It will be their deaths when the time comes." Liutites began pacing in front of Temalus. He paused and looked at his brother, seeming on the verge of saying something, then resumed his pacing. "Is he really so much different than the Overlord?"

It was Temalus' turn to study the floor. He wondered if Lord Saeson was the noble penguin he made himself out to be. If Saeson truly cared for peace and for the safety of those in his care, would he really send them to their deaths if it came to that? What if their agreement was a ruse and Saeson planned to seize power with Antaean gone? There were so many variables, but none of them mattered now. There was no backing out. If Lord Saeson had ulterior motives, then they'd deal with that when the time came. Talus trusted him, and that was good enough for Temalus. The first step would be to eliminate the Overlord.

Liutites clicked his beak when Temalus didn't reply. "You worry that I don't want to protect you. I assure you I want to protect what little I hold dear. I will protect it by all means available to me. When I become the supreme commander, I will have the resources I need at my disposal to finally be rid of our father." Liutites inhaled deeply and was about to continue when Temalus cut in.

"And what assurances do you have that those resources will be available to you?" Temalus' voice carried a sense of urgency. He could see that Liutites was on the verge of giving in to his passion for power. "What if the warriors refuse to fight for you while Antaean lives? What then? Regardless of your misgivings, we need Lord Saeson's help."

"Mearna has assured me that the warrior caste will answer to me." Liutites turned away from his lie, looking at the blank wall.

"I don't trust Mearna. She has her own agenda. And she will say whatever she needs to see that agenda to its end." Temalus looked around, realizing his voice had grown too loud. "You shouldn't trust her."

"I don't," Liutites said with a hushed voice. "That's why I told her Talus planned an insurrection. And she did exactly as I expected. She went to Antaean."

Temalus threw up his flippers in disbelief. "It was you who caused Talus to leave? He could have been killed. He could have been a great ally."

"Talus is an ally to no one. And if the Overlord truly wanted Talus dead, he would have sent a legion of soldiers to kill him. Antaean needs Talus. But now that he's gone, you will have someone to show you how to survive on the plains. You need to go as well, before it's too late."

*Before it's too late.* Talus had said the same thing. He wondered how many times he would hear it before it actually became *too late*. Temalus shook his head. It wasn't too late yet. "No. I'm not going until I see our father dead and I'm sure that you won't repeat his poor choices."

"I won't. But I will be Overlord. And I promise this war nonsense will not come to pass. You will be safe on the ice plains. Safer than here anyway." Liutites met Temalus' eyes. "There are things that you don't know and, for your protection, probably shouldn't know."

"You saying that tells me you think I should know."

Liutites stared at Temalus for several moments before speaking. "Mearna is with egg. And before you ask, the answer is yes. It is mine." He turned away as if expecting a lengthy reproach from Temalus.

Temalus didn't give him one. He stared at the back of his brother's head knowing that he was now lost to him. Liutites' allegiance would be to Mearna, and if she wanted him to be Overlord, then Liutites would become that, and he would do it under the banner of protecting his hatchling. Liutites now had an excuse to justify his desire for power. "Congratulations then, my brother. If you truly want to be Overlord, you must first be supreme commander. You should prepare yourself for the match tomorrow."

"I'm as prepared as I will ever be," Liutites said. He raised his head toward Temalus. "Do you have nothing else to say?"

"What can I say that you don't already know? I'm sure you will win your match with Persus, but I have less confidence that you will win against our father. If you do, I pray to the Ancients that you do not follow in his footsteps." Temalus turned his back on Liutites and began to walk away.

"Are you leaving?" Liutites asked, sounding hopeful that Temalus would be free of the danger of Pack Ice Command.

Temalus paused and inhaled deeply. "Your offspring, like me, will be your weakness, too." Liutites didn't reply. Temalus knew one of the reasons, if not the only reason Liutites wanted him gone, was to be rid of the moral compass that had kept him restrained this long, so he could do his work free of eyes that expected better of him. He turned slightly toward Liutites. "I will leave here, but not today. I have work to do, too." Temalus could feel Liutites' glare as he exited the room.

# CHAPTER 32

The steady rising chatter of hundreds of penguins echoing through the halls awoke Liutites from his uneasy slumber. He grumbled to himself, wondering why the Chinstraps had to wake every other being within the compound when the first hints of daylight appeared. He longed for the winter solstice when day was as dark as night. Rotating his head, stretching his tight unrested muscles, Liutites noticed Temalus hadn't returned. Hoping his brother had reconsidered his options and had gone, he made his way toward a morning meal.

He rounded a corner and saw that Temalus hadn't reconsidered. "I was hoping you had the sense to leave," he said, not masking his disappointment.

"And miss your ascent to supreme commander?" Temalus said, sounding spryer than he had the last time they were together. He joined his side and walked with him to the commissary. "Besides, you need someone in your corner. Who else would be there for you, Diutes?"

"I'd sooner have a Gentoo."

"That could be arranged if you prefer," Temalus remarked, and the two shared an uneasy laugh.

After the moment passed, Liutites regarded his brother. "While I appreciate you being here for the match, it is unnecessary." He looked around the room as they made their way to the farthest trough. "The fight will be…brief."

Temalus looked at Liutites with one eye while swallowing an ice fish. "You always told me not to underestimate my opponent, and you shouldn't, either. Persus is no pushover. He's clever and strong."

"I'm not concerned. It will be over before it begins." Liutites raised his beak high and gulped down a beakful of tiny squid. "I've had enough to eat. I should go."

Temalus looked around the room, clearly confused. "Since when is one bite enough for you? And the match isn't for a while still."

Liutites stood under his brother's watchful gaze. The look in Temalus' eyes had changed. Only a week before, Temalus looked at him with respect and admiration. Liutites wondered when the change had come. Was it really only a week ago? Or had the change begun earlier?

Liutites had always played the part of protector of Temalus. He had protected him from Diutes' jealousy, their father's ire, and he had even gone as far as to beat one of Temalus' opponents prior to a match so badly that he could barely stand when entering the arena. But now, looking at Temalus, he could see that even if he still needed protection, he had grown past accepting it. If anything, it was Temalus who was doing his best to protect Liutites.

But he wouldn't accept Temalus' protection either. Liutites wanted only one thing—to become supreme commander. And Liutites accepted his truth. He didn't want the mantle of Overlord to protect his future hatchlings. He'd already decided that once his chick hatched and fledged, he or she would be sent to the warrior caste or to serve as a crèche minder, and remain anonymous to him and all other penguins. Attachment was too dangerous. Nor did Liutites want to become Overlord for Mearna's sake or approval. He wanted the dais for his own power and glory, and to become more powerful than his father had ever hoped to imagine.

"I'm going to the arena to wait," Liutites finally said.

"I'll go with you." Temalus snagged another bite and made a motion to follow.

Liutites raised a flipper. "Alone." He caught the hurt on his brother's face, and then saw it transform to acceptance at being rebuked. Pain swelled inside Liutites' gut, but he swallowed it, placing it deep inside, hoping for it never to surface again. Attachment was too dangerous, even deadly. He turned his back on Temalus and left him standing alone.

∧∧∧

An hour had passed before the first spectators began to amble their way from Pack Ice Command to the shallow bowl of the arena. Instead of the usual loud chatter, the audience talked in low murmurs. A certain sense of wary anticipation, on the edge of unease, seemed to subdue the crowd, as if what they were about to witness would set their course for the future whether they knew it or not. General Liutites stood on the edge of the battleground awaiting the moment when his desires would come to fruition. He watched the crowd, knowing their apprehension was well placed. This day would mark the beginning of the end of the life they had known, and their new Overlord would soon rise to take control of their destinies.

Overlord Antaean, accompanied by his usual retinue of Clayfus, Mearna, and several elite guards, waddled to the front of the provisional dais and a hush fell over the already subdued crowd. He stared across the arena floor, his eyes falling on Liutites for a moment, and then to Lieutenant-General Persus, who had entered the battleground accompanied by Captain Astramachos.

Clayfus stepped to the edge of the dais and began his usual proclamations. Liutites stared at Persus. It was time to become supreme commander. He calmly walked forward, ignoring Clayfus' pomp, eyes focused on his opponent, determined to end this fight before it began. As he moved closer, he saw Persus and Astramachos exchange confused looks. *Good*, he thought. No one had warned them. Liutites hadn't dismissed the idea that Mearna would forewarn Persus, if not personally, then through her network of informants. At two meters away, Liutites heard Clayfus begin to sputter his announcements. At one meter, he heard Clayfus call his name, and saw Astramachos take a step toward him.

Liutites brushed Astramachos aside with the easiest of effort, and stood face to face with Persus.

"What are you doing, General Liutites?" Persus asked. His eyes shifted toward the dais, where Antaean stood clutching his staff, staring intently at the proceedings.

"I am becoming who I was meant to be," Liutites said. Immediately and without the least hesitation, Liutites lunged, driving his beak into Persus' chest, piercing his heart, and killing him instantly. He stood over Persus, watching his surprised and horrified eyes grow placid and dim, accepting the inevitable.

Death was always so anticlimactic. Killing was dramatic and violent; adrenaline coursed through one's veins, enhancing focus until the death blow was dealt, followed by the victim's spasms and gasps as the body refused to accept its fate. But the passage from life to death was subtle—a simple twitch, or a quiet exhalation, followed by stillness—and then nothing. In that moment of quiet nothingness, Liutites found clarity, bringing with it a determination to kill Antaean so intense, it became part of him, bound to the essence of who he was.

He turned toward the dais and saw his father staring back at him with smug, seemingly mocking eyes. Liutites stole a glance at Mearna, who returned a nearly imperceptible nod. He scanned the throng of spectators and spotted Diutes. Diutes watched him, carrying an almost gleeful countenance. Liutites ignored him and continued to scan the crowd until he found Temalus. His brother shook his head, lowered his beak against his chest, and stepped back, disappearing into the crowd.

A steady murmur coursed through the multitude of onlookers until Overlord Antaean raised his staff. Silence fell over the arena. "General Liutites." The Overlord's bellowing voice rang across the battleground.

Liutites took several steps toward the dais, then raised his beak, awaiting the proclamation that would advance him to the rank of supreme commander.

"You have defeated Lieutenant-General Persus for the right to advance to supreme commander." The Overlord paused as Liutites stiffened in anticipation. He glanced at Mearna, then found Diutes in the crowd, before fixing his dark gaze on the general. "However, the Ancients have deemed that these traditions should be carried out in good faith and fair play. You, Liutites, have shown neither. Therefore you will not be promoted to the rank of supreme commander."

Liutites lowered his salute, barely listening to the Overlord's rambling, ready to accept his promotion. When the Overlord's words finally registered in his mind, his body went still, numb with an anger so intense and so pure that all other sensation vanished, as if stolen by the unceasing wind. He stared at the ice beneath his feet, eyes narrowed with a hint of confusion. His brief confusion faded as he fully grasped what had happened.

His body began to tremble with rage. It took all of his self-control to beat back the fury threatening to spill over. Liutites lifted his head to find Antaean staring back at him with black eyes telling him that he had beaten him. A sickening dread roiled through his gut. This wouldn't be the end of it. The Overlord had more in store. Liutites knew that when Antaean defeated an enemy, whether real or perceived, he didn't stop at merely defeating them, he would crush them with absolute totality.

He scanned the crowd once more, searching for Temalus, but he was nowhere to be found. Worry for his brother mingled with his sense of dread, threatening to send his last meal spilling on the icy ground. He had to get word to Lord Saeson. It was the only way for him to save himself and Temalus.

"General Diutes," the Overlord said, not taking his eyes from Liutites.

Diutes did a double-take, clearly surprised by his promotion. He raised his beak in salute to Antaean when realization crept over his slow mind.

"Have Liutites escorted to my chamber." He paused while maintaining eye contact with Liutites. "And find Temalus."

"Yes, my lord," General Diutes said. He raised a flipper and motioned for several warriors to follow.

Liutites ignored the proceedings. Instead, he focused on Mearna. She stared back at him for several moments before lowering her head. She turned away and followed Antaean as he left the dais. Liutites looked around the arena, watching the crowd disperse, and listening to the steady chatter of the multitude. The words *shame* and *embarrassment* rose to meet his ears. Liutites met several faces who quickly averted their eyes. He made a note of who he'd kill when this was over. The mindless masses may have thought this was the end of him, but it wasn't. No matter what, Liutites would see that this wasn't the end.

General Diutes approached Liutites, his chest puffed, carrying a cocksure posture. He motioned for his warriors and looked at Liutites, and his beak parted as if he were about to make a boastful remark.

Liutites snapped his head toward Diutes. "One word from you and I'll kill you quicker than I did Persus."

Diutes' smug countenance vanished in a heartbeat. His eyes shifted between the warriors and Liutites. He seemed as if he were about to forego better judgement, his beak parted once more, but then closed, self-preservation apparently winning out over any thoughts of rubbing Liutites' beak in his defeat.

Liutites allowed himself to be escorted from the arena with thoughts of killing Antaean filling his head.

# CHAPTER 33

Temalus slid through the halls of Pack Ice Command. He had heard the murmurs of penguins leaving the arena that Antaean wanted both him and Liutites in his chamber. Some had even looked at him, as if they would tell the nearest guard his whereabouts, but thought better of it when they saw Temalus' warning glare.

Temalus spat a continuous string of old penguin curses as he continued on his way. Liutites' foolishness had cost them. All his brother had to do was proceed with the match, kill Persus, and become supreme commander. But even as he considered what may have been, Temalus had doubts that their father *would* have promoted Liutites. It seemed the Overlord had different ideas and had likely known of their plans. Even though he was sure Antaean had a network of spies, he didn't know for certain how the Overlord had known, but Diutes being promoted to general gave him an obvious clue. He would worry about the how and why later. Time was short and he had to get word to Lord Saeson to let him know that the time to act was drawing near.

Alternating between sliding on his belly when the halls were empty and walking when they weren't, Temalus hurried to the corridor leading to the lower reaches. Blood still stained the floor at the site of Talus' massacre, and looking at the remnants of the carnage, Temalus wished the rogue had stuck around. He could use his help. But an old Gentoo adage popped in his mind: *Put wishes in one nest and guano in another, and see which fills fastest.* Gentoo may not be the most eloquent of penguins, but they had a way of seeing the world honestly.

Temalus looked either direction of the crossway and spotted guards lurking in the shadows. He considered making a dash across the intersection, and hope that Lord Saeson would open the door before the guards reached him, but he had to guess that the door would be guarded as well. There had to be another way. Doubling back, Temalus weighed his options. He knew that Saeson had his own network of spies and messengers; the problem was that he didn't know who they were. Most were Chinstraps or Adélie, but they all looked alike to him. He could tell them apart by voice, but it would take the better part of a month to find and speak to every Chinstrap within Pack Ice Command.

He continued to travel back the way he had come, when a voice called to him from a small antechamber to his left. Temalus peered into murky room, and the answer to his problems presented itself. "Are you the one I spoke to in…um, down there?" he asked, tilting his head in the direction of the passage to Lord Saeson's realm.

A Chinstrap penguin stepped closer to him. "I am. If you had bothered to ask my name you could have asked another Chinstrap for me and saved yourself the trouble of wandering aimlessly through the halls."

Temalus rolled his head in frustration. "I thought it best not to know your name in case things went wrong."

"Was it for my safety or because you didn't care?" the Chinstrap asked.

Temalus firmed his beak, fighting back his impatience. "Of course I care. I'm not like the others." Looking at the Chinstrap, he admitted the truth to himself; he had dismissed him as a servant. "Maybe you're right, though. What is your name?"

"It's best you don't know… For my own safety."

Temalus slapped his flippers against his side in exasperation. Taking a calming breath, he stooped close to the unnamed Chinstrap. "I need to get a message to Lord Saeson."

"That's why I'm here. But it's not as easy as it was before. Talus' spectacle has made things more difficult."

"Then how can I communicate with him?"

"I said it was more difficult, not impossible. There are air passages that lead to the lower levels. They're a tight fit for a Chinstrap, but it can be done, as my being here attests." The Chinstrap waved his flippers at the gloomy room.

"Ventilation? If the Overlord wants to kill Saeson, why would he allow the ventilation shafts to remain open?" It didn't make much sense to him, and Temalus wondered if the Chinstrap was a spy for Antaean or someone other than Lord Saeson.

"Open your eyes, Temalus." The Chinstrap scooted closer. "Lord Saeson is a threat every Royal Emperor here knows of. Why would the Overlord need warriors and guards if there were no threat? He needs the Lord of the Misshapen to justify an army. That is, he needs him until the war with the humans begins."

Temalus had no doubt the Chinstrap was speaking the truth. It made sense, it was just more lies and deceit from the Overlord. All of the efforts, all of the patrols, and hunting were nothing more than a show to give the appearance of protection. And all the while, Antaean had built his forces for their true purpose: to subjugate the other clans and rule the Southern Realm. He wondered if his father had sent him and Liutites to hunt for Lord Saeson with the hope that they'd be killed. Whatever Antaean's purpose had been no longer mattered. What mattered now was telling Lord Saeson that the time to act was upon them, and then all of Antaean's scheming and lies would die along with him.

Temalus drew a deep breath. This ended today. "Tell Lord Saeson—"

"Tell Lord Saeson what?" General Diutes' voice hissed from behind Temalus.

Spinning around, Temalus saw Diutes standing alone, with his eyes narrowed in a sneer. He stared back at him for a moment, weighing his options to find a way out of his predicament. Temalus looked down at the Chinstrap. He considered lying, but even though Diutes was a slow-minded brute, he knew his brother could not be so easily fooled. There was only one way. "Run," he said to the Chinstrap.

"When?" the Chinstrap asked.

"Now," Temalus said and rushed toward his brother. He hit Diutes bodily, driving him against the far wall of the corridor. It was then that Temalus saw Diutes wasn't alone. A half dozen elite guards stood on either side of the entry with spears at the ready. Temalus knew at once that his chances of escape were slim.

Diutes hit the wall with a thud. Shaking the impact off, he returned the attack, pressing his body against Temalus, driving him back the way they had come. Diutes stole a glance and noticed the fleeing Chinstrap. "Catch the Chinstrap. Don't let him get away." Three guards brought the spears down, blocking the Chinstrap's escape.

The distraction was all Temalus needed. Shifting his weight, he let Diutes' momentum carry him forward, giving him a hard slap as he slipped past. Diutes stumbled, but didn't fall. Temalus turned to go, but was met by the tips of the remaining guards' weapons. Turning the other direction, he was greeted by Diutes and a flurry of slaps. Letting Diutes drive him toward the wall, he weathered the assault until he felt the wall against his back. He looked into his brother's eyes. "You're strong, Diutes, I'll give you that. But your mind is as sharp as sponge."

Diutes pressed close. "This sponge of a mind was sharp enough to trap you and Liutites. Think about that when you're dead and swimming in the Great Sea."

"Trap?" Temalus dug his beak into Diutes' chest and shoved him away. Glaring at him with the intent to kill, he wondered how Diutes could have found a way to ensnare them. "I'm not trapped. And you don't have the foresight to plan one day ahead of yourself."

Diutes chirped a laugh. "I admit it didn't take much." He slapped at Temalus, followed by a weak stab with his beak that Temalus neatly avoided. "I heard you talking and simply informed the Overlord."

While returning a pair of slaps of his own, Temalus remembered the day he had told Liutites of his plans and recalled getting a sense of someone skulking nearby. He'd dismissed it at the time, but could it have been Diutes lurking in the shadows? It appeared he had been. He had always dismissed his brother as nothing more than a petty, jealous annoyance, and whose acerbic unlikableness, combined with a soft mind, was no more of a threat than an ill-tempered seal pup. As Temalus slapped at Diutes, he realized he had been wrong. Not only in his judgement of his brother, but also his treatment of him. *No wonder he wants to see us suffer.*

He had to try to make amends and appeal to whatever sense of good still dwelled within him. "Diutes, listen to me," Temalus said through heavy breaths while leaning against him. "We can end the Overlord's tyranny. No more challenges to the death, no war with the humans. We can stop it all. And you can be part of it. Together, you, me, Liutites, we can stop the madness."

Diutes pulled away and regarded Temalus. Some of the fury had faded from his expression.

"I was wrong about you," Temalus continued. "I admit that. I treated you unfairly, and I know nothing can change that. But if you join us, I promise I'll do everything I can to make it up to you." The brothers stared at one another, heavy breaths giving way to slow breathing.

Diutes nodded. "You're right, Temalus. You were wrong about me. Not just yesterday, or the years before that, but now as well. You think I'll join you in your little insurrection—at the moment of my triumph over you and Liutites? I'm going to enjoy watching you die—seeing your smugness fade away with your life. I've been waiting for this moment since the day you fledged. You want me to help end the madness." Diutes leaned close enough for their beaks to touch. "I love the madness. I live for it."

The venom in Diutes' words gave Temalus the clarity he needed. It wasn't his fault that Diutes had turned out the way he had. If anyone was to blame, it would be Antaean. Or maybe it was more than that. Maybe it really was the nature of the K'tha to conquer, and to destroy those around them. He had seen it in nearly every K'tha he had known—in Liutites, and even himself to some degree. Didn't he want to conquer and destroy the Overlord? Hadn't he entered into an alliance with their greatest enemy to see that to its end? There would be no swaying Diutes, and there would likely be no swaying Liutites either. Temalus knew that if he wanted to survive, his only chance now was to escape and get word to Lord Saeson.

Firming his beak, Temalus looked to the Chinstrap being held under the guards' spears. "Run!" Temalus shouted, slapped Diutes hard, then turned to run as well.

The Chinstrap pecked one of the guards in the gut, dodged a thrust, and fell to his stomach with the hope to scoot away to safety. Diutes absorbed the blow and saw what the Chinstrap intended. He stabbed his beak toward Temalus, then motioned to the guards. "Don't let the Chinstrap get away. Kill him!"

Looking back at the Chinstrap, Temalus made his choice; he wouldn't let him die because of his mistakes. Letting his anger wash over him, Temalus rushed toward Diutes, pinning him against the wall, flailing his flippers wildly, and stabbing with his beak. Diutes dodged each stab until Temalus found his mark and drove his beak into his brother's shoulder.

Diutes howled with rage, twisted away, and landed a stab of his own against Temalus' chest. The imprecise strike pierced the fatty flesh and hit bone, saving Temalus from a quick death. Undeterred, Diutes continued his assault, slapping with powerful flippers and lunging repeatedly with his deadly beak, driving his brother back, with the intent to kill.

Temalus had never seen such fury. He blocked and parried as best he could, weathering the assault until he felt the firmness of the opposing wall against his back once again. Temalus laughed to himself. As strong as Diutes was, he never learned. He had just escaped the same situation only moments before. Temalus used his beak to bat away each of Diutes' attempted stab, and was about to shift his weight to free himself when he heard the Chinstrap cry out. Both combatants turned to see a Royal Emperor guard drive his spear into the fleeing Chinstrap.

Diutes looked back at Temalus. His eyes narrowed with a sadistic mirth. "No help will come to you now…*brother*."

Temalus watched with impotent horror as the guard stabbed the Chinstrap a second time. There was nothing he could do to save the penguin, his last hope to get word to Saeson and escape. And now it seemed there would be nothing he could do to save his own life either. But as he turned his attention back to Diutes, he saw him for what he really was, a reflection of the twisted, authoritarian society the Overlord had built, one that brought other clans down to lift itself up, a society he himself had helped to grow. Temalus made a choice; he would do what he could or die from the effort.

"Your friend was quite stupid. Did he really think a Chinstrap could kill a Royal Emperor?" Diutes said while pressing against his brother.

Temalus almost laughed at Diutes' weak attempt to taunt him. "Not as stupid as you, Diutes." Temalus parried the strike he knew was coming, drew back and thrust his beak at Diutes' face.

Diutes angled his head to the left and Temalus' beak scraped across his right eye. He howled in pain and stumbled backward.

Temalus looked at Diutes and considered killing him, but now was his chance for escape. Instead of finishing him, he dove to the icy floor and slid toward the guard standing over the Chinstrap, knocking him over in the process and causing the two others to stumble away. He looked for signs of life in the unnamed Chinstrap as he slid to a stop. "I'm sorry," he said softly and was surprised when the Chinstrap's eyes parted open.

"Don't be," the Chinstrap said through a whisper.

"You're alive? I'll get you out of here. Come on." Temalus nudged him with his beak. "I won't let you die here alone."

The Chinstrap raised his head slightly. "We are never alone." His eyes motioned toward the end of the corridor.

Temalus looked the way he had been shown and caught a fleeting glimpse of another Chinstrap duck behind the wall. There was still hope. Looking back to the injured Chinstrap he saw that his life had faded. He heard Diutes barking orders, and Temalus kicked away, intending to toboggan away to safety, when he felt the sharp end of a spear jab him in his back, followed by two more. There would be no escape.

The guards watched closely as Temalus got to his feet, keeping their weapons firmly pressed against him. With nowhere left to go, he faced Diutes.

Diutes strode toward Temalus, stopping well out of striking distance. He stared at him through his one good eye; the other dripped with blood. "I should kill you."

"If you think you can, then do it," Temalus said, hoping to goad Diutes into accepting the challenge. He looked at the guards; none lowered their weapons.

"No," Diutes said with a derisive snort. "I would like to see what our father has in store for his traitorous son." He waved a flipper at the guards. "Take him to the Overlord."

Temalus obeyed the prodding spears and began walking. He looked down the long corridor and once more spotted the fleeting form of the other Chinstrap. Hope still lived.

# CHAPTER 34

Liutites stood unguarded before the Overlord's empty dais. To the side stood Clayfus, looking toward the entry, not making eye contact. Liutites shook with disgust. It wasn't anything he could put his beak on, but being in Clayfus' sickly presence made him feel ill, like the aide's frail visage would somehow infect him. And the feeling made Liutites want to rip the head off the Overlord's sycophant and feed his body to the sea stars. He vowed to do just that after he killed Antaean.

The sound of a door sliding open from the dark recesses at the rear of the chamber pulled Liutites from his murderous designs. The Overlord waddled from the shadows, with his cloak dragging on the floor and staff in his rudimentary grip. Ascending the dais, not taking his eyes from Liutites, Antaean carried the air of a penguin who was on the edge of unbridled violence. Liutites met his glare, body tense, as ready for violence as his father, hoping for it.

"General Liutites," the Overlord said with a calm tone juxtaposed to the rage simmering in his eyes. "Our customs hold a purpose. Ascension by combat was put in place to keep peace between the Royal Emperors who desired to rise above their station. Before I sanctioned the competition, officers assassinated one another in their sleep, killed their competitors while their backs were turned, murdered each other when the opportunity showed itself; it was chaos. I have instilled order. It was by my command that any who sought promotion should have the opportunity with equity."

Liutites rolled his head. Listening to the Overlord ramble on about his just cause always prompted his head to ache. "And yet you choose who is to fight whom, and when."

"If you are a Royal Emperor officer within the Penguin Defense Alliance, you forfeit your right to choose." The Overlord puffed his chest and took a single step forward. "You are under *my* command and you will carry out your orders without question. To do otherwise is to court chaos."

Liutites bristled at hearing the Overlord remind him of his dominance over him. "Is this an edict from the Ancients?" he asked in a scathing tone.

The Overlord grunted. "Where were the Ancients when our kind was nearly wiped from this world? Where were they when the Council of Thrace ordered our ancestors executed? Where were they when the seas warmed? Where were they when men came to our seas and killed penguins by the millions? Where are they now as the seas warm once again? The Ancients." Antaean paced the dais, snorting at the name. "Let the masses keep the Ancients. I have no need for them. I am the only deity the Royal Emperors need."

*Deity?* As Liutites watched the Overlord, he finally understood the depths of his father's madness. Did he really think he was god, or was it all bluster and show? He had always thought Antaean had spoken to the Oracle, and that her proclamation saying that he would be the one who would lead the penguins to unity and peace had been the basis for his alliance. Strange how the Oracle, Lapasia, hadn't been seen since the Overlord's alleged meeting with her. More lies and delusions. Now there was an even greater reason to kill him. The chamber was free of guards, and only Clayfus stood between him and the Overlord. Maybe now was the time to end the Overlord's reign.

Before Liutites could make his choice, Clayfus stepped off the dais and hurried to the entrance. The choice was made for him; his father was alone and unguarded. Liutites stepped closer, carefully watching his target, gauging the best angle of attack to finally end his father's madness. It was time.

The Overlord sighed. His head lolled sideways, showing his disinterest. "Before you do what you think you want to do, there is something you should see." Antaean nodded toward Clayfus. The attendant chirped something indecipherable in reply and the door began to open.

*What I think I* want *to do? More like what I'm going to do,* father. Liutites gauged the distance between them. He knew how long the slow moving door took to open. Would he have enough time to move on Antaean, climb the dais, land a killing blow, all before the guards reached him? The element of surprise he had hoped for was gone; the Overlord had already shown he knew what he intended, but he could still pull it off if he was lucky.

"Will you stop your scheming," the Overlord said, shaking his head. "If you were going to try to kill me, you would've acted already. Now watch the door; this concerns you."

Taking a step back and turning slightly to keep an eye on both the Overlord and the door, Liutites felt an odd and confusing emotion rise up within him. The way his father had spoken to him was different, strange, almost how he had imagined other penguin fathers would speak to their offspring, if not for the talk of killing. True, it was contradictory to his proclamation that he was an Ancient incarnate, and his words were dismissive, as always, plus it showed another layer in the depths of Antaean's madness, but it was oddly calming. He still wanted to kill the Overlord, there were no questions about that, but he had to wonder if his father, somewhere in the deep recesses of his twisted soul, had experienced a slight change in how he viewed him. Or was his father only toying with him before unveiling some new and sick way to punish him? The door ground open, revealing what waited on the other side, and Liutites saw that it was the latter.

A line of elite guards held Temalus at spear point. They prodded him forward, jabbing his back hard enough to draw blood. When they reached the foot of the dais, one of the guards whipped Temalus on the back of head, forcing him to fall before the Overlord.

Any vague feelings of goodwill along with any hope of reconciliation between Liutites and his father vanished, gone without any thought of returning, forever and completely. Liutites rushed to his brother's side, but was held at bay by a guard's spear.

When it appeared as if Liutites would forego better judgement and kill the guard, the Overlord shot him a waring glare, then spoke, "General Diutes, you have brought Temalus as I requested."

"Yes, my lord." Diutes stepped forward and raised his beak high. "I have brought the traitor to you."

The Overlord waddled toward Temalus. "These are serious accusations, General Diutes." He tilted his head and examined Diutes' swollen, blood-red eye. "What evidence do you have?"

Diutes lowered his beak. "When I found Temalus, he was speaking to a Chinstrap, a spy in service to Lord Saeson. He was telling the spy to inform Lord Saeson that the time to act was upon them. Temalus is in league with our enemy, my lord."

Antaean stood over Temalus, gripping his staff tightly, as if he were about to strike. "Commandant Temalus, what do you say to these accusations?" He motioned for him to rise.

Temalus stood under the close watch of the guards and looked at Liutites.

Liutites closed his eyes. Any hope of becoming supreme commander, Overlord, or even living fled from his thoughts. His body sagged. All hope was lost. He knew they would be executed or forced to take the long walk to the marker, from where no penguin returned.

Clearing his throat, Temalus faced the Overlord. "I don't know what traitorous act Diutes is speaking of. I was merely speaking with a Chinstrap messenger to find out what happened to General Liutites. As I'm sure you know, my lord, I left the match early."

"Lies!" Diutes shouted. "You were talking to him about overthrowing the Overlord. I heard you. We heard you." Diutes waved a flipper at the guards.

The Overlord looked at the guards. "Is this true?"

One guard came forward. "My lord, we were stationed outside the room where Temalus was found. We heard no such thing."

"What is this treachery?" Diutes blurted and nodded at another guard. "You were there. You heard it."

Antaean snapped his head toward Diutes. "Are you questioning my elite guard's loyalty, General?"

Diutes stopped his accusations. "No, my lord. I know they are loyal to you without question. I hoped that one heard—"

"Where is the Chinstrap? Perhaps he can be persuaded to illuminate me on the subject of treason." Antaean swung his head toward the first guard when Diutes didn't respond.

The guard raised his beak. "General Diutes ordered us to kill the Chinstrap, my lord."

Liutites watched the proceedings with amusement. Diutes' stupidity never ceased to amaze him. He stifled a laugh and noticed Temalus do the same.

"And did you?" The Overlord let his gaze fall on Diutes, who shifted nervously beneath the withering glare. When the guard answered that they had, Antaean slowly nodded. "General." Diutes stood at attention. "From what you tell me, you killed the only witness to your accusations—a suspected spy for Lord Saeson—a spy we could have interrogated."

Diutes' good eye shifted. "I'm sorry, my lord, was that a question?" He scratched his claws at the ice like a nervous fledgling.

This time Liutites did laugh. It was remarkable. Was Diutes being facetious, or was he really that dumb? His laughter drew a reproachful glare from the Overlord. Coughing a less than sincere laugh for the benefit of the Antaean's annoyance, Liutites stepped back and watched the Overlord. With his father's attention on Diutes' buffoonery, it might've been a good time to strike, especially with Temalus there to help. But with the guards collaring Temalus with their spears, it wouldn't work—they would only have to thrust their weapons forward a little and the only brother that mattered to him would die. Liutites felt a flash of anger at Temalus for not having listened to him—he should've been gone from PIC by now.

Overlord Antaean turned his attention from Liutites' amusement back to the matter before him. "General Diutes…" After a long pause, he continued, "You are strong, there is no doubt. And because of that, and because I also know your weakness, whether you know it or not—and I suspect you do not—I expect half as much from you as I do the other commanders in my alliance. And every time, without fail, you perform half as well as I expect."

Diutes aimed his beak at the ground, trying to puzzle out the Overlord's insult. "My lord," he said, raising his head to his father, with fleeting eye contact.

"You can say nothing in your defense. Had the Chinstrap survived, we might have discovered more of Lord Saeson's spy network. Or the Chinstrap would have died with the information—there is no way to know." Antaean surveyed the brothers before him, his eyes resting on each momentarily. "The three of you have risen higher in the ranks than any of my other offspring. And you have done so without the Grip. And you all share the same mother." Antaean watched the floor for a moment, as if reflecting on the past. "I should have let her live, but as she produced no offspring *with* the Grip, I couldn't allow it."

The three brothers shifted in unison, united in the hatred of their father. Liutites fought against his urge to attack. Antaean could insult him all he wished, make them feel like not having the Grip was an infliction. But he would learn soon enough that it wasn't the case. That one without the defect of rudimentary hands would rise up and take his place on the dais.

"As surprising as it is," the Overlord continued, "that the three of you have done so well with your disadvantages, you disappoint me equally. Diutes, with your weak mind, you fail to see beyond the tip of your beak. Liutites, your loathing of me and lust for power imprisons you to a lifetime of hate. And Temalus, the most intelligent of the three, your empathy for the lesser clans weakens your resolve, and shackles you to their fate. You could have been so much more than your limited vision has allowed."

*More?* Liutites clicked his beak. There was no *more* other than seeing his father dead. He'd had enough of the Overlord's lectures for the day... for a lifetime. "Are you finished with your analysis of our shortcomings? You've already dressed me down about the match, Diutes has proven his incompetence once again, and there is no evidence that Temalus has entered into a conspiracy with Saeson." It was obvious that the promotion to supreme commander was no longer an option and if the Overlord was going to have him executed, he should get on with it or at least try. "If there's nothing else..." Liutites began walking toward the exit.

"There's plenty more, Liutites," Antaean said. He turned his attention to the youngest guard of the group. "Ceocilus, escort General Diutes back to his quarters. See that he remains there."

The young guard motioned toward Diutes with his spear. Diutes shifted nervously and looked as if he was about to protest, but remained silent. He sullenly allowed Ceocilus to escort him from the room, head down, not looking at his brothers.

Liutites watched the proceedings, paying close attention to Ceocilus. The guard, large and strong, recently returned from the two-year trials at sea, his coat still glossy with a youthful sheen, reminded Liutites of his younger days when he was ignorant and looked at the world with different eyes. If he'd known then what he knew now, he might have followed Talus' lead and left PIC far behind. But Liutites was far from old, and though his eyes no longer saw the world with wonder and hope, they saw it for what it was: a world of cruelty and maliciousness, where only the strongest and deadliest survived.

The Overlord's voice called him back to the here and now. "Ceocilus, close the door on the way out." The guard nodded and did as instructed. Liutites faced Antaean with a sudden sense of dread and wondered what was in store for him and Temalus.

# CHAPTER 35

The sound of grinding ice terminated with a dull thud as the door to the Overlord's chamber shut. A silence fell over the room, broken only by the scrape of Clayfus' claws on the ice as he shuffled to the back of the chamber and disappeared into the shadows. Antaean motioned with the slightest of nods toward the remaining guards and they released Temalus. The Overlord watched his sons for a moment, then turned his back and walked to the center of his dais.

Temalus rolled his head, working out his cramped neck muscles after holding it still under the guards' spears. He exchanged a glance with Liutites and knew their thoughts were the same: five guards remaining, they could work together, overcome them, then attack the Overlord before anyone could get the door open and call for help. Liutites blinked in confirmation.

"As I said earlier, Liutites," the Overlord began speaking without his usual preamble. "We have rules in place, and you know the reason for these rules."

Liutites raised an eye at his father. "*You* make the rules. *You* break the rules every day. You create the rules as you go. This display of authority is nothing more than a thin veil of ice to hide the fact that you didn't want *me* to become supreme commander. In fact, the rank was likely just bait, getting us to swim after a fish that could never be caught. I'm through with your games."

"Games?" the Overlord barked. "Games. I wouldn't call it games, General. The rank of supreme commander is very real and it awaits whoever proves himself worthy of second in command to me. Which could have been you, if not for your defiance. Games..." He turned to Temalus. "You've been rather quiet through all of this. Do *you* believe the rank is real, or am doing as your brother said and *playing games?*"

There was something in the way the Overlord spoke. Nothing overtly threatening, but a calm, easy tone that belied something more sinister. Temalus couldn't put his beak on it. He wondered if Liutites had picked up on it too. Judging by the way his brother puffed himself to show his bravado before their father, he might have a clue, but then again, Liutites might just be readying himself for their attack on the guards.

Temalus stared at Antaean. No, he wasn't playing games. Toying with Liutites, yes, but not games. Temalus realized that, as it stood, they couldn't win. There was more to come, and whatever awaited them, it would be worse than they imagined. He clung to the small hope that the Chinstrap who had watched his capture would find a way to get them the help they needed before it was too late.

He sucked in a deep, resigned breath. "No, my lord. You're not playing games." Temalus turned to his brother, who seemed confused that he would agree with their father. "He has something much worse than games planned."

The Overlord took a moment and watched Temalus before speaking. "As insightful as always, Temalus." He turned sharply toward the back of the room, his seal-tooth necklace rattling with the effort of his corpulent frame. Antaean rumbled a clicking noise in his throat and Clayfus returned trailed by a half dozen guards and a pair of warriors.

Temalus lowered his head and looked sideways at his brother, noticing his shoulders slump. There would be no insurrection. They would both be executed here and now, or forced to walk to the marker, or taken to the Phocids. The Overlord ground his staff and Temalus awaited his fate.

The newly arrived Royal Emperors positioned themselves around the brothers with weapons held at their sides. Clayfus lurked behind Antaean, pacing nervously. "Temalus, I know you are in collusion with Lord Saeson." He raised a flipper when Temalus opened his beak to protest. "I knew before Diutes bumbled his way onto your plans. You must know that I have a network of informants...spies...throughout Pack Ice Command. And I learned long ago that Chinstraps shift their allegiance much too quickly and are therefore unreliable for such work." He turned his attention to Liutites and snorted.

Temalus wondered if the Overlord knew of Liutites' cavorting with Mearna. Perhaps he did, maybe he didn't, and he didn't care.

"The supreme commander would have access to my spies... If I ever find such a penguin to fulfil the duties of the post." The Overlord let his gaze linger on Liutites for a pair of heartbeats then looked back at Clayfus. Clayfus stopped his nervous pacing, met Antaean's eyes, then lowered his head.

The Overlord was still dangling the rank of supreme commander in front of Liutites' beak. Temalus wondered what his motives were. Was it simply to torment Liutites with what could have been? And then there was Clayfus. The sickly attendant usually strutted around the Overlord's chamber with an air of confidence, even arrogance. Was there a discord growing between the two? Whatever it was, Temalus had the feeling he wouldn't like what was coming next. In fact he knew it.

"I'm sure by now you're both wondering why I haven't ordered your executions," the Overlord continued, his tone returning to the boisterous authoritarian the brothers were accustomed to. He watched them both for another moment. "Liutites, you have proven yourself qualified to become supreme commander."

Temalus snapped his head toward Liutites. His brother's body instantly transformed from sunken and defeated to puffed up, filled with pride. "Don't get excited just yet, brother," he said to himself in a voice less than a whisper. The Overlord turned to Temalus. *Here it comes.*

"You, Temalus, have also proved yourself worthy. Your willingness to go to any extreme to get what you want proves that." The Overlord stared at him for several moments, until Temalus turned away.

The ground became very interesting to Temalus. He noticed the contrast in shades where claws had gouged the surface, some deep, some light. The faint lines from the workers who had spent countless hours throughout all of Pack Ice Command dragging their talons across the ice to create grooves for better traction so penguins wouldn't spend their days slipping in the vast ice compound. It had all been so well thought-out. He wondered if the creation of the compound had been the Overlord's insightfulness—the passages, tunnels, corridors, chambers, antechambers, feeding troughs, latrines. It would take a great deal of planning and foresight. Did Clayfus help with the planning, or the Adélies—they seemed to have a natural talent for design—or some other penguin no one knew of? Maybe even Saeson had been there at the beginning. But it had taken a great amount of thought and planning. It was planning Temalus realized he himself wasn't capable of.

He had entered into an alliance with Lord Saeson on a whim, had planned the coup in no less than a few hours, and it had crumbled within the same time span. His father was right. It was all to get what he wanted: to protect his brother, be rid of his father, and all at the expense of the safety of those around him. Even the Chinstrap, the one whose name he had never known, had died because of his desire to end the Overlord's reign. It was all done with the best of intentions—to bring a different kind of peace, a *real* peace to the penguin clans of the Southern Realm. But as it happened so often throughout history, during the Great Auk War and other times, the best intentions end up having the direst of consequences. Temalus raised his head from his scrutiny of the icy floor. Whatever came next, he would embrace his chosen path.

"Therefore," the Overlord continued to prattle in a voice that made

Temalus feel like a harangued chick, which increased his desire to kill him even more, "since I have two qualified contenders before me, it will come down to combat. The survivor of which will become supreme commander of the Penguin Defense Alliance." He spread his flippers wide and stared down at his sons with a satisfied glint in his eye.

"No!" Liutites demanded, taking a step toward Antaean. The guards responded by training their spears on him. He glared at each of them. "I will remember your faces and I will kill you all myself." He brushed aside the spears and took another step. "We have rules in place, the same precious rules you recited to me, that siblings are not allowed to fight one another in the ascension combat."

"They are the same *precious* rules that you so willingly discarded when you thought it served you," the Overlord roared back. "And as you said, I make them up as I go along. It is my right as Overlord." He looked back at Clayfus, who didn't return his gaze.

Liutites lunged forward. Temalus saw his brother and tried to do the same, but the guards quickly pressed their spears against him, preventing any movement lest he be stabbed through the throat and chest. Liutites was quicker and knocked away any attempts to stop him, climbed the dais, and rushed toward their father. But the Overlord was faster than his ample physique suggested. With a single quick stroke, Antaean swung his staff, smacking it sharply against Liutites' skull, sending him flailing to his back.

The Overlord came forward and delivered another blow in case Liutites had any ideas about continuing the fight. He motioned toward Temalus, who knew better than to attack. Satisfied, he stepped back up on the dais, never taking his eyes from his sons. "The basic *rules* still apply. If you refuse to fight, both of you will be executed. If either of you try to escape, both of you will be executed. If the victor does not finish the fight, both of you will be executed."

Temalus lowered his head to his brother after the guards released him. Liutites shook his head clear, rolled over, and found his feet. The look in his brother's eyes told him that they would both end up dead. That he wouldn't kill him. That their father had indeed won. Both turned their heads toward Antaean, who lorded over them with a gleefully malicious countenance.

"Escort them from my sight," the Overlord said, waving the pair away. The guards and warriors brought their spears up once more and motioned toward the door. He turned away and waddled toward the dark recesses of the room.

Clayfus stepped off the dais and led the escort. As they waited for the door to open, Clayfus moved between the brothers. "Combat will take place in the Overlord's chamber in twelve hours." He leaned into the pair and spoke just above his breath. "This is not the will of the Ancients, but your father will not be swayed. Use your time wisely. But remember, his spies are everywhere and they are not familiar to you."

Temalus and Liutites exchanged furtive glances then allowed themselves to be guided from the chamber.

# CHAPTER 36

Liutites and Temalus walked together through the main hall and stopped in front of the giant crystalline stalactite. They stood in silence for several minutes, each lost in their own thoughts. "I will not kill you," Liutites finally said.

Temalus said nothing. He continued to stare at the stalactite, watching the colors fade to blue, then grayish white as the sinking sun fell beyond the reach of the compound's window-like apertures. A scattering of lanterns flicked to life, bathing the main hall in a sickly yellow gloom. He exhaled a long resigned sigh and looked to the tip of the stalactite, watching a single bead of water, freed from the ice by the collective heat of penguin bodies, pool at the end then fall away, landing against the waiting stalagmite where it froze instantly and rejoined the ice. "Yes, you will."

"No," Liutites said with a jerk. He leaned toward Temalus, angling his head so that they were nearly face to face. "I said I won't. And I meant it. We'll do whatever it takes to end this. The Overlord has to die. Once that happens, we'll be free of him."

Temalus shifted sideways. "I know we will. You want him dead, I want him dead, and by the sound of it, Clayfus isn't particularly happy with him either. I will do what I can to contact Lord Saeson—he's our last hope." He twisted his head, looking for anyone nearby. Finding no one within earshot, he continued, "But if that fails, it'll be up to you."

"We'll make sure it won't." Liutites plucked a feather in frustration.

Temalus watched the pin-feather waft to the ground. "You should be supreme commander already. And I… I should have listened to you and left when I had the chance. I'm sure by now every possible exit from this place is guarded along with any access to the lower reaches." Temalus looked away. "This is what you wanted, to be supreme commander. If things go wrong, you'll have to do it. And in time, when you're ready and you have the resources, you'll usurp the Overlord, and kill him."

Liutites nodded his head slowly. "It is what I want." He turned away, then looked back. "But not like this."

Temalus watched him walk away. He turned his attention back to the stalactite, watching the ugly yellow manmade light flicker against its beauty like a stain. He turned his back on the only thing in Pack Ice Command that gave him a sense of peace and went in search of a way to contact Lord Saeson. If all went well, peace would be forgotten for a while.

ᴧᴧᴧ

Liutites walked in the vague direction of Mearna's quarters. He no longer trusted her, and admitted to himself that he never had. But if there was a way around his father's plans, she might be the only one who could guide him.

Taking a tired breath, he scanned his surroundings, paying extra attention to the narrow ventilation holes placed near the floor running along the walls. If there were spies nearby, and if they weren't Royal Emperors, they could be small enough to use the small tunnels as a means to remain unseen. He examined them closely, straining his eyes in the dim light, looking for signs of claw scratches near the openings. Nothing. If the Overlord's spies did use them, then those penguins would have to be smaller than a Chinstrap or Adélie. A Rockhopper could fit…maybe, but there were few Rockhoppers around Pack Ice Command. And besides, the Rockhoppers were fiercely independent and wouldn't allow themselves to be subjugated to such duties. Liutites knew of no other penguins that would be small enough other than those who lived farther north, and he had never heard of them coming this far south. They could be one of Lord Saeson's aberrations, but he had never seen them.

Leaving the issue of the Overlord's spies for another time, Liutites began a slow trudge up the passage to Mearna's quarters. Halfway up the sloping walkway he heard voices ahead. He stopped and tilted his head, trying to discern who it was. One was definitely Mearna, the other he didn't know. The voice sounded familiar, but he couldn't quite place it. Listening to the quiet voices, he picked out a few words: *soon* and *there will come a time,* and something that sounded like *you are our future.* Liutites felt a simmering rage building. Mearna had already found his replacement. Did she really think that the Overlord would kill him? That he could? His first instinct was to march straight up there and kill the interloper and perhaps Mearna as well. But that wouldn't serve him at the moment. In the future, perhaps, but not today.

With the greatest of effort, Liutites swallowed his pride and rage. He listened for a second longer and distinctly heard the words, *my son.* For a moment he felt foolish. It wasn't a usurper, but her son. He knew she had a few eggs with Antaean, but thought that, unlike himself and a few others from the Overlord's earlier broods, they were hidden away, placed in the fold of nameless faces for protection in case they were to be used against the Overlord. Liutites had to laugh at the thought. His father used his own offspring for his gain, their protection being the last thing on his mind. He vowed that he wouldn't be like his father, and that his own offspring would know their importance. That was, if he survived to see them. With that thought, he continued toward Mearna.

Walking with his head swiveling, still nervous of being followed or watched, he saw who Mearna had been talking to hurrying away in the opposite direction. The penguin looked familiar, and he carried the spear of an elite guard. Pairing the information with the voice, he still couldn't place it. Whoever it was, he was still young, with the sheen of youth on his coat. He thought of Ceocilus, but hadn't he been given orders to take Diutes to his quarters?

He had other things to worry about. And one of them was standing in the shadows, as if waiting for him.

"I expected you sooner," Mearna said. She turned away and clicked on one of the scavenged lights.

Liutites looked down the hall and entered. "Are you so sure?"

Mearna turned toward him sharply. "You made me look like a fool," she said, ignoring the statement. "Talus? Was it a test of loyalty or your way to be rid of your competition?"

Liutites walked slowly toward her. "Either way, I got what I needed."

Mearna stared at Liutites for a second. She took a step back and looked toward the doorway.

"Your son is gone. He can't hear you," Liutites said, continuing his slow walk. The amorous tension between them that Liutites had felt so often when he caught her eye from a distance or the many times they had crossed paths in a quiet corridor was gone. He could feel her fear and he enjoyed the sensation it gave him. He would need that fear in the future. But right now, it was a hindrance to get what he wanted. Liutites let go of his rising anger. "That was your son, wasn't it?" His voice was calm, with a curious tone.

Mearna remained silent for a moment, as if gauging Liutites' sudden mood change. "Yes," she said, still eyeing him cautiously.

"He's young...strong. You should keep him near you. Dangerous times are ahead. You could use protection."

"I am quite capable of protecting myself."

"Are you so sure?" Liutites felt the power of threat rising in him again and quickly swallowed it. It was becoming too easy. "Things will become chaotic once I kill the Overlord, and there are those who see you as inseparable from him."

"As I said...I can take care of myself." Mearna took a cautious step toward Liutites. "And how will you kill the Overlord now? With Lord Saeson's help—the enemy to all Royal Emperors? You said it was Talus who had formed an alliance with him, not Temalus."

"Did you honestly think I would betray my brother?"

"I hoped you would see how he holds you back. And now you will have to kill him yourself or die."

Mearna already knew of the Overlord's edict. She obviously had her spies. Liutites fought back a sharp reply. "I hope to do it without Saeson's assistance. But that depends on you."

"Me?" Mearna said a little too loudly for Liutites' ears. There was still the issue of the unknown spies. "There's nothing I can do for you now. If I try to convince the Overlord to change his mind about the match, he will dismiss me, if not have me executed. He's already lost faith in my ability thanks to you. And I have it on good word that Clayfus had even tried to convince him otherwise. You see how well that worked. I'm surprised he suffered him to live. No, Liutites, you created this, and you have to fix it."

"There's no way you know of for Temalus to escape? I know you have resources that not even the Overlord knows of. There has to be a way." Liutites realized he sounded like a pleading fledgling, but he didn't care. He wouldn't kill his brother. Diutes, yes, eventually, but not Temalus.

Mearna shook her head. "I'm sorry. No. The Overlord has locked down every exit I know of. You'll have to face Temalus or you'll both die."

"I won't." Liutites absently preened his feathers, thinking. There was only one option left open to him.

"Then what? Will you really seek Lord Saeson's aid?" Mearna came closer. "I am nearly ready to lay our egg. Is that how you want your first hatched to come into this world? During a civil war? Because that's what it will be if you lead the Basileios against the Overlord."

"I will do what I must."

"Then what of the Basileios afterward? Surely you don't think they will placidly sit by as you become Overlord?

"The Cu-kisc, I mean Basileios…that's such a stupid name—they will see me as the hero who freed them. And I will have a powerful ally." Liutites stepped close enough for their beaks to nearly touch. He thought of the first time they had come together. But it was different now. It felt awkward, unnatural. "You leave me no other option. As you said, I have to fix this." He looked away, then back to Mearna, staring into her eyes, searching for the spark that had once been there. Not finding it, he clicked his beak in frustration. "Take care of our egg," he said, then abruptly turned away and left.

ᴧᴧᴧ

Mearna followed Liutites to the exit and watched him go. She watched him fall to the floor and quickly toboggan away, sliding on his stomach, until he disappeared into the darkness of night in Pack Ice Command. She stood in the entryway, watching the empty hall.

She had her secrets. Liutites was right, she knew of more than one way out of Pack Ice Command that not even the Overlord knew of. She could have told Liutites, and Temalus could have escaped, or both of them. But where was the fun in that? She needed Liutites so that she could be rid of Antaean. Her son, Ceocilus, was the better candidate for Overlord, but he was still too young, both physically and mentally, for the burdens of leadership, and he was still too full of the idealism of youth. That would change in time. For now, Liutites was her best bet. And she would be damned if she would let Lord Saeson interfere with her plans.

A twinge in her stomach pulled Mearna from her scheming. "Not now," she said through her clenched beak. The egg was coming. She cursed the timing, and Liutites for putting it there. She called to Ceocilus. It would be up to him now to prevent Lord Saeson from coming to Liutites' aid.

# CHAPTER 37

Temalus wandered through the dark halls of Pack Ice Command, hoping that a messenger, spy, or anyone connected with Lord Saeson would present himself. Three of his twelve-hour reprieve had already passed with no sign of help. If he didn't contact the Lord of the Misshapen soon, he would have to think of another way. But if there was another way, he was sure he would have thought of it before. He wondered why the Overlord had even granted them the time. It would have made more sense to do it then and there. It could only be that Antaean had his spies about with the hope to weed out Saeson's network. But Temalus had no choice other than to proceed with his plans.

Meeting Liutites in combat was a prospect Temalus didn't want to face. He carried no animosity toward his brother. Disappointment, yes, for the way he pursued the title of supreme commander and his desire for power, but it roused no hatred in him. Every time he had given up on Liutites, a small spark of hope appeared and encouraged him not to quit just yet. And there was no power on Earth, the Overlord or otherwise, that could make him want to take Liutites' life.

Coming to intersecting corridors, Temalus stopped and scanned the gloom, hoping for a sign of someone or something to help. The only sign of Lord Saeson's presence he had seen were a pair of Misshapen dragging makeshift brooms made of Petrel feathers and attached to their torsos via crude harnesses made of seal leather, going about their business cleaning the empty halls. He tried to stop them and ask how to contact their lord, but was met with a series of untranslatable honks. The Misshapen had turned away and continued their work. They weren't what he was looking for anyway. They were servants to the Overlord. No, not servants, but slaves. Their solid white plumage, stubby beaks, and large, round, dark eyes, were endearing, contrasting to the image of monsters so many held of the Misshapen. He watched them with an aching pity in his heart until they disappeared into the darkness.

Unsure as to which way to go, Temalus turned left for no reason in particular. His search had quickly become aimless wandering, and though he had gone that way before—in fact, he had nearly traversed all of Pack Ice Command—there were few places left to check. Taking no more than few steps into the darkened corridor, he nearly bumped into yet another patrolling guard. They were everywhere, put on high alert in case of insurrection or attempted escape by either him or Liutites. The guard grunted and shoved him aside. Probably bitter for pulling an overnight watch, Temalus thought as he recovered from the mistreatment.

"They are watching you," a quiet voice said from somewhere low to the ground when the angry guard had passed.

Temalus spun around. "Who's there?" He waited, but no reply came. The guard was long gone and the voice didn't sound like a Royal Emperor anyway. "Hello?" Temalus said quietly.

"Stay on your current path. Do not speak," the whispered voice said.

Straining his eyes, Temalus tried to see where the voice had come from. But it was impossible, the darkness was almost complete. He decided to heed the unseen penguin's words and continued on without speaking.

Several meters later he came to another junction with faint light coming from either direction. "Great. Now which way do I go?" he muttered.

"Left," a soft penguin voice said from somewhere near the floor.

Temalus turned right.

"Other left," the voice admonished a little louder this time.

He was nervous, tired, and not thinking clearly. Taking the *right* left this time, Temalus continued. With more light to lead the way, he saw the ventilation holes every twenty meters or so and remembered the Chinstrap telling him they used them as a means to go to and from the lower reaches. His spirits lifted at finally getting some sense of purpose. Walking along, he noticed that every third hole was slightly larger than the others. When he approached another after a sharp turn, the voice returned.

"Stop," the whisper said.

Temalus did as instructed. He looked back around the corner, nervous of whoever was following him. A minute passed with no further word. Feeling antsy, Temalus took a step to go.

"Wait," the voice said. Temalus froze. Several seconds passed, and the voice returned. "Walk ten meters ahead. You'll come to another crossway. Turn left. Make sure you take the right left. Go."

Temalus bristled under the anonymous penguin's sarcasm. Ten meters ahead he came to the crossway, and turned left. With no further instruction, he kept on his path. Walking along, he spotted an open doorway on his right. He remembered coming this way earlier and the doorway hadn't been there. In fact, he had never before seen any indication of a door in this passage. He slowed his pace, guessing this was his destination.

"In here," a voice said just above a whisper. Temalus was happy he had guessed right.

The door closed suddenly behind him and Temalus was plunged into complete darkness. He listened intently for any sounds and heard the faint rasp of claws scratching against the ice from somewhere in the darkness. "Who's there?"

"Quiet," a voice, different from the one who had guided him, said.

A minute or two passed, then a soft click brought the room to life beneath the pallid glow of dying flashlight. Temalus squinted against the comparative brightness. A Chinstrap penguin stepped from behind the light.

"I apologize for the covertness, but the Overlord's spies are out in force tonight," the Chinstrap said.

"I understand. No need to apologize. I've been looking for you for a while now. I haven't much time." Temalus thought of the Chinstrap who died earlier and decided he wouldn't make the same mistake twice. "Do you have a name?"

The Chinstrap stared at Temalus for second before shaking his head. "I am simply a messenger." He walked across the room and examined the door, making sure it was sealed.

Temalus watched him and it was then that he noticed a Misshapen penguin standing in the corner. The penguin was covered with black feathers from head to toe, and a long pointed beak, which looked like the tusk of a narwhal, protruded from beneath tiny black eyes similar to the ones he had seen in Lord Saeson's layer. Temalus looked the penguin over and the only thought that occurred to him was to wonder how the creature ate.

"We can't be too safe," the Chinstrap said. "Like I said, the Overlord's spies are out and they were keeping a careful watch over you."

"Who are his spies? I saw no one following me."

"Blue penguins. They're small. About half my height." He raised his flipper about twelve inches from the ground. "They come from farther north. Though I don't know how the Overlord got them here without them dying from the cold. Regardless, you wouldn't see them. They use the ventilation chambers just as we do. In fact most of the vents you see are false. They're there solely for the Blues to use. Fortunately there aren't many Blue penguins here, so they can't be everywhere at once. Now about Lord Saeson..."

Temalus waved his flipper to bypass any lengthy discussion. "I haven't much time. We need to go through with our plans. The Overlord has ordered Liutites and I—"

"We already know what the Overlord intends. Lord Saeson has a few Misshapen in place already. The workers you see aren't there for the benefit of Pack Ice Command. Antaean thinks they're his servants, but I assure you they're not. Most aren't fighters, but they can create chaos when the time comes."

"The time is now," Temalus said, losing his patience.

"The time is when Lord Saeson says it is."

Temalus felt a flash of irritability. He swallowed it back, not wanting to lose his only ally. "I've already discussed this with him," he said in a slow, even voice.

"And a Chinstrap has already been killed," his coconspirator said, matching his tone. "Not to mention that the Overlord has guards patrolling every possible entry point."

Unaccustomed to anyone other than a Royal Emperor speaking to him in such a way, Temalus bristled under the Chinstrap's commanding tone. His air of authority was undeniable, and he briefly wondered what would happen if the Chinstraps, the second most abundant species of penguins in the world, were to organize a rebellion. He doubted that would ever happen and dismissed the thought for more pressing matters. "Then what do I do?"

"Nothing for the moment." The Chinstrap swallowed a long breath. "Carry on as normally as possible, given your circumstances. When your match with Liutites begins and the Overlord's attention is focused on your fight, that's when we'll strike. The Misshapen workers will cause a distraction and Lord Saeson himself will lead the attack. There is only a single point of entry we can use. So it will take some time for him to reach the Overlord's chamber. When you hear the fighting, you must take that opportunity to kill Antaean. If you don't kill him, then..." The Chinstrap hesitated.

"Then what?" Temalus had a feeling he wouldn't like what he was about to hear.

"Then Lord Saeson will retreat and await a better opportunity. Not to sound trite, but you must cut the head off the beast for this to succeed. Lord Saeson will not sacrifice his loves for a losing cause." The Chinstrap stared at Temalus in the dying light. "Make certain your brother knows what needs to be done. Saeson doesn't trust Liutites, but he does trust you…to make the right choice."

"The right choice?" Temalus thought he was making the right choice, or at least hoped he was. He let his wings slap against his side, and shook his head with a spit of laughter. In his current situation, what other choice did he have?

"If you defeat Antaean, and Liutites becomes Overlord and continues the same path as your father, you must stop him." The Chinstrap turned his head toward the back of the dark room. "You made a promise to Lord Saeson that the Overlord's madness would not continue, no matter who holds the title."

Temalus nodded. He had promised, but that also meant he would have to remain at Pack Ice Command. He inhaled deeply, trying to breathe through the tightness gripping his chest. Thoughts of freedom now seemed so far away. The truth that Lord Saeson had made him face about himself also meant accepting his responsibility to their pact. He would be bound to this place, and wondered if it was worth the price. He also wondered if Lord Saeson would try to destroy the K'tha once he found freedom. While it was true that Talus had vouched for him, where was Talus now? The more he thought about it, the more the deal made him feel like he had made a deal with Cuasan. But there was no going back. His options were spent. He regretted not leaving when he had the chance.

"I'll uphold my end," Temalus finally said. "Make sure Lord Saeson upholds his." Not in the mood for any more discussion, he turned and stood before the door.

"Are we done?" The Chinstrap asked with a hint of surprise that the conversation ended so abruptly.

"Yes," Temalus said, his voice as cold as the walls around him.

"You know the plan. Move when you hear the signal."

"I will." Temalus stared at the door, waiting for it to open.

The Chinstrap nodded to the Misshapen who in turn jabbed his elongated beak into a hole near the floor. The door slid open much quicker and quieter than the other doors in PIC and Temalus stepped outside. He felt the rush of the breeze as the door closed quickly behind him. He turned, took a few steps in the dim hall, and came face to face with an elite guard.

# CHAPTER 38

The two Royal Emperors stood looking at one another in the gloom. Temalus knew he had seen the guard before, but owing to the dark conditions couldn't quite place him. The guard tapped the end of his spear against the ice a few times then turned the same direction as Temalus. They began walking side by side.

They walked in silence for a while until the guard spoke. "I don't think soliciting the aid of Lord Saeson is a wise choice."

Surprised by the statement, Temalus didn't reply right away. He recognized the voice, but where had he heard it? The guard was still rather young, so what could he know about such things? Temalus wracked his brain, trying to match the voice with the face. There were so many Royal Emperors in Pack Ice Command, the chore was taxing his already stressed mind. Recalling a flurry of images of the day, the name came to him. "What makes you say that…Ceocilus? That is your name, right?"

The guard stopped and cocked his head, listening for something. He straightened and looked at Temalus. "I would prefer you not to use my name in the open areas like this."

Temalus peered at the vents. Not only were the Overlord's spies near, but probably Lord Saeson's as well. No wonder the Overlord knew everything. Was there no place in this accursed command center where one could speak without someone listening? "You're right. But again, why do you think Lord Saeson's help isn't wise? It's not like I have a choice at this point, unless you know of another way." If Temalus had learned anything beyond not trusting anyone, it was also not to discount any information, no matter the source; there was always a grain of truth, even in the biggest lie. But there was something about this Royal Emperor that seemed like he had the rare attribute of honesty, or at least a form of it.

Ceocilus motioned for them to walk. They traveled a little farther down the corridor, walking in silence, and keeping a wary eye on the vents and for other guards. They entered a narrow side passage where the vents were few and far between. Ceocilus walked with his flipper nearly touching Temalus' and leaned closer still. "I believe Lord Saeson has plans to conquer us. You would be the first step in his plans, if not the only one if you succeed."

"How could you know this? You're young enough to have just returned from the Trials." Temalus knew age wasn't a determining factor in knowledge—after all, his father had become Overlord when he was very young—but then again, there were only a few K'tha at that time. But that was then. Now it took years of intrigue and clawing to rise to a position where one could build a network of informants.

"I have…" Ceocilus stopped walking and looked down either direction of the dark corridor. "I have access to a vast network of spies, for lack of a better word. I'm part of a group that seeks change. We're still too small to bring about that change. But one of our informants has not only infiltrated the Overlord's group, but Lord Saeson's as well. And from what the mole has learned, Saeson is on the path to seize control. And not only that, but Talus knew of it, too. Though how much he knew is hard to tell."

Temalus studied Ceocilus' face in the hazy light. If what he said of Talus was true, then why would the rogue leave just before Saeson revealed his ambitions? And why would he have encouraged him to seek Saeson's aid? While Ceocilus appeared to believe what he heard was true, it was obvious that he didn't have all of the facts. And Temalus couldn't dismiss the thought that the young guard could be trying to convince him to abandon the idea just to save the Overlord casualties in case of a prolonged coup, or perhaps he had another motive.

"And the leader of the group you belong to, would he take control of the alliance if we killed Antaean without the assistance of Lord Saeson? Would he become the next Overlord?"

Ceocilus hesitated before answering. "No. I don't believe so. Our aim is to be rid of the Overlord's tyranny."

"You don't *believe*? You don't sound confident."

"There are never any certainties. I would hope it wouldn't come to that. But power is very intoxicating. I would do what I could to prevent that end should it come to pass."

Whoever this phantom rebel was, Temalus was reasonably sure it was a Royal Emperor. He couldn't see a Royal Emperor, no matter how righteous, working for a clandestine group led by a Chinstrap or any other clan. Whoever the mysterious rebel was, he had to be well connected, too, or else he wouldn't have access to a network of spies. He didn't sense any deceit in Ceocilus, but he doubted the Royal Emperor at the head of the group was so altruistic. He was probably taking advantage of the young penguin's naiveté. If Lord Saeson was really in this to seize power, then they'd have to climb that iceberg when they got there.

"I appreciate your warning. But unless you have an alternative..." He waited for a reply, hoping there was another way. When Ceocilus remained silent, he knew what he had to do. "Then this is where we part ways. I hope you hold true to your ideals. Our future might depend on penguins like you."

Ceocilus nodded. "I had to try."

"I know," Temalus said and began to walk away.

"Just so you know, I was told to kill you if you didn't change your mind."

Temalus twitched to a stop. "I appreciate you not doing so," he said without looking back, then continued on his way.

# CHAPTER 39

After spending several hours wandering and searching his thoughts for another way out with no results, Temalus returned to his quarters. Upon entering, he found Liutites resting with his head tucked in against his chest. "Are you asleep?"

Liutites lifted his head. "Far from it."

"Did you find a way out of this?" Temalus ruffled his coat of thick feathers and took a spot beside his brother.

"No. Did you?" Liutites craned his head back, stretching his tense and tired muscles.

Temalus stared at the ground, absently plucking loose pinfeathers on his chest. "Not without Lord Saeson's help."

"I'm loath to accept his aid. But if it's the only way…" Liutites preened loose pinfeathers as well.

"I take it Mearna was no help."

Liutites lifted his head. "You take it right."

Temalus would have been surprised if she had. Mearna was dangerous, probably more dangerous than Antaean. She worked in the shadows, and being female, few would suspect her capable of intrigue. She had certainly sunk her claws into Liutites. Temalus wondered who else she had taken hold of—maybe she had control of this mysterious rebel leader Ceocilus had mentioned.

"She has her own motives."

He desperately tried to think of another way. But they had to face the fact: they would have to face each other and hope Lord Saeson would come to their rescue. And after that, they would have to hope he wouldn't try to seize control as Ceocilus had warned him. Temalus considered telling Liutites of what the idealistic guard had said, but dismissed the idea. If Liutites thought Saeson would try to overthrow him before even taking the dais, he would back out of the arrangement and they'd be back where they started. He also considered telling the Overlord of Lord Saeson's supposed plans, and setting a trap. But he was certain his father would see it as a desperate attempt to save his own life. And if he did tell the Overlord, and they failed to stop Saeson, he doubted the Lord of the Misshapen would be forgiving of his betrayal.

Liutites snorted his resignation to the situation before them. "I'm certain Mearna has her own motives, as well."

Temalus had to think for a second to remember the context of what his brother had said. His thoughts were racing from one to another and he was having trouble staying focused. "Then we work with Lord Saeson, and hopefully this will all end."

Liutites stood fully erect and shook away his fatigue. "Then tell me the plans in detail. Leave nothing out."

Temalus nodded. He would tell him everything he needed to know. But there were things he didn't need to know. Not yet.

∧∧∧

After a long recitation of the plans, Liutites paced the room. It seemed like it would work. He agreed that Lord Saeson shouldn't be part of the killing of Antaean, but he didn't like the idea that he would stay out of the Overlord's chamber until the deed was done. If the guards didn't desert their posts, they would have a difficult time getting to the Overlord. "He will likely be expecting something like this. He knows you are in league with Saeson."

"I don't doubt that," Temalus said, watching Liutites make another circuit around their quarters. "And I'm sure that's why he delayed the match—to see if we would expose our secrets. Our only other option is to try to escape. We might be able to overpower the guards near one of the exits."

"The guards are ten deep at the exits. Plus, most of the command center is on alert. While I have no doubt we would eventually get through the guards, it would take time we don't have. We'd have fifty warriors on our backs before we got to the door. And then there's the problem of opening the doors." Liutites stopped and tapped his clawed feet on the ground, then shook his head. "No. Our only chance is the plan you have in place. It's too late for anything else."

"And what if the plan fails?" Temalus asked, his voice growing somber. "What then?"

Liutites stared at his brother. What then indeed. One or both of them would have to die. The hatred for their father grew burning hot in his gut. "I won't kill you. We'll fight. We'll make a show of it until the moment is right. But I won't kill you. I promise you that."

Temalus sighed. "You can't make that promise."

"I can make any promise I please," Liutites shot back, not masking his irritation. "Besides," he said, trying to take on a lighter tone. "You're quicker than me. Smarter, too. It might not be me who needs to make that promise."

"If I was the smarter one I would have left when I had the chance," Temalus said with a regretful sniff. "But if it's any consolation, I promise I won't kill you either." They both shared a tense laugh.

The tap of a spear at the doorway pulled their attention away. An elite guard stood at attention, backed by a half dozen others.

"Is it time already?" Temalus asked. The guard responded with a nervous nod. "Are you ready?"

Liutites glared at the guard. The fleeting moment of good cheer disappeared into the cauldron of hatred in his heart.

The brothers looked at one another in silence. Nothing more needed to be said. Both knew the stakes and both knew the consequences of their actions. They walked toward the guards, who raised their weapons in case the brothers tried something foolish. Liutites made a contemptuous snort and let the guards lead them away.

# CHAPTER 40

Temalus and Liutites followed the guards at an unhurried pace. Neither spoke, and neither had thoughts of seeing the compound or penguins neither cared about for the last time. Their minds were focused on the task before them, with no room for such distractions. They entered the main hall and a contingent of warriors joined the procession. All along the way, seemingly at every turn, elite guards and warriors followed or led at a distance, as if expecting the pair to attempt a desperate escape or act of defiance. There would be no such attempt. Their plan was set and there would be no deviation.

Crowds of penguins went about their business, seeing to tasks in the early morning bustle of Pack Ice Command. Most kept their heads down, doing their best to ignore the Royal Emperors marching through their midst. A pair of Kings raised their heads to watch, whispering quietly to one another. A passing Royal Emperor warrior shot them a warning glare and the Kings quickly turned away. Had it not been for the hush over the usually chattering penguins, it would have seemed like any other day for the inhabitants of the penguin stronghold. Most were oblivious to the possible upheaval about to take place.

Temalus stole a glance to his right and noticed a Chinstrap penguin standing still amongst the crowd. The Chinstrap raised his beak with the slightest movement, then disappeared. Satisfied that help would come, he returned to walking with an unfixed stare.

The brothers kept their eyes forward as they passed the crystalline stalactite. Temalus made no attempt to admire the prismatic shafts of light bathing the room in ever changing color. He no longer found any beauty in that or anything else in Pack Ice Command. All he saw was ugliness; the ugliness of his father's designs and the ugliness of death that would soon stain the ice like it would stain his soul.

They entered the wide corridor leading to the Overlord's chambers. The eyes of the finely carved penguin reliefs, sentinels of every known species, unwitting servants to the Overlord, seemed to watch them as they passed. There was a time when Temalus had thought of them as the representation of penguin unity. Now he saw they were subjects in the Overlord's burgeoning empire—tools to be worked until they were no longer useful, only to be discarded. The Adélie sculptor had gone, and with her, the words telling him he had a choice.

Diutes stood tall at the entrance to the Overlord's chamber, carrying a countenance of arrogance and satisfaction. The brothers ignored him as they had through most of their lives. He seemed on the cusp of making a boastful remark, but a passing guard nudged him aside, relegating him back to his station of insignificance.

Liutites and Temalus stood at the threshold of the Overlord's chamber, their feet in the shallow depression where the large ice slab of a door would lay when closed. They studied the room, as vast and bloated as the Overlord himself. The trophy pedestals had been moved to the walls, and armed warriors surrounded the room, leaving only a single gap before the dais. The brothers each made a quick count of the Overlord's protectors. Fifty, with more likely lurking in the shadows behind the dais. If even a quarter of the procession of guards that trailed them entered, that number would swell to seventy or more. It was clear that the Overlord was taking no chances.

A nudge against their backs prodded Liutites and Temalus forward. The guards ushered them toward the dais, and when their spears crossed their path, they stopped, standing halfway between the dais and the doorway. Twenty guards entered the room behind them and moments later the slow grind of the door began, ending with a thud, sealing the occupants from the outside world.

The room fell silent. The armed Royal Emperors stood at full attention, unmoving except for the rising of their chests through their nervous breaths. A faint sound crept from the shadows behind the dais: clawed feet scraping against the icy floor, the bony clink of seal teeth rattling on a necklace of trophies, and the steady whoosh of seal-leather gliding along the ice. The Overlord appeared from the darkness like the phantasmal form of Cuasan, becoming incarnate in the realm of the living. He stopped on the edge of the dais, and the surrounding penguins ground their spears and raised their beaks toward the ceiling in one uniform movement.

Liutites and Temalus stood motionless and unimpressed, both refusing to raise their beaks in salute. They had seen enough of the Overlord's displays and pomp to grow tired of the redundancy. Every event was the same: Clayfus would make some ridiculous proclamation and their father would rise, walk forward, or grind his staff, followed by him making some outrageous claim that he was about to impart the will of the Ancients. The mindless crowd would cheer and then someone would die. They expected nothing less today, but today they would both be wrong.

Antaean watched them both from the elevated platform of his dais. Clayfus was nowhere to be seen, and the Overlord made no wild gestures with his flippers, staff, or otherwise. "General Liutites, Commandant Temalus. You have both been charged with treason. Because of the serious accusation, you are ordered to face one another in combat. You do not do this for the will of the Ancients, you do not do this for glory—you do so at my whim, for my entertainment alone. The one who dies will receive their punishment. The one who survives will carry the murder of his brother on his conscience for a lifetime, a punishment I look forward to seeing."

Though both Liutites and Temalus' outward appearances showed they were unmoved by their father's words, their innards trembled with hate, threatening to spill over at any moment. They both remained still, waiting for the moment to strike their father down, and rid themselves of his burden.

"However, I am not without good will, or perhaps a sense of irony," the Overlord continued for the sake of his audience. "Since you are both qualified in your own ways, the victor of this bout will become supreme commander, second in command only to me. And as such, you will be answerable to me in all things. If you refuse the rank," his eyes shifted between Liutites and Temalus, "you will be killed."

Temalus paid attention to the wording, noticing that his father had used the word *killed* instead of executed. He wondered if that meant Antaean would perform the deed himself. Temalus hoped the Overlord wouldn't survive long enough to for him find out what he meant. He stole a glance at Liutites, then prepared himself for what was to come.

Antaean awkwardly waddled backwards, stopped and looked at the brothers. He clicked his beak sharply, and nodded to the guards. "The fight begins now." The guards brought their weapons forward in unison, creating a deadly wall of spears in case either brother thought to turn the fight on them.

Liutites and Temalus looked at each other, both confused by the proclamation. Neither raised beak or flipper to strike at the other.

"You will fight or you will both die," the Overlord announced from behind a wall of warriors when neither began the fight. Every guard took a step forward in unison, making the ring of spears that much smaller.

"Should we make a show of it or wait?" Temalus asked, hoping to save his strength for the fight against Antaean, which he was sure would come.

Liutites looked at guards, spotted Diutes hiding behind the wall of soldiers, and turned back to Temalus. He slapped his brother hard enough to knock him off balance, then butted him with his chest, putting him on the ice.

Temalus quickly got to his feet and watched Liutites, surprised by the blow. He made a tentative jab with his beak, then moved toward him until their bodies were pressed against one another. They pushed and shoved with their chests, claws scraping against the ice, as both tried to maintain their balance.

Liutites pressed his yellow-gold cheek against Temalus' and whispered, "Just like our sparring matches. Fight to make it look good until help arrives."

Temalus got the idea, shifted right, and slid past Liutites, delivering a slap of his own against his back as he stumbled forward. The brothers faced each other, and Temalus saw a glint of joy in Liutites' eyes, telling him the sparring was about to escalate as it so often did when they trained. Liutites came at him, walking in with an exaggerated waddle, his body swinging left, right, left, right, picking up speed until he was nearly on him. Temalus knew the tactic and it almost always ended with a left winged slap, almost without fail. He braced himself and ducked, intending to head-butt Liutites square in the chest, a counter that had worked before.

But Liutites didn't do as expected. Instead, he ended his nearly comical attack with a flurry of slaps that Temalus had just ducked into. The slaps stung, but were largely ineffectual. Liutites hadn't put his strength into it. Had he done so, Temalus was certain he would have been seeing stars.

Liutites relented as Temalus backed away. He snorted a laugh. "Did you think I would fall for that twice?"

"I hoped," Temalus said with equal humor. Had their lives not hung in the balance, it would have been like old times, when they were younger. Liutites had taken it upon himself to train his brother, preparing him for the inevitable challengers that lay ahead. They had sparred almost daily for three years, until the responsibility of Liutites' rank began to steal more and more time from him. The sparring turned to weekly training sessions, then to Liutites recruiting hordes of Adélie and Chinstraps to challenge him. Through it all, Temalus had never won a match. Fighting seemed to come naturally to his older brother. Not so for Temalus. Despite all of the training and lectures, he just didn't have the fire Liutites had. He was capable, above adequate, as his match with Reticles had proved, but he wasn't the born killer his brother was.

"You should know better by now," Liutites replied. The brothers circled each other, looking for an opening. Antaean hammered the butt of his staff against the dais and the guards took another step forward.

Liutites moved in quickly, and again the brothers butted each other and jostled for an advantage. "He knows we're not giving it our all," Temalus said against Liutites' ear. "If the guards keep coming at us, they'll end up doing what our father wants us to do to each other."

"Let them come. If they get that close, their weapons will be ineffectual."

"And if one of us should fall against them? That would end our sparring really fast."

"Make sure that doesn't happen then." Liutites met his brother's eyes. "Time for a little stab and parry exercise."

Stab and parry. It was Temalus' least favorite part of his training. One false move, one mistimed lunge, and somebody could lose an eye, or worse. He had more than a few scars to prove just how dangerous his training had been. But they needed to continue with the show. He had hoped to hear the calls of alarm signaling Lord Saeson's attack by now. Clearly, they had to give it more time.

Liutites swung his beak at Temalus, who dodged it with ease. Temalus returned the swing with a feint and half-hearted stab, which Liutites deftly blocked, then followed up with another flurry of slaps, putting Temalus on the defensive. Liutites then stabbed his beak toward his brother's face, who parried with a stab of his own. The two continued this way for several minutes; strike, parry, feint left and stab right, going back and forth in an impressive display of skill.

Tiring, Temalus lunged forward with a misguided stab that grazed the side of Liutites' neck, exposing a streak of flesh. Liutites' responded instinctually and immediately. He swung with his right flipper, trailed by his left, with a blow so hard, it took Temalus off his feet. The years of fighting and training kicked in, and without thinking, he reacted. He stood over his brother, breathing heavily. It took a moment for him to realize what he had done.

Temalus looked up at his brother from the floor, shocked by the blow. He saw that Liutites was equally shocked. Somewhere from the back of the guards, they heard Diutes cackle with laughter. The Overlord jammed his staff against the dais twice, and the guards took two steps forward. Temalus stood and they faced each other once again.

The pair came at one another again, and once again fell against each other. Neither made any real effort to continue their sparring, and they no longer cared if the Overlord ordered the guards forward. "Where is your accomplice? This is taking too long. If we keep this up, we won't have the strength to kill Antaean," Liutites said between ragged breaths.

"I don't know. They should have attacked by now. Something must have gone wrong," Temalus said with equal fatigue.

"Enough!" the Overlord bellowed. The guards parted and Antaean stepped to the edge of the dais.

The brothers jerked away from each other and stared up at their father.

"It has become apparent that neither of you has the will to fight. Liutites, you could have easily finished him more than once. And Temalus, you had your chance as well. That will change." The Overlord looked to his left and Clayfus made his first appearance.

The gaunt penguin scurried from the dais, his head down, looking sullen and defeated. He hurried past the brothers, and the penguins near the door parted to either side. Clayfus looked back at Liutites and Temalus, took a deep breath and faced the door.

Temalus watched the proceedings along with Liutites. He waited and watched as the door began its slow grind. A sickening feeling of dread washed over him. Something, perhaps instinct, told him he wouldn't like what was the other side. When the door finally opened, he saw that his instinct had proved correct.

Escorted by a squad of Royal Emperor warriors, the Chinstrap messenger to Lord Saeson and two of the Misshapen were ushered into the chamber.

Temalus watched them as they were prodded forward. When they passed, he met the Chinstrap's eyes, who glanced at him briefly, then lowered his head. There would be no rebellion, no rescues, and there would be no escape. Temalus let out a long, defeated breath. "The game is over, my brother."

Liutites stared at the Overlord standing on the dais with his chest puffed proudly and carrying a mirthless glint in his eyes. "It will be over when our father is dead."

# CHAPTER 41

Overlord Antaean stood as still as the sculpted reliefs, his eyes never moving from his sons standing before him with their heads held steady, unflinching beneath his gaze. The room carried the tense silence of expected tragedy, with only the quiet pitiful moans of the two Misshapen penguins breaking the stillness.

"Bring me the Chinstrap," the Overlord said, his voice calm, revealing no emotion or motive. A Royal Emperor officer nudged the Chinstrap forward. "Are these the only insurgents you captured, Captain Astramachos?"

"Yes, my lord," Astramachos said with his beak high. "Two of Lord Saeson's Misshapen were killed when they resisted. And we found these two near the crèche."

"And has the door been sealed?"

"Yes, my lord. The remaining entrance to Lord Saeson's lair has been sealed, the lock destroyed, and their ventilation shafts have either been sealed or destroyed as ordered," Astramachos said, standing tall and proud of his accomplishment.

The Overlord turned his attention to the pair of Misshapen. It was the same pair Temalus had seen cleaning the floors only hours before. Their puffy white plumage, dark, round, innocent eyes, and nubby beaks made them look more like walking fur-seal pups than dangerous insurgents. "Do you speak?" Antaean asked, cocking his head.

The Misshapen made pathetic bleats and looked around the room full of Royal Emperors until they spotted the familiar face of Temalus. They honked and tried to go to him. The guards quickly stopped them, and the simple-minded Misshapen honked in confusion.

The Overlord watched them try to get to Temalus and laughed. "They like you," he said, his voice oily and venomous. His eyes narrowed.

"No!" Temalus shouted, seeing what was coming. "They are innocent workers in your service. They had nothing to do with this."

The Overlord tilted his head, keeping his gaze on Temalus. "Guards... kill them." Six elite guards moved in and immediately began stabbing the Misshapen, who, confused by what was taking place, didn't react until the first spear found its mark.

Temalus tried to go to them, but was held in place by Liutites. "I have to help." He looked past his brother and saw the fluffy penguins fall beneath the onslaught. Their mournful wails echoed through the chamber and Temalus turned away.

"There's nothing you can do for them except get yourself killed." Liutites didn't watch the carnage; instead, he kept his sights firmly set on Antaean.

When the last dying wails of the Misshapen faded away, the Overlord returned his attention to the Chinstrap. "Do you have a name?" The Chinstrap stood with his beak shut, looking past Antaean. "Very well. We know that you are a spy for Lord Saeson, the enemy of the Penguin Defense Alliance. You were seen making contact with Commandant Temalus, and I know that you relayed information through a series of ventilation shafts to Lord Saeson regarding his alliance with my son, and his plans to depose me."

Still the Chinstrap remained silent.

The Overlord sniffed a laugh at the penguin's defiance. "Look at the Misshapen lying dead behind you." When the Chinstrap made no attempt to do so, Antaean slammed the butt of his staff on the dais. "Look!" He screamed so loud that every penguin in the room jerked from the violence in his voice, Liutites and Temalus included.

Slowly, the Chinstrap turned and looked at the bloodied corpses lying on the ice. Their once pristine white plumage was now marred by gouts of crimson and their dark eyes were either wide with the shock of death or gouged out by a guard's spear.

"Is this what you want?" the Overlord continued. "If you do not speak, I promise you that this will be the fate of every Chinstrap in Pack Ice Command. One by one, every one of your kind will die, whether they are innocent or guilty, until you speak." Antaean waited while the Chinstrap digested what he was told. "And to show that I am not without mercy, I give you my word before all those who stand before me that no harm will come to you or your kind if you testify against Temalus and Liutites."

Temalus waited and watched the Chinstrap, while Liutites kept his steely gaze on Antaean. The Chinstrap stared at the ground, and Temalus noticed his chest rising and falling through heavy breaths, the weight of hundreds of lives resting on the penguin's shoulders. The Chinstrap peered over at Temalus, and the two stared at one another, each knowing their fate rested in what came next.

The Chinstrap turned away with a jerk and raised his head, almost defiantly. This was it. The Chinstrap would take his secrets to his death in service to the greater good, and without his testimony the Overlord would likely still kill either both Temalus and Liutites or one of them, but it would be done on suspicion and nothing else. It would stain his authority, and perhaps that would be enough to create greater doubt in his leadership. And maybe, one day, penguins like Ceocilus would rise against him and finally end his reign. It was a small consolation to take to the Great Sea, but a consolation nonetheless.

The Chinstrap spoke, "My name is Volité. I was in service to the Penguin Defense Alliance until I was selected to be sacrificed as bait to lure Lord Saeson from hiding. Lord Saeson took me in and now I am a spy in service to Saeson, Lord of the Misshapen." Volité looked at

Temalus once more, then recounted the events leading up to his capture by Captain Astramachos. He told the Overlord everything: from Temalus' first meeting with Lord Saeson to every detail, as far as he knew, of their would-be insurrection. When he finished, Volité stood on wobbly legs, his body sagging with relief and regret.

The Overlord kept his icy glare on the Chinstrap. "And what was General Liutites' part in this?"

Liutites had no reaction to the question. His gaze remained fixed on Antaean, as if entranced by plots of murder and how it would play out.

"None, as far as I know. I only had reassurances by Commandant Temalus that General Liutites would comply. Though Commandant Temalus seemed less than confident in that assertion." Volité seemed to know the implications of what he said. He looked at Temalus from the corner of his eye, then brought them toward the floor.

That was that. Liutites hadn't been implicated in the conspiracy except by hearsay, and Temalus now stood alone as guilty in the plot to kill the Overlord with the aid of Lord Saeson. Temalus was surprised to find that he felt no particular animosity toward the Chinstrap. Had he actually cared about the K'tha, and someone had threatened their lives, perhaps he would've done the same. But he didn't care. The Royal Emperors were all as equally loathsome as his father, compliant to his tyranny whether knowingly or blindly, as he had once been. The question was no longer how would he survive; it was how would he be killed?

# CHAPTER 42

Volité was escorted from the chamber and the door closed behind him. When silence had once again fallen over the room, the Overlord motioned for Clayfus to come forward. Antaean whispered something in his ear, and the attendant looked at Liutites.

"What do you suppose that's about?" Temalus asked his stoic brother, trying to make light out of the hopeless situation they found themselves in. "You think he's the executioner?"

Liutites inhaled deeply. "Things will be worse than I feared."

"Worse?" Temalus exclaimed. "What's worse than dying?"

Liutites finally pulled his eyes from Antaean. "For you, my brother, nothing."

"You're being really cryptic when I need you to be clear. We either find a way out now, or we die." Temalus scanned the guards, trying to decide which one to attack first when the time came. He had accepted that he would die, but would be damned if he wouldn't take a few guards out with him, and at least attempt to kill the Overlord.

Clayfus stepped off the dais and slunk his way to the brothers. He leaned close and spoke in a low voice, "As I said before, I tried to convince your father that this was not in keeping with the will of the Ancients. But he would not be swayed."

"Get on with it," the Overlord shouted from behind him.

Letting out a resigned sigh, Clayfus straightened his frail frame. "In accordance with the will of the Overlord and the Ancients alike, Liutites, you are now supreme commander of the Penguin Defense Alliance. Do you accept this title?"

Temalus' body deflated. Any hope of a last stand was now gone. Liutites had what he wanted, and with that, he would abandon any remaining loyalty he felt toward Temalus. Liutites' beak parted, but he seemed to hesitate. Temalus knew what had to be done. He motioned for Clayfus to give him a minute. When the Overlord didn't object, he faced Liutites.

"Take the title. Become who you were meant to be. Use it. And when the time is right, you'll know what to do."

Everything Temalus had done was under the guise that it was to save Liutites. Even if that was no longer true, it was the catalyst which had sent him on this journey and led him to where he was now. He wouldn't let Liutites refuse the title. It would have all been for nothing. "Accept it."

^^^

Liutites faced the Overlord. He was about to get all that he had yearned for, and yet it meant nothing to him. He knew the consequences if he accepted the rank. He would use that rank to build his own army, loyal to him. And when the time came, he would strike at the Overlord and end the pain he was about to embrace for all time. "I accept, my lord."

Overlord Antaean raised his staff. "You are now Supreme Commander Liutites, commander of the Penguin Defense Alliance and protector of the Southern Realm against all threats, foreign and domestic, within and without."

Supreme Commander Liutites closed his eyes and raised his beak in salute to his Overlord. He waited for what would come next.

"As protector and enforcer of our laws, your first duty is to execute Temalus for the crime of treason and conspiracy against the Penguin Defense Alliance." Antaean lowered his staff and stared at Liutites. His eyes were cool and indifferent as if he had just ordered the killing of a Petrel.

Liutites stood, unmoving and staring at his father, eyes imploring him to rescind his command or have it fall to another.

Antaean was unmoved. He raised his staff once more. "Fulfil your duties or accept your fate."

Fate. Destiny. All lies one told themselves to deny the responsibility for their actions. Liutites knew the possibilities if he tried to usurp the Overlord and failed. The fact that it wouldn't end with his own death had nothing to do with fate. It was strength of will. Strength to do what was hard. Strength to do what seemed impossible only the day before. Strength to embrace the pain he would feel for a lifetime. He looked at his brother. He didn't think of the times they had shared, their disagreements or the shared laughs. He thought of the future.

"Liutites…" Temalus said in a soft voice, carrying a final plea to find another way.

Liutites struck. The strike was quick, below the breast plate, up, and piercing the heart, just as he had taught his brother. The quick kill was the most difficult to achieve.

Temalus fell back and Liutites fell with him. They looked into each other's eyes for a final time. "Don't let this destroy you," Temalus said. His eyes closed and he faded into the Great Sea.

Supreme Commander Liutites watched him die, and with his death the fire in his heart was replaced with a cold hatred, icier than the world he had to live in.

# CHAPTER 43

Four months after the death of Temalus, Supreme Commander Liutites stood atop a low rise with a view that stretched to the horizon, where the endless white landscape met with endless blue sky. Somewhere out there, where the land and sky met, was their offspring, the sea, or so the legend of creation said. He wondered if he would ever again feel the cold embrace of the ocean, or use his wings for what they were intended, flying through the sea, feeling the thrill of evading the predators of the deep, and the satisfaction of snaring his own meal.

Liutites thought of the daughter he'd never named and would never know. He thought of the day when she became old enough to feed without her parents' aid, and how Mearna had abandoned her to the crèche to be protected by anonymity. He felt no remorse, nor did he miss her. In fact, Liutites felt nothing other than a frozen fire of hatred for his father, the Overlord.

He examined the months-old blood of his brother still staining the white of his breast. He had refused to preen the encrusted feathers away, which he wore as a badge of remembrance to the brother he had killed, and as a testament of what it took to rise to the rank of Supreme Commander. Liutites had remembered the faces of each guard who had brought Temalus before the Overlord and he had given every one a painful and gruesome death. With each murder, he saw the face of Antaean in their frightened eyes, and he had plucked those eyes as a proxy to the eyes he desired to take. He had intended to do the same to General Diutes, as well, but the Overlord had forbidden it and sent Diutes to Forward Command for his own protection.

A voice from behind him took Supreme Commander Liutites from his memories and thoughts. "Yes, Lieutenant?" he said without looking at the voice's owner.

"Supreme Commander, sir. The human machines we've been tracking have stopped just outside Pack Ice Command. Shall we attack?" the nervous Royal Emperor lieutenant asked.

They had spotted the treaded vehicles the day before as they made a circuitous trek near the compound. But the brief winter days brought the night quickly and the vehicles turned back. The humans operating the machines had gotten an earlier start this day, and now it appeared they were about to stumble upon their command center.

"Have they exited their machines?" Liutites asked, still not looking at the officer.

The lieutenant nodded until realizing his mistake, then spoke, "Yes, sir. We counted four men. Shall we attack?"

Liutites stared at the horizon and wondered how the men had missed General Diutes' Forward Command. But the outpost was small and unobtrusive, and would likely appear as nothing extraordinary to anything other than the most observant eye. "No, Lieutenant. Wait for them to enter and then come in behind them. Let the Overlord deal with them."

"Yes, sir." The lieutenant began to salute, but saw there was no need as Liutites' eyes still looked away. The lieutenant fell to his stomach and quickly tobogganed away.

A gurgle from the ground before him finally pulled Liutites' eyes away from the vista. His beak parted and a piece of ice-laden blood flaked away. "You're still alive."

"The Overlord promised," a Chinstrap penguin lying with his back against the frozen ground coughed, choking on his words. His ragged, torn flesh trembled with each breath and with each word he spoke. His left flipper lay two feet away in a frozen pool of blood as if waving farewell to the body it had once been a part of. His remaining eye scanned the sky, unseeing. "He swore before you all…"

"I am not the Overlord," Liutites said, his tone even, carrying the threat of more violence. "Let this be a lesson to you, Volité. A good spy takes his secrets to the grave." Supreme Commander Liutites leaned down and tore at the Chinstrap's throat, stabbing and ripping repeatedly until the former spy's head rolled off his shoulders. Liutites stood and shook the blood from his beak, and examined his work. He stared at the empty eye socket of the separated head. "And never trust a Royal Emperor."

Supreme Commander Liutites turned away from his kill and began a slow trek back to Pack Ice Command. More death awaited him on the horizon, which he was eager to meet.

# About the Author

Steven Hammond is a Sci-fi/fantasy author, artist and photographer. He has written six books in the *Rise of the Penguins Saga* including *Rise of the Penguins, The Warlord, The Warrior, The War, Crosscurrents, Whispers of Shadows, The Royal Creed,* and *Order of Kings*. He also penned *The Staffs of Omia series,* which includes *The Talents of Bet,* and *The Journey of Bet.* He is currently working on two new titles in both series.

Steven lives in California's Central Valley, his home since birth, where enjoys spending time with his family. When not slapping at his keyboard like an enraged Siamang, while his Buster Dog curiously looks on, he can be found working on any number of art projects, or enjoying a good movie.

To learn more about Steven, visit his Web site at:

www.stevenhammondbooks.com

# More from Rockhopper Books

THE RISE OF THE PENGUINS SAGA

Rise of the Penguins - Book 1

The Warlord, The Warrior, The War - Book 2

Crosscurrents - Book 3

Whispers of Shadows - Book 4

The Royal Creed - Book 5

Order of Kings - Book 6

THE STAFFS OF OMIA SERIES

The Talents of Bet

The Journey of Bet

www.ingramcontent.com/pod-product-compliance
Lightning Source LLC
Chambersburg PA
CBHW031235120726
47905CB00002B/602